The Cottage

ISBN 9798421813071

This is a work of fiction. All of the characters are fictitious and any resemblance to real persons is accidental and unintentional.

CHAPTER 1

NOW

It's torture. The blackness absolute. The plip, plop of dripping water, innocuous yet insidious in its relentless persistence, torments more with each passing minute. The pulse in the eardrum, synchronous with the sound, hurts, intensified by the blindness, the disabling of one sense heightening the sensitivity of another. Cramp revisits; the muscle in the foot tightening, pain spreading, crushing the ankle bone as if in a vice. Clench teeth and whimper and stretch the leg but there's nothing to do but let it subside, as it will. And after a while, it does, and the plip, plop returns, reasserting its authority.

Curled up on a coarse mattress, shivering, bare outstretched arms, pain induced sweat drying in the musky air, shuddering in a vain attempt to shake off the chill. Cords burn wrists, hemp assaulting delicate skin with the slightest movement, efforts to loosen them long since abandoned, tied securely as they are to the metal frame. Sense of smell acute, pricked by the pungency of damp and body filth. The aroma of death and decay.

It couldn't be helped. When I could hold it no longer, I swung both legs off the mattress and peed through my jeans onto the floor, weeping at the indignity. Clothes still damp, thighs chafed, and I stink. Tongue like leather, lips cracked and dry, the urge to weep again, irresistible. How long has it been? Twelve hours? Twenty-four? Lost track; can't think, the utter darkness, the plip, plop, the stink, the pain, vying for control of remaining senses.

Now, a new terror; a scuttling sound. The pitter-patter of tiny feet. An animal; a rat, most likely, the ultimate nightmare. Draw legs in because feet are furthest away and vulnerable, yet at the same time, the only weapon of defence.

Sit up, constrained but alert, blind eyes searching forlornly in the black void. Breath deepens, sweat reforms, chill returns inducing the urge to scream, but throat is parched and raw. The scuttling stops and I'm left with my friend, the plip, plop, but only for a few seconds when, smelling fear, the animal starts again with snuffling purpose. Tug on the cords and the bed-frame rattles and squeaks and the scuttling stops, for a few seconds more.

Stay calm; stay logical. I need hands, but they're securely tied. I tried hours ago until the pain was too much but now the pain doesn't matter; the lesser of two evils. I move fingers to re-examine metal, rusty and rough. I slide a right hand, up and down, six inches between horizontal bars, identifying crude welds where they meet the vertical. Top and bottom are both smooth. Try the left. The bottom is smooth, but the top, ragged and split. A sharp edge. A tentative touch paints the picture. I twist the arm so the underside of the wrist faces up. Can't risk cutting a vein. Picture the relative proximity of soft flesh and coarse rope to jagged metal and wait for the stab of pain to direct me. It does.

Try again until the cord snags on the edge. Work in tiny movements, splitting micro fibres until the cord breaks free of its hook and must be found again. I learn, snagging the cord on the ragged edge, picking and tugging, and when it fights back and flesh meets metal, squeal in pain and despair at the unjust punishment.

The scuttling demon is attuned to the noise, unmoved by the creaking of bed springs or the muted gasps of its occupant. I stop and hold breath and it stops too. I listen, super-sensitive hearing primed. A scratch, a scrabble, vibration on the mattress, tiny menacing footsteps. A tickle of whisker on ankle. Suck in the foul air until lungs are full.

Scream.

Kick both legs into the void, feet flailing in air until there's impact, hard toe against soft mass. One shriek, and then the thud of collision with a hard surface and the splash before it goes silent. I'm breathing heavily, teeth bared in the dark, eyes useless, ears straining. Silence but for my own panting.

The plip, plop, resumes. It's back to work. Metal stabs again but I'm inured to pain and it's no longer a deterrent. The cord snags easily now, fraying in the mind's eye and I tug harder, each time rewarded by the pop of tiny threads tearing and separating. But still it won't yield. A finger feels for the ragged edge and it's less sharp now, the rusty metal fragile like the cord. A tug on the rope in frustration and the pain shoots up the arm from a wounded wrist, invisibly bloody and bruised. I allow breath to settle and listen for a scuttle. There is none. I'm now skilled in snagging the cord. I may be blind, but I can still see. Change technique. Saw rather than tug, with minute oscillations. It could take forever but this is my only task and it could be my last.

It takes time. I don't know how long. An hour? But I sense a change and pull hard and the metal shrieks. *Or is it me?* Untethered hand collides with vertical strut and the pain is exquisite. Stay calm. The rope is loose but still shackling me to the frame. I work the wrist around and soon, the knots unravel, and the hand is free. I touch my face, stifling euphoria. It's not over yet. Lips cracked, tongue dry, hair matted, and neck wet with sweat. Roll over and reach for the other cord. Tease open the knot a fraction at a time until it slackens and yields. Both hands are free.

Lie back, exhausted.

CHAPTER 2

THEN

I slide on the aviators, adjust the floppy straw hat and step into a delicious warmth that caresses my bare shoulders. It's gone two and the village smoulders quietly in the unseasonal heatwave.

The weather has drawn me outside for the first time in three days. There are still boxes to unpack, but no rush. It became stiflingly hot in the cottage, moving furniture and possessions from one place to another and back, but the essentials are in place and what remains encased in cardboard can stay there until it's required.

There's been little opportunity to explore my new surroundings, so engrossed was I in the chaos of moving. Clare and I drove around the village back in February, the day I came to view. It was wet and gloomy, and I got little sense of belonging or indeed, that Oakdale was even the place for me. How could I? I'm a city-dweller.

Not that I've never seen the countryside. We lived on the edge of Wimbledon Common. I played there as a child, and growing up, spent many a Sunday picnicking in nearby Richmond Park. It was country as far as we knew it and it was right on our doorstep. It didn't compare to the Dales though. We once had a holiday here. This is real country where pockets of civilisation are spaced out, and the folk speak a strange language. And so, here I am now, reliving childhood memories.

It's not just the sights, it's the sounds. Wailing police sirens, low-flying aircraft, the clatter of train on track, the constant hum of traffic; all absent. Here, there's relative silence. Trees rustle audibly, birds sing harmoniously and only the occasional tractor signifies industry of any kind. It's not why I came, but I'm glad I did. This is a new experience and I'm loving it.

An elderly lady with a Westie totters along the road ahead and I look forward to the introduction, but she turns down a side-street before I can get there. Halfway along the High Street, there's a crossroads, one leg heading left to nearby Thurston, one to the right signed Church Street, and bordering it, a grassed area with a war memorial to the fallen of Oakdale. Beyond the memorial is Oakdale mere. I saw it last time when the sky was overcast, but today in the late spring sunshine, the vibrant greens of the trees against the blue sky are mirrored in the water and families of duck and swan float serenely, leaving the barest ripple on the surface. I take the path around the mere and head towards the church, its steeple standing proud amongst oak and beech. I push at the wrought iron gate and its hinges squeak, discordant in the tranquillity.

The churchyard is deserted, devoid of the living, its ancient headstones leaning drunkenly one way or another, the grass between them long and lush. I sit on a decrepit oak bench and admire the 12th century Church of St John the Baptist. I'm not religious, and apart from weddings and funerals never went to church in London. But it feels right here, and I resolve to attend the next Sunday service. I might meet some of the locals.

An old gentleman with a stick is shuffling up the path, favouring one leg. Despite the heat, he's wearing country clothes; cloth cap, tweed jacket, corduroy trousers and stout boots. I remove the sunglasses and smile, but he ignores me, grim and determined, eyes focussed on the path and the task ahead. He comes alongside and I venture a greeting.

"Good afternoon." He stops and turns his head towards me in slow motion, grimace unabated. I shift uncomfortably on the bench, wondering what he could have found offensive. Maybe it's his bench? I try again. "Lovely day, isn't it?" He doesn't respond immediately. He could be deaf.

"You'll be in Farrier's Cottage," he grunts, the trace of a sneer on his stubbled face.

"Yes!" I say enthusiastically, relieved to have elicited a response, however peremptory, and somewhat honoured he knows where I live. *The village is small, Kate, everyone knows everything.* He sniffs and wipes his nose on a sleeve, looking like he's said all he wants to say. He's the wrong side of eighty I'd guess. Not a great deal to be cheery or enthusiastic about at that age, with or without a gammy leg, so it's up to me to make the running. "Catherine Duvall," I proffer. "Kate."

"Is that right? You'll be another one of them city types comin' here buyin' up all the houses, makin' it so's the locals can't afford nothin'. You rich folk and your second homes," he says, tutting. I'm stung by the criticism and dismayed the first person I meet is so unwelcoming and aggressive. He's also completely wrong and I can't let it go.

"This is my only home, and I can assure you I'm not rich enough to buy, just renting." I regret it immediately. It sounds petulant and shows he's struck a nerve, which was probably his intention.

"Is that right?" he says again, a trace of smugness exacerbating my irritation. "You won't be here long. Last girl wasn't. Six month and she was gone, back to Chelsea or wherever. Good riddance that's what I say."

"Is that right?" It's a childish riposte, especially with arms folded in defiance. He curls his top lip and shuffles off up the path towards the church. "Nice to meet you!" I shout after him, but he pays no heed to my sarcasm. I stifle the urge to weep. My first encounter with one of the locals has been an uncomfortable and mildly distressing experience. *What if they're all like that?* I pull myself together. It's just bad luck, and anyway, there's no going back now.

I stroll around the graveyard, reading the headstones, imagining the people whose bodies are buried; their lives, their loves, their families and the times in which they lived. Their triumphs and disasters, the battles fought, the illnesses suffered, the pleasure they gave others. They laughed and cried and ate and drank and went to weddings and funerals and had babies. I've always been fascinated by graveyards; they dispel the myth the world was made for me and my time,

"I knew Jackie had moved out, but not who was moving in. Welcome to Oakdale. You're not from around here?"

"No, I'm a Londoner, I'm afraid."

"Nothing to be sorry about. I'm sure you'll love it here. Everyone's very friendly." I think of grumpy old man but decide it's not worthy of mention; Reverend John Lee has redressed the balance.

"You knew the previous tenant?"

"Yes," he says. "Not very well," he adds a little too briskly. "I met her a couple of times, but she wasn't a churchgoer; kept herself to herself. I suppose she found it difficult to fit in."

"Well, let's hope I don't."

"Might you be joining us this Sunday?"

"Yes, I think so."

"Eleven a.m. Look forward to it. Have a nice day." He turns to go.

"Reverend Lee?"

"John."

"John. Where does Mr Fitzgerald live?" I don't know why I'm asking.

"Lord Fitzgerald," he says, with mock deference.

"Of course."

"Oakdale Manor. If you go up the High Street and turn down Horse Lane, you'll find it about two hundred yards along there."

"Thanks."

He looks at me quizzically. "Er, you're not thinking of paying him a visit?"

"No, just curious. And no, I'm not a Fitzgerald."

CHAPTER 3

"Sounds idyllic. Send me some pics will you? Can't wait to see it once you're properly settled." Mandy goes over the top as ever, even at thirty. She was like that at school, she was like that at university and even now, fully grown-up with a husband and a mortgage and a Cockapoo, she's hyper about everything. My ex-flatmate says she will never leave South London. She loves her advertising job in the West End, she's addicted to the myriad bars and restaurants, the clubs and theatres and the whole cosmopolitan vibe. She'd love the idea of spending a weekend in the Dales with her best friend, drinking Prosecco and gossiping about old times, but she wouldn't last twenty-four hours before going stir-crazy. I know she won't come.

"How's Phil?" I ask because it's only polite. Phil and I were together until I brought him back to the flat and he met Mandy, after which I was history. He's another reason she won't come because she can't leave him to fend for himself. I know he's helpless, at least in a domestic setting. He did have the decency to introduce me to Mark as consolation, and that worked for a while. Five years, in fact, before I came to my senses.

"He's fine," says Mandy. "Sends his love." *I bet.* "Useless as ever, of course. Kettle, fridge, TV remote, that's the limit. Beyond that..."

"Mark was the same."

"They're out tonight."

"On a Saturday?" I say, surprised Phil has abandoned his new wife on a weekend.

"Bit of male bonding." Mandy chuckles, but I sense edginess to the humour. I can tell. I've known Mandy for fifteen years and I know when she's covering up. I bristle at the thought my last two exes may be out there swigging beer and talking about me. Mark telling Phil I wanted too much, and he was well out of it. *You had a lucky escape there, mate.*

I know why you palmed her off onto me, you've done well for yourself with Mandy. If only I'd got there first, blah, blah, blah.... I'm the common denominator, and Mandy won't like that. Worse, her best friend has shipped off to the back of beyond and left her alone in bloke-land. It's not that she doesn't have any other friends; it's just she and I have a special relationship that means I'm always there when she needs me and sometimes, she reciprocates. "It's a real shame."

"What is?"

"You and Mark."

I bristle again. "Don't go there Mand. It wasn't meant to be."

"Yes but…"

"Leave it. I should have done it years ago." It's true. I realised early on Mark loved himself more than anything else and I learned to tolerate it. He could do five things to annoy me and just as I was ready to kick him out, he put it all right with one small romantic gesture. I fell for it every time until one day, I didn't.

"What's got into you?" he says, as if it's all my fault or I'm just having a period.

"I think we should take a break."

"What do you mean? Why?"

"Because I'm sick of living like this."

"Like what?" *Don't weaken Kate! First, he's going to bombard you with questions to undermine you and make you think you're being irrational and then he'll turn on the charm and if past experience is any guide, you'll give him another chance and you'll hate yourself afterwards.* "Look…" he's skipped the preamble and gone for the placatory smile. He knows he's screwed up again and he knows all it takes is a little TLC and a nice dinner. *He thinks he knows.* "C'mon, Katie. Let's go and have a pint and a curry and talk it over." *I'm feeling resolute and for some reason, empowered. There's no going back.*

"I'm going home for the weekend and when I get back, I want you and all your things gone. Stick the key through the letterbox."

"So where do I go?" He now knows I'm serious. Aggressive pose, hands on his hips, a hint of anger mixed with fear.

"You'll think of something."

"Just tell me what I've done." Arms spread wide, the innocent victim. Mr Reasonable will attempt contrition if I demand it, but I'm in control now and I don't need to explain. The decision's been made. He's already a stranger. I'm not even sorry.

"I just don't like you anymore." I've already packed a soft bag. I pick it up, leave him in the flat and go to mum and dad's.

"Well, I can't say I'm sorry," says mum. "Never took to him much. Always thought he was a chancer."

"Yes mum."

"Who wants a G&T?" asks dad. Anything to avoid getting sucked into the conversation. *Good old dad.*

"Is Mark seeing anyone?" I say to Mandy and regret it instantly because it makes me sound pathetic and because I already know the answer. The delay says it all.

"Er, I think so," she says, but she's fooling no one and I feel sorry for her. It's difficult for a couple when their friends split up and both halves stay in touch. They never know how to share out loyalties and avoid taking sides. Most of the time they have no idea who's to blame and most of the time it's neither, so they're forced to play along with both. Mark has been round to Mandy and Phil's with his new girlfriend, and they've had a great time and probably repaid the compliment. For all I know Mandy's become great friends with her and is now feeling guilty on all fronts. I resist the temptation to ask what she's like. Mandy's talking again. "Maybe you'll find a nice young man up there? A rich landowner or farmer or something."

"Maybe." I couldn't care less. I'm happy to enjoy a bit of solitude, for a while at least. It's liberating.

"OK Kate. Gotta go. You take care." She's had enough of feeling guilty, however misplaced.

"You too."

Before the solitude takes hold, I call mum.

"Hello darling." She sounds weary. She's only sixty-six but the last few months have taken it out of her. The only world she's known for forty-five years is crumbling, right in front of her eyes, and there's nothing she or anyone can do about it.

"How's dad?" I know it's not going to be good, but it gives her an opening. Get it off her chest. She wouldn't ring me to have a moan; she wouldn't want to worry her baby. Her youngest has a life of her own and a very important job; doesn't have time to be distracted by old people's problems.

"He went down the garden for some runner beans and he was taking ages. I found him sitting on the bench by the greenhouse, staring into space. He'd forgotten what he was doing there." It's depressing but predictable, a further step down the slope. I saw it for the first time the weekend I walked out on Mark. Dad not returning with the G&Ts and me finding him in the kitchen staring intently at three full glasses.

"Slice of lemon?" I ask, and his eyes light up.

"I knew there was something missing!" he says triumphantly and finishes the task. It isn't the first bit of absent-mindedness we've noticed and until now we've all had a good laugh about it, but somehow this time, the alarm bells are ringing.

"Could be ten months or ten years," says Dr. Taylor. "It all depends."

"Depends on what?"

"Ordinarily, he'll deteriorate slowly over time and if you only see him every few months you'll notice the change, unlike your mum, who won't. But if he has a seizure…"

"Meaning?"

"Some are prone to epilepsy. An epileptic seizure can cause a significant and irreversible deterioration. Like dropping a few rungs down the ladder, so to speak."

"Here, you speak to him," says mum. There's mumbling in the background, a rustle and finally a familiar voice.

"How's my favourite daughter?" It's something he says to us both.

"Great dad. How are you? Are you behaving yourself?"

"What do you mean?" he replies with faux indignation. "Don't I always? Getting a bit forgetful I suppose, but that goes with the territory, doesn't it?"

"I suppose." I'm not sure exactly what he means and hesitate to bring up the subject of mental health. Best we all pretend it doesn't exist.

"It's not going to get any better, that much is true." I feel a lump in my throat. "Anyway, never mind me. How's the new house? Is it as charming as it looks?"

"It's beautiful, thank you. I'm really chuffed. You'll have to come up here and see for yourself." It's a hollow gesture. He's forbidden to drive, mum's too nervous and Eastbourne is too far for me to collect and return in one day. Nor would they stay over; out of their comfort zone. I'm suddenly dismayed, realising he may never see it.

Years ago, he wanted to lend me the deposit on a flat. *Get yourself on the property ladder – we don't need the money, there's nothing we want we haven't already got.* But I stubbornly refused; wanted to do it myself but also wanted them to enjoy their money in retirement. *Forget that, it's going to come to you eventually. You may as well have some of it now.* So, I stayed renting and while Mandy was sharing with me we were fine, but then she went off with Phil and Mark moved in instead. Seemed like a good idea at the time. Years later, I kick Mark out and it means I either get a new flatmate which, at my age, I consider risky and undesirable, or else downsize. It was a seminal moment. I chose relocation and found I could upsize to a house, even if I don't own it. Dad's talking again.

"I don't know that part of the world. Went to Pontefract once," he mused. "Can't remember why. Anyway, how's the new house? Is it as charming as it looks?" It's a classic symptom. He's forgotten he just asked the same question.

"Lovely thank you."

"Your mum and I must come over and see it sometime." *Oh God.* "As soon as you're settled."

"That would be nice. Can I speak to mum again?"

"Jean?" he shouts, unnecessarily.

"Graham, go sit down and I'll make us a cup of tea," I can hear mum in the background taking the phone off him. "Don't you worry darling. We'll be just fine. You've got lots to think about."

"He's getting worse, isn't he?"

"No, he's fine. Just a bit confused. He gets frustrated and cantankerous sometimes."

"What can I do?"

"Nothing darling, we're fine."

She sounds teary and with good reason. If I dared think about it, she might be going the same way. But I can't go without asking. I take a deep breath and try to sound jolly.

"How's Clare?"

Her voice begins to break. "Oh, she's fine darling. Comfortable, the doctors say."

"How are you getting there?"

"There's a volunteer service. They're very nice. You just pay for their petrol."

"That's good." I've got to make time to go home and see them all. "I'll be down there as soon as I can. I'll call you in the week. Love you."

CHAPTER 4

I was last into the church and I'm last out, bringing up the rear as the fifty or so members of the congregation meander their way towards the door and into the sunshine. I had a pew to myself at the back and in between hymns, sermons, and announcements I amused myself casting an eye around the worshippers, imagining who they all were, where they lived and what they did. No one made eye contact, even when they were leaving.

They're mostly retired folk, one youngish couple with kids and a couple of young women who look like twins the only ones under sixty. I'm wondering what Reverend Lee gets out of this gig, or rather, what the congregation gets out of him. Did he choose it? Is he climbing his way up the ecclesiastical ladder, or has he been despatched to a rural backwater as penance for some misdemeanour? He's there at the door, shaking hands and exchanging pleasantries, bidding them all a good day. He greets me warmly, but I'm not brave enough to ask why Oakdale has a hippy vicar.

"Kate! So pleased you could join us. Did you enjoy the service?" He's deliberately putting me on the spot. I thought people went to church to pray for forgiveness, redemption or a lottery win; something guilty people did out of conscience rather than desire, to ensure God has kept them a place in the afterlife. None of those apply to me.

"I confess church is a novelty for me."

"We don't do confessions here, unless of course you insist." I'm staring into deep brown eyes. *He's flirting with you, Kate.* I open my mouth to speak, unsure of what might come out, but he spares my blushes. "The real question is, will you be back next week?"

"Yes, I think so. It was nice to see other people even though I haven't had a chance to meet any of them."

"They either rush off to The Crown or straight home for Sunday lunch. You've met George, I understand?"

"George?" I know who he means. Grumpy old man looked like a George.

"Friday in the churchyard. I fear he was less than welcoming towards you."

"It really doesn't matter."

"Don't take it personally, he's like that with everyone. He doesn't mean anything by it. Just bitter and twisted." I turn to the sound of footsteps coming up behind. It's the organist. Late forties, greying hair, slightly overweight, attractive once. "Sara, this is Kate. Kate, my wife Sara." I try to suppress the look of surprise but fail miserably.

"He's my toy boy," she says cocking a thumb at John and offering a warm smile that counters any embarrassment. She's probably used to it. "Nice to meet you, Kate. You're new in Oakdale?"

"Yes. Moved in on Thursday."

"Farrier's Cottage?" I'm nodding, feeling my privacy is again under threat and she puts a hand on my arm. "Don't worry, it's our job to know these things, keep track of comings and goings. Where do you hail from?"

"South London."

"And what brings you here?"

"Lifestyle, I suppose. Just wanted to break free from the tyranny of city life."

Sara nods in understanding. "I was brought up in Wandsworth, but I don't miss it. What is it you do?"

"I'm a writer. Magazine and newspaper articles, commentary, general interest stuff, corporate brochures, anything I'm asked to do."

"Novels?"

"Yes, two so far, although hardly bestseller material. I'm hoping Oakdale can bring me some new inspiration."

"Good luck with that."

"Kate wants to meet some of the locals," says John, "we'll have to introduce her."

"Parish Council meeting on Wednesday in the hall. Seven thirty. Why don't you come? Lots of good material there.

You'll be able to observe some of the village's more colourful characters expressing their views."

"Complaining, she means," says John.

"Now John," she says in reproach. "There's no reason to malign the good people of Oakdale."

"Yes dear."

"I might do that."

***

I pick up a Sunday paper from the only shop in the village, *N&N Newsagents*, reads a sign above the door. Papers, cards, general provisions, off license and a wide range of handy homewares; a veritable Aladdin's Cave. Open seven days except for the tiny post office counter in one corner which is closed on Sunday. There's a smiley Asian woman behind the front counter; forty something, streaks of grey in otherwise raven hair and lots of bangles.

"You must be the new lady in Farrier's Cottage," she says, beaming and I can't be offended, but no less unsettled everyone seems to know me and my house, while I know nothing. "I'm Naira and my husband is Nirvaan. Welcome to Oakdale."

I'm touched to find another kindly face and extend a hand.

"Kate. It's lovely to be here. Very quiet and peaceful compared to London."

"Oh, my goodness, you moved here from London?" she says with rather more interest than warranted, given she probably arrived from much further away. I'm tempted to ask, just to be courteous, but I feel awkward asking foreigners where they come from. It's not that I'm not interested, quite the contrary; it's just that it risks implying they belong somewhere else and might sound condescending or worse, racist. I take the easy way and say nothing. "That's a big change for a single person. I hope you won't be too lonely by yourself."

I'm aware my mouth is open but nothing's coming out. She knows I'm the new girl in town, she knows I have neither husband, wife, child, partner, cat nor dog and she probably knew my name and where I came from before I said anything. Her knowledge of me is accurate and perfectly innocuous, but I can't help feeling perturbed. *It doesn't matter Kate. It's just gossip. You'll be a curtain-twitcher yourself before long.* "Not at all. I'm looking forward to meeting the neighbours."

"You will find everyone very friendly," she says.

"I knocked on doors on either side but got no reply."

"The Old Forge belongs to a couple from London. I think they only come two or three times a year. Use it as a holiday home." George's remonstrations about rich folk ring true.

"What about the bungalow on the other side?"

"That's Mrs Frost. She's been in hospital for several weeks now." Naira looks around and lowers her voice. "Between you and me I'm not sure she'll be coming back."

"Oh dear."

I bid Naira good-day and turn left up the High Street rather than right towards the cottage. In a few minutes, I find Horse Lane, which has rows of terraced cottages on either side, petering out after a hundred yards. To the left, lush pasture extends almost to the horizon and on my right, beyond a dry-stone wall, dense woodland. The pavement runs out and I continue on the road heading out of the village, when a driveway appears, the entrance barred by ten-foot-high iron gates. The drive on the other side curves out of sight but a few metres further on I'm rewarded with a good view of what lies beyond.

An imposing Georgian manor house sits a hundred metres distant, a large expanse of well-kept lawn stretching from the stone wall to the house, the landscaped garden peppered with oak, beech, and conifers. The house is red brick with multi-paned sash windows over two floors, plus dormers set into a tiled roof and chimney stacks that tower above each gable end. At this distance, there's no sign of life. I admire the vista, soak up the warmth of the sunshine and listen to the occasional chirp of blackbird and robin. From high up in a conifer, a pigeon coos with an air of sophistication its verminous, city dwelling cousins could not hope to emulate. I guess this must be the Fitzgerald residence, and it looks familiar, so I pull out my phone and take a picture.

"What are you doing?" A man's voice booms angrily, shattering the peace. I turn my head left, right and perform an inelegant pirouette to see if there's anyone behind me.

"Hello?" I say feebly, searching in vain for the source of the outburst when I detect movement behind the dry-stone wall.

"Who the devil are you, and mores the point, who gave you permission to take a photograph?" says a bedraggled figure from the other side of the wall, pointing an accusatory finger in my direction. He's elderly, wearing a black twill shirt, brown corduroy trousers with braces and a crumpled felt hat. He's leaning on a garden rake, staring at me with a toxic combination of anger, suspicion, and contempt. I try my best to smile, but a quivering voice betrays my discomfort.

"I'm sorry if I'm intruding."

"You are intruding."

"I didn't mean any harm. The house and garden are so beautiful, I thought they deserved a picture."

"That may be so, but it does not give you the right to take one!" he bellows as if I have committed some mortal sin. I've now met two grumpy old men in Oakdale. *Maybe he's a relative of George?* I attempt placation.

"Kate Duvall. I live in the village."

"What's that to me?"

"You asked who I was."

He raises his eyebrows and sighs as if addressing an imbecile. "I'm not interested in your name. I simply wanted to know what your business was, snooping around private property."

I purse my lips. I object to be harangued by a belligerent geriatric gardener. "I am not snooping! This is a public road.

If the owner wants to keep his home out of sight, then I suggest he builds a bigger wall."

"Don't be ridiculous! His Lordship is entitled to privacy. He doesn't tolerate strangers stealing images of his estate."

In a fit of rage, I stab a few times at my phone and hold the screen up towards him. He can't possibly see it from thirty feet, but the point is made. "There! I've deleted it. Are you satisfied?"

"So you say."

A simple 'thank you' would have ended the matter, but the attack on my integrity has crossed a line. I lift my chin in defiance. "I want to see the owner."

"Why?"

"I will apologise to him directly, ask permission to take a picture and lodge a complaint about you for being insufferably rude and objectionable."

"It won't help you."

"Is he at home?"

"His Lordship is always at home."

"Then I insist on seeing him."

"You can't. He doesn't receive visitors."

"Why not?"

"That's none of your business."

"Then I shall climb over the wall, go up to the house and knock on the door until someone with an ounce of civility answers!" I rarely get angry, but this bad-tempered old man has got under my skin. I glare at him, waiting for an answer. He sighs theatrically and shakes his head.

"Alright. If you must. But I can assure you it will be futile. Go back to the main gate," he says, dismissing me with a wave of his hand. He lays the rake on a wheelbarrow full of leaves and pushes it across the lawn towards the house. I stride purposefully back to iron gates that are already swinging open and head up the drive, rehearsing my speech as I go.

I find the wheelbarrow abandoned by the main entrance and the front door wide open. I step tentatively into the porch, waiting to be invited in, but when nothing happens, press the white ceramic doorbell. A mediaeval clang sounds from within. "It's open!" someone bellows irritably and I step nervously over the threshold into an oak-panelled hallway. The flagstone floor is worn smooth by centuries of footfall and on both walls, generations of Fitzgeralds stare down at me in disdain. I wish I hadn't bothered making a fuss but it's too late now; the only alternative is to cut and run and that's unthinkable. I remove my hat and lay the Sunday newspaper on a table. Grumpy old gardener appears in a doorway to the right and points across the hallway to another open door. "Go in there and wait. His Lordship will be with you presently; that is, if he's not too busy."

"Thank you," I say curtly, still bristling from the earlier exchange yet encouraged I haven't been summarily dismissed. I step into a drawing room that has sash windows looking out onto the front garden and a door at either end. Mahogany bookcases line one wall, shelves filled with ancient leatherbound volumes. Brown leather Chesterfield sofas face each other across a mahogany table and a marble fireplace is topped with a gilt mirror. Ancient oak floorboards are dressed in oriental rugs, and numerous oil paintings hang on flock-papered walls. A crystal chandelier hangs from a ceiling decorated with intricate plaster mouldings and coving. Apart from four standard lamps, the only electrical device I can see is an old-fashioned wireless housed in a walnut cabinet. The room has the appearance of a museum and probably hasn't changed for decades.

I hear footsteps on the oak floor and swing around, expecting to meet an imperious Lord Fitzgerald in tweeds or velvet smoking jacket. But it's just the gardener, and he's carrying a silver tray.

"Please take a seat, Miss Duvall," he says, laying the tray down on the mahogany table. It contains two crystal champagne glasses and a bottle of Veuve Cliquot. I remain standing, contemplating a quick exit but am now too confused to make a decision. He carefully unwraps the foil, twists off the wire cage and deftly pops the cork. Before I can summon up the courage to speak, he's standing before me with a glass in each hand. "It is after twelve."

"You're not the gardener, are you?"

"I can assure you I am."

"I mean, you're Lord Fitzgerald."

"The one and only," he says with a hint of irony, "but that does not preclude my being the gardener." I take the wafer-thin glass from him and marvel at its intricate pattern. "Bohemian crystal," he says. "Czechoslovakia, as was. Nineteen-ten." He clinks them gently and I twitch, fearing they'll shatter. He takes a swig, rolls the precious liquid around his mouth and swallows. "Aah, excellent stuff the twenty-twelve; almost as good as the eighty-two. They come up with a gem every ten years so they're due another about now. Down to my last two dozen. You're not drinking?" he asks, draining his glass.

I'm still flummoxed and want to be annoyed, but holding a vintage glass of vintage champagne, somehow, I don't have the will to fight. I take a small sip and make a supreme effort not to grin foolishly at the exquisite sensation that only the best champagne can offer. The scent and taste of alcohol has the desired effect and I'm emboldened enough to ask.

"Why the charade?"

He frowns. "Charade? You jumped to a conclusion, and I elected not to disabuse you of it."

"You referred to his Lordship in the third person."

"I always do that. You simply assumed the scruffy old fool sweeping up leaves could not be a member of the landed gentry." He refills his glass and sits down, gesturing to the Chesterfield opposite. "You took me by surprise, and I overreacted. I'm an irascible old buffoon who doesn't take to strangers. The default response is to give them short shrift and most scurry away, but you stood your ground and I admire that."

"Is that why we're drinking champagne? To toast my courage."

"Not at all. It's just gone twelve on Sunday. It's what I do."

"You drink expensive champagne at noon every Sunday?"

"No. I keep the expensive stuff for special occasions. But a ten-year-old Veuve is perfectly adequate, don't you think?"

I'm not sure what to think. We're not of the same world and it's all rather odd. If I weren't enjoying the deliciously soporific effect on my brain cells, I might make my excuses and beat a hasty retreat. But if I were honest, it's curiosity that brought me here in the first place and now, it's been further piqued. "You're not a church-goer then?"

"Certainly not! Charlatans and hypocrites, the lot of them," he says with another wave of the hand. "Don't tell me you're one of the happy-clappy brigade."

"I'm not a regular but I did go to the service this morning."

"Why? You don't look like someone who needs divine inspiration. You're far too self-assured for that."

I'm not sure if that's meant to be a compliment, but it's clearly presumptuous and a not wholly welcome observation. "Reverend Lee invited me, and I felt it would be churlish to refuse. I also thought I might meet a few of the villagers."

"And did you?"

"No. They all 'scurried away' before I got a chance. But I met his wife, Sara. They both seem very nice."

"Yes of course," he says with heavy sarcasm. "They would be. Can't have the new vicar or his lovely wife corrupting members of the congregation, especially new ones. I take it you have arrived recently in the village?" He raises the bottle to refill my glass and I think of refusing, but only for a second.

"I can't believe you don't already know that; everyone else seems to."

"I'm not party to village gossip nor am I surprised word gets around. It's a very close community, suspicious of outsiders. You'll find half of them try to ingratiate themselves so they can find out all about you while the other half are just plain hostile."

"And in which half do you belong?" I know it's provocative, but I don't care, and the quip elicits no reaction.

"Neither. I'm in a minority of one. I have no interest in anyone's affairs and I expect others to keep their noses out of mine."

"Hence the short shrift." I know I'm on dangerous ground. I've already determined his Lordship is a truculent so and so, but wonder if, like similar characters I've come across in the past, he has a sense of humour.

"You could say that. It was the camera that did it."

"It's a phone."

He looks bewildered. "You pretended to take a picture with a phone?"

"I did take a picture with a phone." I can see how ridiculous it would sound to someone who'd been stranded on a desert island for the last twenty-five years. Lord Fitzgerald could well be Robinson Crusoe as he appears none the wiser. I fish the device out of my bag and hold it up. "This does phone calls, emails and texts, takes pictures, plays music, connects to the internet…".

"Good lord."

"… is a calculator, a watch, a radio, a TV…"

"Stop!" He holds both hands up in surrender. "My brain is already full to capacity. I have no room for useless information." His bark has swept away any semblance of humour. "I saw it as a threat, that's all." For the first time, he sounds more vulnerable than irritable.

"I was simply walking by," I offer innocently and then remember why I'm here. I raise my glass to add an air of gravitas to my announcement. "Lord Fitzgerald, please accept my apologies for invading your privacy. I assure you it was not intentional, and I meant neither harm nor disrespect."

He eyes me grumpily before raising his glass in return. "Apology accepted."

I notice with some consternation the champagne bottle is almost empty and decide this is an appropriate time to take my leave. I place my glass carefully on the silver tray, stand up and smooth down my floral dress, acutely aware of a lightness of head. "Thank you for your hospitality. It has been a pleasure to meet you." It's all I can do not to giggle.

"Stay for lunch!" he says.

I'm thrown. "Er, no. Thank you, that's very kind, but I have work to do this afternoon. Preparations for tomorrow." It's not quite true, but I can't think of anything else to say. I'm not sure I can take another hour or two of his Lordship, especially if he's going to hit the Veuve again. It's the prudent thing to do.

"Work? On a Sunday?"

"So you respect the sabbath after all?" Mouth has run ahead of brain, and body tenses in anticipation of the backlash, but to my relief, he conjures up the flicker of a smile, a twinkle of contrition.

"Touché, Miss Duvall."

"Kate, your Lordship."

He shows me out onto the porch, and I turn to offer a hand which he takes, bows stiffly and gently kisses the back. That has never happened to me before and my confidence overflows.

"Lord Fitzgerald? Would you mind awfully if I take a picture of your beautiful house and garden? As a personal keepsake, you understand."

"Be my guest." I set off down the drive, but I've only gone a few steps when he bellows after me. "Where do you live, by the way?"

"Farrier's Cottage."

"Ah yes, I might have guessed."

"Do you know it?"

"Should do. I own it."

CHAPTER 5

I had to get back to work; deadlines were approaching and where the press is concerned, can't be missed. The latest draft of a plc annual report that's due to publish in two months is less urgent, but I've been asked to do a regular piece for a provincial free-distribution magazine and have yet to come up with a theme. I managed to get up do date within a couple of days despite being distracted by recurring thoughts of my curious encounter with Lord Edmund Fitzgerald.

I glance at the phone for the hundredth time; the picture I took as I left Oakdale Manor on Sunday, this time with the Lord of the Manor waving at me from his porch. I thought it looked familiar and now it comes to me. Three or four years ago I had a client who published several regional titles; free circulation publications full of adverts but incorporating articles of local interest. I wrote something on the challenges of dairy farming and oppressive milk pricing by supermarkets. The client has since sold out, but I'm sure I still have the final proofs on my system and forage around until I locate a folder named *Dales Diary*. It takes three minutes to find the one I want.

Autumn 2018 features an article on Lord and Lady Fitzgerald and there's a photograph of them, smiling, arm-in-arm outside Oakdale Manor. I'm amazed I didn't remember it earlier, but the fact is, my task was to write my own piece and I barely glanced at the rest of it. The article contains the usual trivia; a potted history of the Fitzgeralds from their roots in Ireland, the foundation of their wealth through tenant farming and their diversification into lead mining in the eighteenth century. Notably, the absence of an heir means Lord Edmund, in his own words, is "the end of the line" and four months after the death of his beloved Eleanor, this is now a reality.

I see nothing in the article of the irascible recluse I encountered and wonder if this is a recent transformation, precipitated by circumstance in his final years. Despite our bizarre introduction, I found him charming and hospitable.

***

The church hall is busy, I count eighty people, not including ten councillors seated at the top table. Reverend Lee is there as is Sara who's sitting at one end, shuffling papers and brandishing a pencil, which suggests she's parish clerk. I might have expected Lord Edmund to be Chair or at least in attendance but given his uncompromising views on the Church and his self-imposed seclusion, it's no surprise. I recognise Naira and next to her, a chap wearing a turban whom I assume to be Nirvaan, together with a few faces I remember from church. Grumpy old George is there too, leaning on his stick.

The Chairman brings the meeting to order; apologies for absence, minutes of the previous meeting, financial statements, all passed with little more than a murmur. He looks around seventy, earnest and weary, as if chairing the Parish Council is a chore he could well do without and one he's keen to get over with as soon as possible. The agenda is largely brought forward from last time; progress on the dry-stone walling repairs to the southern perimeter of the village; '*his Lordship should get that sorted – it's been six month now and it's only going to take one of my ewes to get frisky and make a break through that hole and the rest will follow of that I have no doubt,'* says farmer Barry Wilson; correspondence from the district council and Highways over the proposal for speed bumps in the High Street; *'why is Fitzgerald objecting to that? – it's alright for him he doesn't have traffic going past his house does he?'* pipes up Irene Fowler from number twenty three; maintenance of streetlamps, renewal of footpath signs in three locations; *'he don't want folks walking across his land so he's not bothered is he?'* suggests Janet Hughes; planning applications for tree surgery and an update from the police on the recent theft of lead from the roof of the church extension; *'that's the second time that is - funny them pikies don't take no lead from his Lordship's roof ain't it? I reckon it's all a bit strange so I do,'* says grumpy old George whose surname I learn is Hawley. The Chairman bangs his gavel on a sound block.

"I'll thank you to temper your language Mr Hawley. There's no reason to be disparaging about the travelling community." Reverend Lee nods sombrely but there's little consensus from his audience. I note Lord Edmund features a lot in their deliberations and has few supporters.

"Any other business?" announces the Chair after an hour's debate, with little evident optimism silence will prevail. George gets to his feet.

"Yes, Mr Chairman." I can hear groans. "Farrier's Cottage." It's disturbing enough to hear my home mentioned in public, but one or two heads turn to where I'm seated making me feel conspicuous and isolated.

"We've been through this George," sighs the Chair.

"And we'll keep going through it Arthur Needham until I get what's rightfully mine!" says George, rapping his stick on the wooden floor. At least I now know the name of the Chairman.

"And I'll say again, for what it's worth, the title to the property is a matter of public record. It's beyond the power of the Parish Council to do anything about that, so if you have a dispute with Lord Fitzgerald on this or any other matter, then I suggest you take it up with him. Now, is there any other…"

"Now just you wait a minute," interrupts George, pointing a finger in accusation. "I'm not finished. That cottage belongs to my family. I know it, you know it, everyone here knows it apart from Lord Muck and that latest fancy woman he's just moved in!" My pulse rate has been rising steadily and I'm on my feet in an instant.

"Excuse me!"

Heads swivel around, and I scan the sea of faces looking me up and down. Smirks, nods, disdainful yet defiant expressions, challenging me to refute the charge or else offer some salacious titbit by way of confession. The attention is unnerving, but I won't be intimidated. "What right do you have to be so rude? How dare you make such a vile accusation? You know nothing about me, you silly old man!" I regret the last comment immediately but it's too late and anyway, it can't be the first time George Hawley has been chastised. One or two are grinning, but it's not support, it's the look of a baying crowd enjoying the entertainment and itching for a fight.

"We've seen your type before," he grumbles.

I'm incensed. "My type?"

"Let's all calm down please," says Reverend Lee but he's just making it worse and sees me glaring at him. He attempts to backtrack. "I think we all should offer a warm welcome to Kate as Oakdale's newest resident," he says, squirming, but it's fallen on deaf ears. Even Naira, *you'll find everyone here very friendly,* appears to be scowling.

"In my cottage," rages George.

"I will ask you to moderate your tone, George Hawley," says Arthur Needham in exasperation. He catches my eye and addresses me directly. "Miss Duvall, isn't it? On behalf of the Parish, may I welcome you to our village. I hope you will be very happy here," he says, trying to sound sincere. I have a fervent desire to slap someone, but I wouldn't know where to start.

"Thank you, Mr Chairman. I shall endeavour to behave in an appropriate manner and do nothing to offend the sensibilities of its residents." It's deliberately portentous but it's either that or a stream of invective. A few priggish faces turn back to the front. "For the record, I rented Farrier's Cottage in good faith through an estate agent in Bradwell. I had no idea of the identity of the landlord until a few days ago."

"You've been up there already," says George, waving his free hand in a random direction, "schmoozing at the Manor. I know what you're up to!"

I take a deep breath. "I came here for some peace and quiet, that's all." I've said enough. It's time to leave.

"Six month!" I hear grumpy George Hawley bellowing at me as I reach the door. "At most!"

Gavel hits block. "Order! George! That's enough."

***

I wanted to cry, being subjected to unfounded aggression and unjust criticism, made worse by the passivity of the good residents of Oakdale; but I was too angry. Walking home, the anger subsides, and I wipe away a few tears. I thought I would be perfectly happy on my own, but I feel desperately lonely now and it's not the same thing. I've no shoulder to cry on, no one to take my side or give me a hug and tell me it'll be alright in the morning. *Tomorrow's another day.*

I round the mere and turn left towards my cottage. There's a figure coming out of my gate; a woman in a padded coat, middle aged I can tell, even in the dark. I'm across the road, twenty meters away and she pretends not to see me as she shuffles down the High Street then quickly turns left and out of sight. I let myself in and there's an envelope on the mat. Inside, there's a card bearing an embossed coat of arms: *Oakdale Manor*, and a handwritten note; *Come for dinner on Friday. 7pm. Edmund.*

CHAPTER 6

I've spent longer than necessary getting ready. It's not a date in the conventional sense, but I want to look my best and I'm not sure who else will be there. The invitation gave no clue, and appeared more like a summons, consistent with what little I knew of his Lordship's peremptory character. I plumped for silk blouse and trousers in the end, conscious of the chilly night air. I was killing time when I remembered I'd said I'd call.

"Hello darling."

"Hi mum, how are you."

"Oh, you know, we're coping. Not much else we can do is there?" My mother is putting on her brave face and it's getting harder by the day.

"How's dad."

"He's gone to bed, dear."

"At six?"

"Well, he's had his dinner and usually drops off in front of the telly, but he said he was very tired. He's had a bad day."

"How so?"

"He went to the post office this afternoon and Pete Nolan brought him home, said he was standing outside looking lost and lonely. Told Pete he didn't know which way to go."

"Oh dear."

"I can't let him out on his own anymore."

"No, I suppose not. Give him my love. Have you been to see Clare?"

"Not this week dear, not with your father the way he is." Her voice drops and I feel her sorrow. "She won't know."

It's breaking my heart, but there's nothing to be done, just life taking its course. Mum will need assistance soon and that's going to cost. I need to do some research on what help is available.

"And how are you darling? Are you happy?"

"Yes," I say, determined she should have nothing else to worry about while at the same time feeling guilty that my life, despite its challenges, is idyllic in comparison to hers. "I'm out for dinner tonight," I announce, compounding my self-inflicted discomfort.

"Oh, really?"

"Yes, I met a real-life Lord and I'm going to his Manor house," I say with false enthusiasm. *Leave it Kate. You're just making it worse.*

"I always said you should find yourself a rich husband."

"It's not like that mum. He's over eighty."

"Goodness me, you will be careful darling, won't you?" I've worried her now when I was trying to do precisely the opposite.

"There'll be lots of people there, mum."

"Your dad's calling me now dear."

"Ok, give him a big hug from me."

***

I'm using the phone as a torch to guide the way, wary of potholes, puddles and stepping in something unpleasant which would not make a good impression. The gates are already open, and I'm at the front door just after seven, surprised there are no cars on the drive.

"Miss Duvall. You came!" says an ebullient Lord Edmund Fitzgerald ushering me into the hallway. He bows stiffly and kisses the back of my hand, making me feel like royalty all over again. "I wasn't sure you could bear spending the evening with a silly old fool like me," he says, to which I can find no obvious answer.

"It's very kind of you to invite me."

"Let me take your coat." The gardening attire has been discarded in favour of checked shirt and corduroys which, although clean, have seen better days, as has the heavy woollen cardigan with leather elbow pads and buttons. The house is cool, and I give up my coat reluctantly, relieved to have brought a light sweater. "Come through to the kitchen. I thought we would keep it informal. Hardly ever use the dining room these days."

The kitchen is mercifully warm and spacious. An ancient Aga under a copper canopy dominates one wall and a range of antique oak cupboards house more modern appliances. There's an island with marble worktop and Belfast sink, a pine French dresser stacked with crockery, and a heavy oak table with settles either side. A champagne bucket and two glasses are laid ready. I notice there are only two place settings.

"I saw a woman delivering your invitation."

He lifts the bottle from its icy bath and wraps it in linen. "That's Marian, my cleaner. She lives in the next village." He studies the label and presents it to me like a sommelier. "I got out the '82 Veuve. Thought we could start on that," he says, deftly removing the foil and cage, and I nod dumbly as he wrestles with the cork. It yields with a gentle phut.

"Is anyone else coming?"

"No. Is that a problem?"

"Not at all. I just assumed you were having some friends round."

"Friends? Ha! Gave them up years ago. They all turn out to be a disappointment in the end."

"Is there anyone in the village you see regularly?"

"I think you'll find I'm not terribly popular; 'twas ever thus with the Fitzgeralds." He hands me the exquisite Czech crystal and clinks gently. The champagne is crisp, dry, and ice cold and, I reflect, ten years older than I am.

"I went to the Parish Council meeting on Wednesday. You certainly got a mention or two."

"Really? Moaners and whingers, I expect."

"Mostly."

"You mean exclusively. Tell me Miss Duvall…"

"Kate, please." He smiles and bows almost imperceptibly.

"…Kate. Was there anyone at the Parish Council who put in a good word for me or my family?"

"Er, not that I recall."

"Thought not." He takes a mouthful of champagne and reaches for a refill. I've barely taken a sip and lay a hand over my glass. I need to pace myself, but I already feel confident I can be completely honest with Edmund Fitzgerald. He would expect nothing less.

"Then why did you invite me here? And how long before I too become a moaner or a whinger? Or am I simply destined to be a disappointment?"

"Well, that's rather up to you, isn't it? As to why I asked you to come; I like you. You're honest and stood your ground. People are increasingly two-faced these days, hide behind a mask of duplicity, however benign they appear. They will criticise you to others but never say the same to your face. I can spot it immediately and I can't abide it. I don't need to. When you get to my age you earn the right to do and say whatever you like. Tolerance is a waste of time, and I don't have much of that left."

"But you expect tolerance from others?" I'm pushing, but it doesn't feel rude or unduly provocative.

"Certainly not! You don't feel obliged to tolerate me, do you?"

"The night is young." It's meant to be humorous but he frowns and for a moment I fear I've overstepped the mark. Thankfully, he bursts into a wide grin.

"Ha! Yes indeed."

I accept a top-up and we chink crystal again. "Now, on that score, let me be clear. When you've had enough, just get up and leave. No need for excuses or explanations or dilly-dallying; just say, 'thank you very much, I'm off'. Okay?"

"Okay."

"And when I feel the same..."

"...you'll go to bed and leave me to do the washing up."

"Correct!"

We laugh together and I feel at ease, more so than with anyone I've met in the village. I wonder when, if ever, his Lordship and I will have a falling out. At this moment, it seems unlikely but at the same time, inevitable.

"Now, please sit. I have some amuse-bouches." We sit across the table, and he removes the cover from a plate of canapes; smoked salmon, prosciutto, prawns and caviar with stuffed olives.

"Gosh! Did you make all this?"

"Of course not. Do I look like a chef? We have a posh delicatessen in Bradwell. They prepared it all and delivered it along with the main course. All I had to do with that was shove it in the oven and pray."

"There speaks a man of faith." I'm living dangerously, but he laughs and offers a gentle admonishment.

"You know what I mean!"

"Yes, I do."

"Now tell me what went on at the Parish Council."

I hesitate to mention my contretemps with George Hawley. It was as embarrassing as it was distressing, but as the landlord, I feel he ought to know. There's a connection between, George, his Lordship and me and I'd like to know what it is.

"There was a chap there called George Hawley. He was rather rude and obnoxious, I'm sorry to say."

"George is always like that."

"He said the cottage belonged to him."

"He has always maintained Farrier's belonged to his family and he made it his mission to make life miserable for anyone who lived there."

"You said you own it."

"It's been in the family for hundreds of years, since 1652 in fact. Gerald Fitzgerald was granted a peerage and handed a small piece of Dales countryside by the Lord Protector…"

"Cromwell?"

"…for services rendered, subjugating the papists in Ireland. A thousand acres of farmland and a dozen cottages dotted around an area that became Oakdale, including the blacksmiths which is now in the High Street."

"The property next door?"

"Yes."

"So why does George think the cottage is his?"

He looks distracted, casting a glance across at the Aga and wrinkling his nose. I sense a wonderful aroma.

"If you will excuse me for a moment, I had better check the oven." He tops up the champagne glasses, emptying the bottle into mine, and totters off towards the Aga. Much grunting and complaining ensues before he returns with an iron casserole and lays it on the table. "It's a cassoulet so I'm told," he says, retrieving a pair of Spode plates from the dresser. "I hope you're not one of those vegan types, otherwise you're out of luck! Perhaps you could serve?"

I dish out two platefuls while he disappears for a moment, returning with an open bottle of red. "St. Emilion Grand Cru," he announces, sloshing the ruby red liquid into a new glass. Should go well." I'm wondering when or whether he'll answer my question when he puts his fork down and wipes his mouth with a napkin.

"George Hawley's grandfather Jacob was smithy at the Old Forge and he and his family lived in Farrier's Cottage, both rented from my grandfather Lord Julian. We're talking around 1890 or so. By all accounts Jacob was a decent man whereas there is plenty of evidence to suggest Julian was not. He inherited the title at an early age after the premature demise of his father John in Crimea. In contrast to John, who was highly regarded in the community and very supportive of all his tenants, especially the farmers, Julian was a rascal; a womaniser, playboy, gambler, alcoholic, opium addict, you name it. Julian exploited his tenants by continuously increasing rents, no doubt to help fund his debauched lifestyle. He was a regularly attendee at the Lords, but only so that when in London, he could indulge himself in the pleasures of the flesh."

"What a cad."

"Indeed. How's the cassoulet?"

"Excellent." Edmund drains his glass and pours himself a refill. I've only had a sip, wary of losing control.

"Did he not have a family?"

"Oh yes. Wife Mary and two children, daughter Sophia and son Charles, my father. They lived here along with Julian's mother Winifred, but he spent most of his time away, leaving Mary to run the house and an estates manager to liaise with tenants and collect rent. But it was one of his visits home in Christmas 1891 that started it off."

"Started what?"

"The feud between the Fitzgeralds and the Hawleys."

"You've been feuding for a hundred and thirty years?"

"It's been a bit one-sided; I must admit. The Hawleys doing the feuding and the Fitzgeralds ignoring them."

"What happened?"

"Julian was bored by Boxing Day, so that evening and already three sheets to the wind, took himself off to the pub which was packed with locals enjoying a festive night out. He swaggered in throwing his weight around, demanding free drink because he owned the place and generally making a nuisance of himself."

"He owned the pub?"

"Tenanted."

"Jacob Hawley was playing poker with three other chaps when Julian muscled in demanding a game, so one of them stepped aside. Now, despite being the richest man there, or perhaps because of it, he carried very little money and soon, due mainly to his intoxicated state, he'd lost it all. He offered to sign a promissory note but Jacob Hawley, knowing Julian's reputation and bitter about his high rent, demanded the freehold of Farrier's Cottage as collateral. Would you like some more wine?"

I don't hear the question because I'm somewhere else. The air reeks of tobacco and my eyes sting with the woodsmoke from the open fire. The stench of stale alcohol mingles with sweaty bodies and the faint odour of cow dung that clings to the boots of farm labourers. I'm in The Crown, Boxing Day, 1891 and it's so vivid, I shudder and feel a tingle of excitement. I notice Edmund is holding the bottle of St.

Emilion at an angle waiting for me to respond but all I can do is stare at him and speak.

"The stakes have got out of control, Jacob thinks he has a winning hand and shows it in triumph, but Julian astonishes him and everyone else by trumping it. Jacob accuses Julian of cheating, and they square up for a fight, so Jacob is thrown out because the landlord has no choice and knows where his interests lie."

Edmund stands the bottle on the table, looking perplexed.

"Who told you that?"

"No one," I say, but it sounds unconvincing. The truth is, I have no idea where it came from.

"You must have got it from somewhere. It's no big secret the Hawleys hold a grudge against the Fitzgeralds, but it doesn't extend beyond the village."

I wonder if it was in the *Dales Diary* article but think twice about mentioning it. It would reveal I had prior knowledge of Edmund and his wife, and he may not wish to talk about it.

"Whatever," he says, "it's ancient history and utterly trivial."

"It isn't trivial to George Hawley."

"What makes you say that?" Edmund suddenly appears suspicious, and his expression darkens. "So, he told you?"

"No! He claimed the cottage was his but didn't say why." I feel like I'm being cross examined and it's making me uncomfortable. "I met him in the churchyard a couple of days after I arrived, and he harangued me simply for moving in and then he attacked me at the Parish Council. He said Farrier's was his and accused me of being your 'fancy woman'."

Edmund's jaw drops open and then, to my irritation, his anger turns to mirth. "Ha! Chance would be a fine thing."

It's my turn to look severe. "What does that mean?"

He waves a hand in dismissal. "Because my dear, I'm eighty-five and you are, well ...considerably younger."

"Twenty-nine, in case you were wondering."

"No braver man is he who has the temerity to guess a lady's age. It never turns out well."

I take a sip of red wine. It's rather good and it settles me down but further loosens my tongue. "I don't think age should be a barrier to anything."

"My wife would not approve," he says wistfully, examining the deep red contents of his glass. It brings me back to earth.

"Yes, I know you lost her recently. I'm sorry about that."

He shrugs. "Happens to us all."

"I was here, in the village with my sister. The day she died. We were viewing the cottage."

"How do you know when she died?"

"I saw her headstone. The day I met George in the churchyard, I saw the Fitzgerald plot. I was fascinated how a few brief inscriptions could exude such vivid history."

"As vivid as your imagination?"

"Reverend Lee asked if I was a relative. Rather implied you were unapproachable."

"It doesn't surprise me, but that said, he's not too wide of the mark." He puts his glass down on the table and fixes me with a steely look. "Ah, now I see."

"What?"

"Last Sunday, you were snooping after all."

"I was not!"

"Yes, you were! Your obsession with gravestones together with your overactive imagination drew you to seek out his irascible, unapproachable Lordship and see for yourself!"

It's half true. "I admit I was interested to see where the Fitzgeralds have lived for four centuries, but I never meant to intrude. Honestly."

"It's alright my dear. I'm glad you did."

"I saw the article in *Dales Diary* about you and Lady Eleanor." He frowns and I curse the alcohol doing its mischief, making me say things I shouldn't. It turns out he's only trying to recollect.

"I don't remember that."

"I'm a writer. I contributed to that magazine. When I saw your house last Sunday, I knew it looked familiar and I found the article in my files. You made a very handsome couple," I say, wincing at the cliche, but he doesn't notice. "I'm sorry for your loss."

"She'd been ill for a while. It was her time. But I miss her terribly. Married fifty years you know!"

"Gosh."

"And I'm the end of the line."

"You have no children?"

He shakes his head. "The early Fitzgeralds were prolific, but by the nineteenth century became, shall we say, less fertile. Perhaps it was the lead in the water. Mostly single offspring with a propensity to self-destruct or get themselves killed fighting for King and country. I almost didn't happen, being a late arrival for my father. He was 51 when I was born, my mother being his second wife. Eleanor and I would have liked one, but we were just as happy together and I didn't feel any duty or responsibility to continue the family line. There must be some fourth cousins out there, but I've never been inclined to track them down. They'd be complete strangers to me." He stands up and reaches for my plate.

"Let me," I say getting to my feet.

"Thank you. I have cheesecake for dessert."

"Goodness me! The deli has been working hard." I carry the dinner plates to the island as Edmund opens the fridge. "So, what happened next? After the incident at the pub."

"Jacob refused to pay the rent, insisting Farrier's was rightly his, so Julian threatened to have him evicted."

"That must have been terrible for them."

"It gets worse."

"Do I really want to know?"

"My dear Kate, I'm certain even your febrile imagination could not make it up." He carries the cheesecake to the table and plucks two small plates from the dresser. "Go on. Dish it up and I'll get the wine."

He returns with a half-bottle, half-full of an amber liquid.

"Chateau Climens," he announces, tugging at the cork and pouring a small measure into new crystal glasses. "Your good health," he proposes. The wine is super-sweet, velvety, and heady and I blink twice at a label that reads 1962. Edmund rolls the wine around his tongue and swallows, a look of intense satisfaction on his face. But I'm getting impatient.

"You were saying?"

"Was I?" I fear he's toying with me.

"It gets worse."

"Ah yes. This is all the stuff of legend you know. There's no evidence to prove any of it other than the fact my grandfather was a prize scoundrel. My father said so as did his mother Mary and his grandmother Winifred." He pauses, and I look at him expectantly, urging him on because the story is fascinating, but he seems curiously reticent for once. "Under threat of eviction and with nowhere else to go, Jacob's wife Edith went to Julian and begged him to let them to stay in Farrier's Cottage. Julian initially refused her entreaties, but never being one to pass up an opportunity to exploit the weak for his own gratification, he acquiesced, on condition she agreed to pay the rent. In kind."

I suddenly feel sick. "Oh no, the poor woman."

"Indeed. Edith acceded to his demands, and he took his pleasure, until a few weeks later, he grew tired of the arrangement and ordered the eviction after all, whereupon bailiffs and police arrived to throw the Hawleys out onto the street."

It's probably the alcohol, but I feel close to tears, imagining the casual cruelty with which Edmund's grandfather destroyed a poor family, the shock waves resonating to this day. I hear Edmund saying something, but his voice is a mere echo in the background. In the foreground are the shouts and screams inside Farrier's cottage, the smashing of crockery and furniture, the children weeping as their mother and father tear the family apart in a frenzy of anguish and vitriol and desperate sadness. And then despite the cacophony in my head, I'm speaking, interrupting Lord Edmund Fitzgerald mid-sentence as he comments on the quality of a cheesecake and how it's a perfect match with a fifty-year-old bottle of wine.

"Jacob has found out about Edith and Julian, and he's told her to get out of the house, that he never wants to see her again, and that she will never see her children again and she's pleading with him to forgive her, that she did it to save the family and keep a roof over their heads, but he's unrepentant and she's on her knees begging him and when she tells him she's pregnant with Julian's baby, he picks up a breadknife and threatens to kill her and her bastard child if she doesn't get out of his sight, before throwing her out onto the street, where the neighbours, who already know what she's done, throw rotten fruit and vegetables at her, so she picks up her skirts and with tears in her eyes, runs up the High Street, the neighbours' shouts of 'whore' and 'harlot' ringing in her ears and she arrives at the Manor, intending to throw herself on the mercy of Lord Julian but he's gone back to London and his wife and mother, outraged by Edith's vile claims, refuse to listen and slam the door in her face, after which...Edith is never seen again."

Such is the silence, I can hear a heart beating in my ears and for the first time, the kitchen clock, ticking languorously, reminding us we're only passengers on a journey through time. I don't know where the thoughts and images came from and I don't know if they're accurate, but they're as vivid and haunting as those I experienced earlier. I turn my head to look at Edmund. He's regarding me with a mixture of shock and suspicion, such that I'm suddenly afraid I've incurred his wrath and he's about to react badly.

"Astonishing. There are very few left who know any of the gory details; most have either died or moved away. Jacob and his son Albert may well have been traumatised by the whole experience and passed it down to George. He never witnessed it himself, but it has haunted him all his life." Edmund is looking into space, pensive and weary, perhaps from the copious quantities of wine, but perhaps also because he just heard a personal drama relived in graphic detail from the mouth of a stranger. "How do you know all this?"

"I don't know anything. I'm just imagining," I say, protesting innocence because in truth, I'm as disturbed as he is.

"What do you think happened to Julian?" he says casually. He's beginning to frighten me; my genial host has acquired an ominous persona.

"I don't know."

"Imagine."

"I can't," I say, pleading with him, but he's staring at me, and I must respond. I shrug and blurt out the first thing that comes to mind. "Found dead in a brothel. Stab wounds to the heart. Prostitute arrested and hanged for murder."

"Go on." The baleful expression says it all, and the rest comes.

"Soho, 1912. *The Times* reports his murder and the trial and execution of the woman. But it's subsequently revealed Julian was high on heroin, riddled with syphilis and it turns into the scandalous story of the debauched peer and his unseemly end. It's discovered he's run up massive debts to fund his drugs, gambling, and women so as well as living with the disgrace, Mary has to sell off most of the estate to clear them, leaving the Fitzgeralds with little more than this house and Farrier's Cottage."

Edmund sits back in his chair, nodding his head slowly like someone marshalling his thoughts, considering his options.

"Who are you?"

CHAPTER 7

I struggle to sleep, reliving my extraordinary encounter with Lord Edmund, unable to banish the awful saga of the Fitzgeralds and Hawleys from my consciousness. The night could have ended badly had I not invoked the escape clause; I made no excuses, refrained from dilly dallying, thanked Edmund for his hospitality, and left. He kept to his word and offered no resistance, the only proviso being we continue our conversation at another time. But the events of 1891 and its terrible aftermath loom large in my mind and in the dead of night, I imagine Jacob and Edith in this room, staring at the ceiling as I am now, contemplating the challenges they face; Jacob, consumed with bitterness at the injustice; Edith, her abominable secret festering inside and each, harbouring fears for the survival of their family, wondering what the next day will bring.

I'm distracted by a sound, a faint, rhythmic rubbing, like an animal pawing softly at my door. It stops almost as soon as it has begun and I listen intently for it to start again, but it doesn't and eventually, I drift off to sleep.

***

I'm doing some housework when the doorbell rings. It's the postman and he's staring at the door, smiling awkwardly in a patronising way. I open it wide and follow his gaze. The word *'WHORE'* is crudely painted in white over the dark green.

"That's not very nice, is it?" he says handing me a few pieces of mail. "I'd call the police if I were you, can't be having that around here." I must look shocked and unable to speak because he somehow feels the need to go on. "Any idea who done that?"

"No." I say, numb and suddenly weepy. They came in the night with that weird sound. They attacked me with hate in my own home and ran away. It's very upsetting. "Thanks." I say and close the door. I wallow in self-pity for half an hour then throw on my coat and head outside.

The hardware section in N&N has no green paint to match the colour of my door so I settle for white; at least I can cover up the hateful word.

"Doing some DIY?" says Nirvaan, grinning as he scans the small paint pot and brush. I try in vain to discern evidence of guilt in his expression.

"You could say that." I force a smile. "I'm Kate, in Farrier's Cottage."

"Oh yes I already know that. You were at the Parish Council," he says, without introducing himself. I'm tempted to read it as discourtesy but then who else would he be? I'm also suspicious of his easy smile wondering if he's imagining me as Edmund's 'fancy woman' or concealing the fact he sneaked out in the night and daubed abusive graffiti on my door. I decide to confront the issue head on.

"Someone painted 'whore' on my front door last night."

"Really?" He looks genuinely shocked, and I feel uncomfortable doubting him. "There are lunatics everywhere it seems. I don't know what the world is coming to."

"Neither do I. How much is that?"

"That will be no charge, Kate. I would come and paint it for you myself, but I have to look after the shop."

"That's very kind but you don't need to."

"I know, but it's only neighbourly to help."

I'm touched. "Do you know who might want to do that?" It's a leading question. The finger points squarely at George Hawley who was quick to threaten the 'fancy woman' living in 'his' cottage

He shrugs but he's read my mind. "Do you think it was George?"

"I can't believe he feels so strongly about it."

"Oh yes. That goes back a long way. You are not the first to suffer you know."

"Really?"

"Yes, the lady before you received similar treatment."

George alluded to this before and John Lee mentioned her too. Edmund didn't, but then he didn't know I was his tenant so was probably oblivious to my predecessor. I make a mental note to ask him.

"Do you mean Jackie?"

"Yes. Jackie Thomas. Nice girl, but she decided to go back to London when it got too much for her."

"Too much?"

"Oh, you know. She felt unwelcome. We tried our best but one day out of the blue, she decided to leave."

"Do you know where she went?"

I can tell he's thinking about it. "She filled in a mail redirection request, and we kept a copy, just in case. But I'm not supposed to tell you. Data Protection, you see."

I guess he wants to be persuaded and I give him a mournful look. "She might be able to help me. Tell me what to expect."

"Leave it with me."

CHAPTER 8

There's a commotion outside. It's the incongruous sound that wakes me, a combination of muttering voices, the occasionally repeated instruction, like a gathering of unruly schoolchildren. Lights are flashing blue and amber, passing my bedroom window in both directions and I glance at the clock. It's two in the morning. It takes me a moment to gather my senses; I've been arguing with George Hawley, and Lord Fitzgerald is looking on, raking his leaves and enjoying the sport. I slide out from under the duvet and peek through a gap in the curtains.

Two dozen people mingle on the road next to the mere, held back by four uniformed policemen and two seemingly abandoned police cars, blue lights twinkling forlornly in the dark. Three yellow and white vans with flashing orange roof lights are backed onto the water's edge, men and women in green suits scurrying back and forth. An unmarked car arrives, adding to the parked chaos and two men in plain clothes get out and walk purposefully towards the epicentre of the scene, ducking under a makeshift barrier of striped tape. It doesn't take an expert to realise there's been an incident.

I slip on a tee-shirt and jeans, throw on my padded jacket and step outside, breath condensing in the chilly night air. There's not much to see from the gate so I sidle ever closer. No one takes any notice of me and I'm content with that, nervous of more unwarranted criticism or attention, but they're all talking amongst themselves, engrossed in the activity of officialdom. I reach a group of three women I recognise from church, gossiping, arms folded. The slim one looks up, so I take a chance.

"What's happening?"

She doesn't answer immediately, but the up-down eye movement is less than friendly. She tips her head towards the mere.

"Body in the water."

"My God. Do you know who?"

"They haven't said yet, but we reckon it's George Hawley, like as not."

I've never been this close to a tragedy. In Wimbledon, there were always alarms going off and police cars and ambulances whizzing by, but none ever stopped in my street. Not only is this right on my doorstep, I may also know the victim.

"What makes you say that?"

"His wife," says another who bears some resemblance to the first but is heavier, has multiple piercings, short spiky hair and a tattoo on her neck. "She called them when he didn't come home from the pub. While she was waiting for plod to arrive, her next-door neighbour went looking and saw him in the water. Face down."

"How terrible," I say. George never had anything civil to say to me, but I wouldn't wish him ill. I even feel guilty I called him grumpy.

"You in Farrier's?" asks the third. She's much older than the other two, aged around sixty and doesn't wait for a response. "Well at least he won't be bothering you no more." It's either a callous remark suggesting I would be happy at George's demise, or else some belated show of support for my suffering his abuse, I don't know which.

"What does that mean?" I know I sound overly aggressive, but I've become suspicious of the good people of Oakdale. They've put me on guard.

"He made that girl's life a misery, so he did. Hounded her out of that cottage. And the one before that."

"Best not speak ill of the dead, Ma," says the first one who's in her twenties. "He was a miserable old sod but he don't deserve that."

"Ladies?" John Lee has strolled up alongside. "Hello Kate." I cast a glance at the older woman who's rolled her eyes.

"Hello John." The eye roll has turned into a smirk, and I secretly curse the Reverend for doing my reputation no favours.

"Terrible business. Poor old George."

"Have the police confirmed it's him?"

"No, they've yet to carry out a formal identification, but there's little room for doubt. Mrs Hawley has gone home distraught. I'm going there now to see her."

"Janet over there says he was mouthing off at the Parish Council again," says the older one, "then went straight down the pub as usual. Blind drunk he would be. Only a matter of time before he came a cropper."

"Well, we don't know the circumstances yet Mrs Gibbs. I'm sure the police will get to the bottom of it."

"I wouldn't bet on it, Reverend. They ain't found your lead in three years so don't hold your breath."

"I suspect they'll consider this more of a priority than the mere theft of lead."

Ma Gibbs gives out a snort. "Come on girls," she says. "Back to bed."

"Bye Mrs Gibbs and er…" I say, trying to effect an introduction, but they've already turned their backs and are walking away.

"Margaret and her daughters Melanie and Tiffany," says John Lee helpfully when they're out of earshot. "Mel's the butch one with tats. Live in Old Street. Never ones to miss an event or pass up on a piece of gossip, however gruesome."

"I can't believe it," I say, beginning to feel a chill. "This isn't supposed to happen in a sleepy little village like this."

"What's supposed to happen?" He's picked up a throwaway comment and contrived a question that doesn't have an answer. *He's just making conversation Kate!* I rub my upper arms with a hand. It's a show of nerves.

"I don't know. I mean all this drama with police and ambulances and flashing lights. It's like something out of the movies."

"They like to put on a show. Same everywhere, I imagine. But if you mean the happening of a personal tragedy, then it can happen anytime, anywhere."

"It's just that I was speaking to him earlier and I know we didn't get on, but..." My words tail off and he puts a hand on my arm. I want to brush it away, but that would be rude. *He's just trying to be friendly and supportive, Kate!*

"George was an accident waiting to happen. He's not the first to drown in the mere and he won't be the last."

The ambulances are packing up and leaving and the uniformed officers are shepherding people away. One of them wanders up.

"Evening John."

"Mike."

He checks his watch. "Or should I say 'Morning'?" He casts me a glance. "Ma'am?"

I'm taken aback by the ancient formality, especially from someone still in their thirties, but I guess he's a graduate from the school of plod-speak.

"Are you finished for the night?" says John.

Mike the copper shakes his head. "Not likely. The DI wants us to run a tape around the entire perimeter. Gonna take all night I reckon."

"Really? What for?"

"Can't say," he says, but his smug expression says it all. *Man in authority with a uniform bigging it up in front of a woman.* "Best everyone moves on and goes back to bed. Nothing to see now." He turns and swaggers back towards his car.

"Gotta go. Work to do. Have a restful night," says Reverend Lee touching my arm again, giving it a squeeze for good measure and for some reason, I don't like it.

***

I'm trying to concentrate on work, but I can't get poor old George Hawley out of my mind. I know it's irrational, but I feel partly responsible. If I hadn't been in "his" cottage and not reacted to his aggression, he might not have got himself wound up, might not have gone to the pub, might not have downed eight pints (as was his habit according to Naira) and might not have fallen into the mere. No matter how many times I tell myself I'm no more to blame than anyone else, I regret not being able to mend bridges with grumpy old George before his end came. It will forever linger in my conscience.

But Margaret Gibbs' words linger too, *he hounded her out of that cottage,* clearly a reference to the previous tenant. The graffiti is unpleasant enough, but I can't imagine what else George might have done that constituted hounding. People will exaggerate for effect, but one thing she was right about; I'll be spared that ordeal, whatever it was. John Lee comes round to see if I'm alright, but I tell him I'm busy working and haven't got time for a chat. It may be his job, but I don't need sympathy.

"Police have confirmed it's George," he says at the door. "Thought you should know."

"Thanks," I say, wondering why a man of the Church, on a mission to provide emotional and spiritual support to his congregation, elects to plant self-doubt and confusion instead. *Why should I need to know, John? Two weeks ago, I never knew he, you, or anyone around here even existed.*

"They'll be doing house to house enquiries tomorrow."

"Who?"

"The police."

"Why?"

"Just to see if they can piece together his last few hours."

"Do they suspect foul play?" I wince at my own bit of plod-speak but he seems not to notice.

"I doubt it, but you never know. They're just doing their job."

***

It's Friday afternoon before they arrive.

“Good afternoon, ma’am,” says the middle-aged man in an anorak, opened to reveal a bulging, well-fed torso. Next to him, a diminutive woman police officer in uniform complete with jaunty little cap. “I’m Detective Inspector Stride, Dale Valley police,” he says holding up a warrant card at eye level. The picture is out of date; younger, slimmer, more hair. “This is WPC Jenkins.” She remains impassive. “We’re just following up on a serious incident here on Wednesday night.”

“Would you like to come in?”

“No thank you that won’t be necessary. May we take your name?”

“Yes of course. It’s Kate Duvall.” WPC Jenkins scribbles on a notepad.

“We just wanted to know if you saw or heard anything untoward between the hours of eleven thirty and two that night.”

“No, I’m sorry. I went to bed around ten and was asleep soon after. The commotion and the flashing lights woke me up.”

He smiles in understanding. “Well, if you happen to remember anything, please get in touch.” He hands me a card. “Good afternoon,” he says and turns away.

“Inspector? Was it George Hawley?”

“Yes, I’m afraid it was. Did you know him?”

“Not very well. I only moved in a couple of weeks ago.” His eyes are drawn to the front door, no doubt bemused by the unconventional paint job. “Work in progress.”

CHAPTER 9

I think twice about attending church. I won't be subscribing to religion, nor finding God in the foreseeable future, but I won't have anyone think I can be intimidated by cowardly, juvenile trolls armed with a paintbrush. The sad demise of George Hawley is bound to come up, so if I'm there, at least they'll have less to gossip about. I might even spot someone with a smug expression and white paint under their fingernails.

It's more sombre than usual, despite John Lee's best efforts to give succour to his congregation and promote the positive aspects of George's life. There may be a murderer in their midst but that's no reason to panic. People should go about their normal business and God will watch over them. *Just like he did George Hawley.* The bible appears to have a multitude of phrases to cover tragic deaths and he quotes the best bits, but it's all gobbledegook to me. On a more practical level, he announces the funeral will be delayed until the police have finished their deliberations, and given the circumstances, that will be no time soon. In the meantime, we commit George's soul to God and pray for his family.

I recognise Arthur Needham with a woman I presume is his wife, plus several of those who attended the Parish Council. The Gibbs women are there with a paunchy, middle-aged fellow I guess is Margaret's husband. I glance at hands but there's no sign of paint. I try to catch an eye, but they stare straight ahead, either too worried about their own safety or suspicious of the 'whore' in Farrier's. I wait until everyone's passed by and Sara Lee ambles up, swiftly joined by two children: a boy and a girl both aged around twelve, running up the aisle.

"Sara?" says the boy. "Dad says we can go and play with the horses."

"Did he now?"

"We've got time before lunch," adds the girl enthusiastically.

"Please." The boy puts both hands together instinctively, as you would in a church with clergy for parents.

"Go on then. There are apples in the barn." The children turn on the spot and run off shouting. "And give Bramble a good brush!" she shouts after them, but they're already gone. Sara shakes her head and I'm reflecting on the boy's use of her first name.

"I didn't know you had kids."

"Home for the weekend. Freddie boards at Chelverton and Anna at Broxhall, but they get every fourth weekend at home. We alternate with their mother."

"Ah I see," but I don't, quite.

"They're not mine. I'm Mrs Lee number two. Mrs Lee number one lives in Surrey with her mega-rich husband, but the twins much prefer to be here. Ex-Mrs Lee is more interested in her career and her rich friends than giving children her undivided attention." I sense a latent bitterness, tinged with gold old-fashioned envy. "Still, she pays for the posh schooling. We certainly couldn't afford it on a vicar's stipend." I fear I've set her off and change the subject.

"You keep horses?"

"Yes. Just a couple; an ex-hunter and a pony. They're more like pets really, but they keep the grass down in the meadow behind The Vicarage and the kids love them. I expect they'll grow out of them soon. Do you ride?"

"No."

"I've always had horses, and John was into hunting when he was younger, so he's used to having them around."

"Unusual hobby for a vicar. Hunting."

"He wasn't a vicar back then. He was into corporate finance, just like his wife. They had everything they ever wanted until it all fell apart."

"Where did you two meet?"

"AA."

"Really?" I say, doing my best not to show any reaction. Mild curiosity come friendly conversation has just taken a serious twist. She lets me off the hook. "I'll tell you about it one day, over coffee."

"I keep thinking about poor old George," I say, word association driving my thoughts.

"Awful. Just awful." Sara folds her arms and shakes her head. "It makes me shudder just to think about it."

"His poor wife must be distraught."

"Mm." It's hardly an unequivocal response and I'm interested. "She'll get over it," says Sara dismissively. I don't know whether she and Mrs Hawley are well acquainted but it's a curious remark and Sara instantly qualifies it. "We all do," she forces a smile. "Fact is, George Hawley was trouble and won't be missed."

"Not quite how John put it."

"Just doing his job. You can't deliver a eulogy suggesting the deceased was actually a prize shit. Doesn't go down well, especially in the house of God."

I've never heard a vicar's wife swear, in or out of church and I want to laugh out loud, but the subject matter is beyond humour.

"Police came round yesterday asking questions."

"Doing that everywhere. Just routine. By the way how did you get on with his Lordship?"

It's like an electric shock. Somehow, she knows I've met Edmund. She's probably also aware of the abuse daubed in white paint and thrown George's 'fancy woman' insult into the mix. It's probably in the Parish Council minutes.

"What's that got to do with you?" I'm not prone to aggression or emotional outburst but I'm seething, and she knows it, because she looks anxious.

"Hey." She lays her hand on my arm, just like John did before, and it doesn't help. "I didn't mean anything by it. What you do in your own time is your own business." If she were trying to make things worse, she's succeeding.

"My point exactly. How come everything I do and everywhere I go is common knowledge around here?"

"It's just village gossip, Kate," she says trying to mollify me.

"Really?"

"Yes. We're a close community. Consider it as looking out for each other. There's no harm in it."

"No harm in calling me a whore? How's that looking after each other?" She doesn't recoil in shock which means she does know about it but decided not to mention it or offer any moral support. Instead, she nods ruefully.

"Happened to Jackie too."

"Well, I'm not going anywhere. Enjoy the rest of your day." I turn and take three steps towards the door. She calls after me.

"Kate! Be careful. John knows who you are." I hesitate for a moment and then keep going.

CHAPTER 10

I'm leaning on the front gate. I can see two police cars parked by the mere along with a large white van, rear doors open wide. Three officers and several men in specialist clothing are standing around chatting. Out on the mere, two more in an inflatable dinghy take an object from a scuba diver, before he dives below the surface again. One or two villagers stand around aimlessly watching the proceedings. A car I recognise pulls up. It's the police, the same two as last time plus another one in plain clothes.

"Good morning, Miss Duvall," says DI Stride. "Could you spare us a few minutes of your time?"

"Of course, come in." They follow me to the front door. I'm still not about to explain why anyone would paint a square white patch on a green door. It would be a perfect opportunity to make a complaint, but I don't imagine they've come here about that. I step inside.

"You know WPC Jenkins. This is Detective Sergeant Gerrard," says Stride. Gerrard holds up his ID. "I hope we're not interrupting anything."

"Not at all. Please take a seat." Stride and Gerrard perch themselves on the edge of the sofa while Jenkins stands by the door. There's a pecking order and the woman knows her place. DS Gerrard flips open a pad, pen at the ready.

"It's about the incident in the mere last Wednesday. We've formally identified the deceased as George Hawley. Did you know him?"

"Yes. I mean, I hardly know anyone. I've only been here a short while but George was one of the few I met in the first few days."

"Were you friends?"

"No, not really. In fact, he seemed a bit disgruntled."

"About what?"

"About my being here. In this cottage. He said it belonged to him." Gerrard is scribbling furiously on his pad.

"And does it?"

"I wouldn't know. I pay rent to a managing agent in Bradwell."

"So you don't know who the landlord is?"

"I believe it may be Lord Edmund Fitzgerald."

"What makes you think that?"

"He said so."

"You know his Lordship?"

"I met him a couple of weeks ago." I'm not going to elaborate by mentioning last Friday's dinner. It's none of his business. DI Stride nods slowly and pauses. He's either waiting for his scribbling DS to catch up, wondering whether to pursue this new thread or more likely, just letting my last statement hang in the air to see if I'm spooked into unnecessary embellishment. I've seen enough TV cop shows to know how it works.

"I have information that you attended the Parish Council meeting on Wednesday 14th." *He has information?* He makes it sound like I've been spotted committing some criminal act.

"Yes, I was there."

"What made you go?"

I try an expression that conveys genuine surprise at the question, without appearing disdainful, which is what I really feel.

"I thought I might find out what's going on in the village and meet a few people." He nods again and it's irritating. "It's a public meeting. Anyone can go." *You're sounding defensive Kate.*

"And did you?"

"Did I what?"

"Did you find out what's going on and meet a few people?" I can tell Stride is trying to keep it conversational, so he doesn't have to invoke any formalities, but it doesn't stop me feeling increasingly apprehensive.

"Yes and no."

"Can you elaborate?"

“I saw some people I already know, many that I don’t, learned some names from those who spoke up and that of the Chairman.”

“I understand you had a stand-up row with George Hawley.” It takes me by surprise, which was probably his intention, and all three are looking at me, putting me under pressure. I feel myself getting hot and angry and make a supreme effort to stay calm.

“Hardly. George reiterated his claim to the cottage and made an offensive remark about me in front of eighty people. I was forced to defend myself.” Stride waits for his DS to finish writing, during which time I’ve worked out what the next question will be.

“What did he say?” Gerrard flips back a few pages in his notebook as I look Stride in the eye.

“He accused me of being Lord Fitzgerald’s ‘fancy woman’.” Gerrard exchanges a glance with his boss but doesn’t write anything down. He already has that juicy little nugget. I glance at Jenkins who was smirking until I caught her out and she fakes a light cough as if clearing her throat. “Who told you that?”

“Several witnesses have said something similar.”

“Similar?” I imagine the gossip mongers relishing the retelling of the incident. “Did any of them admit to painting graffiti on my front door?”

“What graffiti?”

I wasn’t going to mention it, but now it may be relevant.

“Whore! Big white letters, in the middle of the night, while I was asleep.”

“No, they didn’t.”

“Thought not.”

“Do you wish to make a complaint?”

“I just did.”

“A formal complaint.”

“Is there any point?”

“Abuse of women in any form is an issue we take very seriously, Miss Duvall,” he says stuffily.

I shake my head, petulant I know. "I'm sure you have much more important things to do." Another thought occurs to me. "Why have you come back asking questions?"

DI Stride sits up from his slouching position, imparting an air of gravitas. "The pathologist report has determined that Mr Hawley drowned following a blow to the head, probably from a hammer or similar. Consequently, this is now a murder investigation."

"Oh God," is my instinctive reaction. Jenkins is smirking again. "That's terrible. In this sleepy little village? I don't believe it."

"May I ask where you were on Wednesday night between the hours of eleven thirty and two a.m.?"

"I already told you that. I was in bed from ten."

"And were you alone?"

"What business is that of yours?"

"Just for corroboration Miss Duvall."

"Yes, I was alone," I say, through clenched teeth.

"Do you know someone by the name of Steve Marshall?"

"No I don't. Look, am I a suspect?" I say, getting increasingly exasperated.

"No more than anyone else," he says. "At the moment we're just trying to eliminate people from our enquiries."

"So, you're not eliminating me yet?" He makes no comment. "Do you seriously think I murdered poor old George because he was nasty to me?"

"And painted offensive words on your door."

"Did he? Do you have evidence it was him?"

"You said you met Lord Fitzgerald a couple of weeks ago," he says, ignoring the question.

"Yes."

"But you had dinner with him last Friday night. At his house."

"What about it?"

"You did have dinner with Lord Fitzgerald didn't you."

"Yes."

"But you didn't feel the need to mention it?"

"It's nobody's business but mine!"

"And Lord Fitzgerald's."

"Look. Aren't you supposed to read me my rights or whatever it is you do?"

"That's just if we interview you under caution. We're just making general enquiries at the moment. Thank you for your time." They get to their feet and Jenkins opens the door. "We'll see ourselves out."

I want to throw something at the door, but instead take a few deep breaths and make myself a strong coffee, reflecting on a bitter irony. I escaped the madness of London, just to step into the mayhem of Oakdale.

CHAPTER 11

I lie low for a few days and carry on with my work, only venturing out at midday for a breath of air. The police have removed the tape from the perimeter of the mere and after my encounter with Stride and his team I presume the divers were looking for a murder weapon. Someone has posted a card through my door with an address in south London, presumably the forwarding address for Jackie Thomas, but it's of little use unless I go there or write a letter, neither of which is terribly appealing. I dial the agent instead.

"Jeremy, it's Kate Duvall in Farrier's Cottage."

"Hello Kate Duvall," says Jeremy Jones in his smooth manner, the preserve of estate agents and car salesmen. "How are you liking the cottage?" He puts the question without any discernible reticence. Either he's a good actor or he's not aware of any problems encountered by tenants present or former.

"It's lovely," I reply, determined to sound content. "It's everything I hoped for, and the villagers have been very welcoming." I imagine a sigh of relief.

"Marvellous! What can I do for you?"

"I wondered if you had the contact details for the previous tenant?"

"Yes, we probably do. May I ask why?"

"Whoever it was, a woman I'm guessing, left some items of clothing in one of the cupboards. I don't know whether she forgot them or meant to leave them behind, but I thought I'd ask her before I chucked them out."

"Why don't you bring them in next time you're in Bradwell and I'll deal with it for you?"

I suspected he might say that, so I'm prepared.

"Er, it's a little delicate. Maybe something best kept between us girls?"

"Ooh, now I am intrigued." His lascivious tone makes my lip curl but as I provoked him, I shouldn't complain. "What if

I call her and give her your number? Data protection, you know how it is."

"Yes of course." It's not ideal but will have to do.

"Everything else alright?"

"Couldn't be better. By the way, I've met the landlord."

"Sorry?"

"The landlord. Lord Fitzgerald. I bumped into him and even had dinner at his house."

"I'm not with you Kate. The freehold belongs to an investment company based in Jersey. I don't know Lord Fitzgerald."

I get a flutter of apprehension. "You must know the Fitzgeralds, they've lived here for centuries?"

"Yes, I am aware of that, but I have never met him, and I don't know why he thinks he's the owner. Maybe he's a trustee or shareholder?" I really want to believe him. I could do without another surprise.

"Yes, that's probably it. Thanks Jeremy."

I end the call, deflated. I set out to do a little detective work, experienced a frisson of pleasure at the mild chicanery, and have been punished by the planting of another seed of doubt. Sara's words as I left the church on Sunday are part of it.

'Be careful, John knows who you are' has more than one interpretation. On a simplistic level, he knows I'm the tenant of Farrier's Cottage, but doesn't everyone? She may be implying he knows what type of person I am, that I won't give in to threats, but he hasn't had time to judge my character, unless his God has blessed him with a keen perspicacity. Does he recognise me from the past, or is she accusing me of being the whore of Farrier's Cottage? If the former, I would surely remember and if the latter, she would have surely used 'what' rather than 'who'. Ultimately, I know who I am and that's all that matters, but it's still unnerving, as unnerving as Edmund asking, *'Who are you?'*.

***

I take a deep breath and knock tentatively on the door of the terraced cottage, part of me hoping no one's home.

"Naira, do you know Mrs Hawley?"

"You mean George's wife? Not very well. George used to come in regularly for a paper and a lottery ticket, but I only saw them together a couple of times. Quiet little soul as I remember. Why do you ask?"

"I wanted to offer my condolences, personally. Do you know where she lives?"

It takes a while and I decide to leave when there's a turn of a key, a clatter of bolts and the door opens a few inches. A bemused, little old lady stands there.

"Mrs Hawley?" She nods without reply. "I'm sorry to bother you. My name's Kate. I live in Farrier's Cottage." No reaction. "I just wanted to say how sorry I am about your husband." A blink, that's all. "If there's anything I can do…" I thrust a small bunch of flowers I bought at N&N and smile sheepishly. "I brought you these." She takes the flowers and looks dumbly at them.

"You'd better come in."

"I don't want to intrude."

"Come in. I'll make us a cup of tea."

I step straight into a sitting room that smells fusty, a blend of coal smoke, stale cooking, and damp. The heavily patterned carpets are shiny and threadbare, the paintwork yellowed and scuffed, the furniture worn, and faded curtains hang limply in front of grey curtain nets. A single light bulb dangles from the ceiling under a frilly shade.

"Sit yourself down," she say, waddling off into the kitchen, and I take a moment to assess which is the most appropriate seat for a visitor. The battered leather armchair by the fire would have been George's I guess, so I sit on a hard chair by the window. She's back in five minutes with a plastic tray, and pours from a brown teapot into ancient, chipped crockery. "What did you say your name was?" she says, lowering herself gently into a ripped and stained wingback chair, cup and saucer rattling in a shaky hand.

"Kate."

"Kate," she says. "Nice of you to come round. Don't get many visitors." I notice the absence of family photographs apart from one on the mantlepiece, a young man in army uniform.

"It's the least I can do. Do you have any family?"

"Boy, but he won't come. Not before the funeral."

I sip the tea. It's very strong and I try not to wince.

"That's a shame."

"Well they didn't get on, did they? Once he was all grown up he was off. Hardly seen him since."

"He didn't get on with George?"

She lets out a derisory laugh. "No one got on with George. He made it his business to pick a fight with everyone round here, including his boy. He would have upset you too, being in that blasted cottage." I decide it's better neither to confirm nor deny; my problems are of no significance compared to hers. "Well, he's met his maker now. He can go and moan on about Farrier's with his father and grandfather."

"I'm sorry for your loss."

"Probably brought it on himself. Probably picked on someone who'd had a few like him and took umbrage and got into a punch-up and, well he was eighty-two you know?" she says nodding in agreement with herself. I was expecting the grieving widow, and either she's putting on a brave face or she really means it. "Used to slap me, you know. After I had Simon. I was covered in bruises and couldn't go out in case the neighbours gossiped. I pulled a kitchen knife on him one day and told him to keep his hands off me. Then he stopped."

"I'm sorry."

"They was a bad lot them Hawleys. I remember his grandad. He had an evil look about him, he did. And his dad was just the same. He never got over his mum so I heard, but that was years ago, before I was born." I'm in danger of getting Mrs Hawley's entire life story, but I don't have the heart to interrupt her or make excuses and leave. "They was all bad towards their women. Oh, they could turn on the charm if they wanted to, but deep down they hated them."

"Women?"

"Misogynists," she declares proudly. "That's what they were. Bitter, twisted, women-hating bastards! Sod the lot of them." I fear the conversation is spiralling out of control and having wound her up, I need to do something to calm her down.

"Where does your son live?"

"Simon? York. He's married with three kids, but I only ever seen them a couple of times"

"Maybe you'll see more of them in future."

"Doubt it. They won't come here. Think the place is cursed so they do and it's all the fault of them Hawleys. He wouldn't leave it alone and Jacob and Albert were just the same."

"You mean the cottage?" My attempt to change the subject derailed, I might as well get another perspective on Oakdale's long-running feud.

"Him and his dad made sure no one would live there in peace. If a Hawley couldn't live there, then no one else would."

"What did they do?"

"Little things at first. Telling them they had no right to be there. Bad-mouthing them down the pub, spreading rumours about the wives. But then it got worse, accusing the men of sheep stealing, letting a fox into their chicken run and smashing the odd window. Once Albert caught a rat and nailed it to the front door. Folks never lasted more than a few months before they were off and then the place was empty for years and years and going to rack and ruin because word got round and no one wanted to live there. Then in the seventies after Albert died, George told everyone the place was haunted by the ghost of grandad Jacob and then folks found strange things happening."

"Like what?"

"You know. Objects moving around. Pipes making a terrible clanking noise in the night and dead crows coming down the chimney. And then there was the signs."

"What signs?"

"Folks had words like 'Thief' and 'Murderer' and 'Child Molester' painted on the walls." It all sounds chilling and not a little familiar.

"What about… 'Whore'?"

"Yes! That girl Jennifer had 'Whore' painted in big white letters on the front door where everyone could see. It was disgusting and I told him to stop it, but he denied it were him and said it was the ghost of his grandad. He wouldn't let it go. Said it was won fair and square and he wouldn't rest until Lord Fancypants gave it up."

"Did you know the girl who rented it before me?"

"No. But I heard he was horrible to her and drove her out. Well, it's all over now. There's no Hawleys left apart from me and my son and we don't want it. You shouldn't have no trouble there now."

I thank Mrs Hawley for the tea and go to leave, again offering my help if she needs it.

"I can live out my days in peace now," she says opening the front door. "And so can you. I'm pleased to meet you at last. You got what's rightfully yours."

***

Another invitation in the same style as before. An envelope pushed through the letterbox containing a card with a minimalist message. *Come to dinner Friday, 7pm. Edmund.* Again, there's no request to RSVP, nor any phone number to accept, decline or communicate at all. It's vaguely irritating; another summons from his overbearing Lordship, but equally, I know if I simply failed to show up, he would take no offence. He would just file me under 'disappointing' and never speak to me again.

I'm less flattered this time. *Who are you?* Edmund's question rings in my ears and I'm no closer to understanding what he means by it. But now I have a question for him. After my chat with Jeremy Jones, his claim to be my landlord has been cast into doubt. I don't believe Edmund would knowingly mislead me; it serves no purpose. If I hadn't gone 'snooping', he would have no idea I even existed, but then if he were the landlord, he would be aware that an agent is collecting rental income, or not.

Jeremy calls me back; the number he dialled for Jackie Thomas is unobtainable. Sorry.

CHAPTER 12

It's a bright, fresh morning to go for a walk and clear my head. I hope getting outside and away from the village for a few hours will change my perspective on recent events and give me space to think. I've written a letter to Jackie Thomas at her last known address, asking her to get in touch. I have little expectation of a response but it's worth a try. I drop it in the post box in the High Street.

Footpaths go off in all directions. I choose one that's signposted 'Willow Dale' and it takes me through a cleft in the landscape with limestone cliffs either side and a meandering stream that runs alongside the trail. It's cool, crisp, and sunny and being in the fresh air gives me a sense of wellbeing. After a while, the ragged limestone subsides, the land flattens out and the stream widens into a small river. In a clearing, I encounter some derelict buildings, ruins of an industrial past. A warning sign advises people to keep away from crumbling structures and be wary of hidden sink holes. Alongside, an information board offers a brief history of lead mining in the area. Inevitably, the Fitzgeralds feature prominently.

It tells me lead had been mined in the area for three hundred years before the Fitzgeralds came to the Dales and it made them wealthy until the mine closed in the middle of the nineteenth century. I'm left to speculate how much of their wealth was squandered by Lord Julian in pursuit of his nefarious activities. But it's another reminder of Oakdale's infamous dynasty and each time, I learn a little more of how it touched the lives of others.

The late George Hawley, his entire life devoted to settling an ancient grudge. *I'll give you six month.* His long-suffering wife Ethel, herself a victim of his aggression, tolerating her husband's obsession until the end. *I'm pleased to meet you at last.* Reverend John Lee, divorcee, and his second wife Sara, their irreverent style incongruous in a village with an elderly population and conservative values. *John knows who you are.* Naira and Nirvaan, the only immigrants I've seen, yet who, in their own words, hail from Bradford. *The lady before you received similar treatment.* The Gibbs family, close-knit, born and bred in Oakdale, ear to the ground and inquisitive. *He won't be bothering you no more.* And Lord Edmund himself, an aristocratic hermit, purporting to keep a distance from anyone and everyone but prepared to engage with someone whose identity is a mystery to him. *Who are you?*

I'm a common thread by default. I have no conceivable connection with any of them; just someone passing through a place in time and who, through circumstance, has become a focus for their attention. I think of my predecessor in Farrier's Cottage and wonder whether she'll reply to my letter and equally, whether I'm prepared for it.

I decide to return home, but something catches my eye; a brick archway built into a grassy hump behind one of the buildings, the entrance barred by a rusty iron grille. I'm tempted to explore further and pick my way carefully across boggy terrain. A crooked sign dangling from the grill warns: *'Danger, Keep Out'* and I peer inside but there's little to be seen other than a few stone steps that disappear down into a black void. I feel a shiver and pull the zip of my jacket up to my neck. Time to go home.

***

The house is curiously dark and if I had not been invited, I would have guessed there was no one home. I ring the doorbell and wait on the porch steps clutching the carnations, staring up at the full moon that shines bright on a warm evening.

A light comes on in the hallway. There's a rattle of keys and a clunking of bolts before the door opens and his Lordship appears. He's dishevelled, bleary-eyed, and from the look on his face, not a little confused.

"Oh, it's you," he says without any semblance of charm. "What do you want?" It's as if the tenuous friendship we established last week never occurred. I've become a disappointment.

"You invited me for dinner."

"That was last week," he says gruffly.

"You invited me again, this week."

"Why would I do that?"

"How should I know?"

"Are you sure?"

I'm hurt and embarrassed and suddenly not in the mood to debate which one of us made a mistake, if indeed that's what it was. I thought it unusual to be asked back again so soon, but I got the impression he liked my company, and he might be lonely. And anyway, I was only obeying orders. I've had enough.

"Of course I'm sure!" I snap back at him. "You sent me one of your curt little summonses and here I am again, as directed, at the appointed hour. If you had the good sense to put a phone number on there, I might have called to thank you and we might have cleared up any confusion at the time. Instead, you've wasted my time and now I'm wasting yours!" I thrust the flowers at him. "Here! These are for you. I'm off. Thank you for a lovely evening." He looks at the flowers but doesn't take them.

"You received an invitation?"

"Yes! Why else would I be here?"

"Show me."

I'm ready to explode. "I didn't know I needed to show it to gain entry. It's not a ticket to a fancy-dress ball, it's just a scribble on a piece of card, like last time. Or do you simply not believe me?" Edmund sighs and shakes his head as if trying to engage his thoughts.

"No. Of course not. That's not what I meant."

"Then what did you mean?"

"You'd better come in." He turns and shuffles off down the hall. I'm tempted to throw the flowers after him and flounce off, but a flounce is all it would be. I swear under my breath and follow the silly old duffer down the hall and into the kitchen. There is no evidence he was expecting me or anyone else. Crockery, glasses, empty bottles, pots and pans are strewn everywhere. A half-eaten loaf of bread sits on a wooden board amongst a pile of its own crumbs next to an open bottle of milk, and a packet of porridge has keeled over spilling its contents onto the island worktop. Next to it, a lump of cheese sits forlornly, dry and cracked around the edges and the butter dish is uncovered, the silver knife embedded in its mouldering contents. The dining table is laden with dirty dishes stacked at one end: soup bowls, small plates and cups jockey for position with Czech crystal and red wine glasses, all gradually encroaching on the single place at the head. Edmund is nowhere to be seen but I hear a tell-tale clink and he reappears with a champagne bottle and two crystal glasses.

"Not for me," I say haughtily, despite craving something to settle my nerves. He ignores me and proceeds to open it. "Cleaner on holiday?" I ask with more derision than is called for. He fills two glasses and holds one out to me even though I'm glaring at him.

"I'm afraid dinner is going to be a bit tricky," he says as I reluctantly take the glass, desperately trying to stifle the urge to grin but it's no good, even if I am still cross.

"I can see that." We chink crystal and as usual, one sip tells me the Veuve is chilled to perfection, something I can take for granted in this house. I take charge. "Right! We're going to tidy up first." He looks at me with a bewildered expression and takes another drink. "Put that down," I say, placing the crystal glass carefully on the table. "Have you got any rubber gloves?"

"Probably." I let out a sigh, sorely tempted to despatch him to get himself tidied up, but that would be too insulting.

"Best you sit down. I'll call you when I need you." Edmund takes no persuading and wanders over to the dining table clutching the champagne bottle. I locate the dishwasher and begin to stack the crockery and glassware, while the sink fills with warm soapy water.

"I asked you to show me the invitation merely so I could establish whether I did indeed write it or whether it's a forgery."

"You don't remember giving it to Marian to deliver?"

"When did you get it?"

"Wednesday, I think." I dump dirty pans in the sink and gather up the foodstuff. The fridge is almost bare apart from some random lumps of cheese and a few wizened vegetables.

"Then it must be a forgery. Marian walked out last weekend."

"Why?"

"Why must it be a forgery?"

"No. Why did she walk out?"

"She wanted more money and I refused."

"Why did she want more money?" I say, scrubbing at scrambled egg welded to a non-stick pan.

"She said that she had to do a lot more work than before and it was taking longer and longer."

"I bet you gave her short shrift."

"I suppose I did. She caught me at a bad moment that's all," he says, but I can sense his contrition. "The truth is, Eleanor used to do a lot of the housework herself, and Marian was just the hired help. But since Eleanor passed away, well, you know, the house has got into a bit of a state."

"So Marian was perfectly justified in pointing this out?"

"Yes, I suppose so."

"So, what are you going to do? Get down on your knees and ask for forgiveness?" I know Edmund is too stubborn for that and he confirms it with a grunt.

"I think that bridge is well and truly burnt."

"Come and dry up." He gets to his feet dutifully and I toss him a tea towel. "I can't believe Marian posted a forged invite through my letterbox in a fit of pique. As gestures of retribution go, it's pretty tame. All it does is embarrass you and inconvenience me. Hardly World War Three, is it?"

"I might be able to tell from the handwriting."

"Well, it certainly fooled me, but it's back at the cottage. Anyway, maybe you did write it and gave it to someone else to deliver."

"Who?"

"How should I know? If you forgot you wrote it, you could have forgotten who you gave it to."

"God help me."

"I wouldn't rely on it. I think you burnt that bridge too."

"I mean maybe I'm developing dementia or something?" It brings me up short, thinking of dad's sudden decline and the impact of his condition on mum and I forget where I am for the moment. Edmund reaches over and gently takes from my hand the frying pan I've been holding over the sink. "Can't be having that. If something is going to take me, I want it to be quick." I snap out of it and carry on scrubbing.

"It's no matter. Help is at hand."

"And very welcome it is too."

I remember suddenly. "Oh gosh! Did you hear about poor George Hawley?" He sighs and his expression turns grim.

"Yes, I did. Terrible business. Police came round to ask if I knew anything. Didn't of course. Have they spoken to you too?"

"Spoken to everyone I think."

"I mean, after that trouble he caused you." It still leaves a nasty taste and I'm reluctant to talk about it. George was beastly to me and went to his grave before we ever had a chance to be friends, if that were ever possible in the circumstances. His time is passed. There had never been nor will there ever be justice for the Hawleys.

***

It takes another hour to return the kitchen to working order and to consume the Welsh Rarebit I made from his meagre resources. We sit quietly, swirling a vintage Claret, listening to the clock.

"Maybe it was a ruse." I say eventually.

"What was?"

"The invitation. A ruse to entice me here and tidy up for you." I'm smirking, but he hasn't seen the joke.

"I would never do anything so duplicitous and dishonourable." I place a hand on his arm and give it a squeeze. It's the first time I've initiated physical contact. *Must be the wine.*

"I'm just teasing Edmund. I know if you wanted me to help, you'd simply ask. At least, I hope you would."

"Tell me about yourself, Kate Duvall. Where you're from, why you're here. Do you have family?" *Who are you?*

Last week's parting comment took me aback, as if he sensed something untoward in my uncannily accurate depiction of ancient events. If he's still suspicious, his questions might be a way of finding out, although my impression is he's simply interested, making conversation. It's fair to say I know a lot more about the Fitzgeralds than he does about me and it's not unreasonable I should share some personal details with him. They're perfectly innocuous.

"Born in Wimbledon, brought up in Wimbledon, educated in Wimbledon, degree in English Lit. from UCL, left home and shared a flat in Wandsworth with my friend Mandy until she selfishly went off and got married. Had several jobs, worked as a freelancer, lived with my boyfriend, broke up with boyfriend, came here instead."

"And your parents?"

"Lived in Wimbledon all their lives but retired to the south coast about five years ago."

"And are they well?"

"No." I could just as easily have said 'yes' and that would have been the end of it; Kate Duvall's potted history in three sentences. But I don't mind talking about it and despite his unpredictability, I like Edmund. I feel I can trust him.

"Dad's got Alzheimer's."

"Oh dear. I'm sorry about that. Forgive me if I sounded flippant about my impending dementia."

"You weren't to know. But he's gone downhill rapidly, and mum is finding it difficult to cope. I really should go back there and help, but she doesn't want me to, and anyway, I'm not qualified. He's going to need specialist help and soon he'll have to go into a home. She will too."

"I'm sorry. Are you an only child?"

Alcohol induced tears are welling up, an indelicate swig of Claret required to cover it, and I find I have to clear my throat before continuing. "No. I have a sister, Clare. She's in hospital, in a coma. She's unlikely ever to come out of it, or so they say. They're just waiting to switch her off."

"Oh dear," he says again because there's little else to say.

"That's why I remember the date so well."

"Date?"

"The day Eleanor died."

"Valentine's day. I'll never forget it either."

"It was the day I came to view the cottage. Clare insisted on driving me, said we'd have a girlie day out. Took us three hours to get here but we had great fun and she agreed with me the cottage was charming, if a little crusty and decrepit. I think she was jealous because she said she was determined to find one the same and get out of London." I'm smiling at the reminiscence and he's smiling back at me, and I want the story to end there, happily ever after, but I know it doesn't.

"We got back to London, it's dark and raining heavily and the traffic is terrible, and Clare is tired and frustrated because she wanted to get back in time for her yoga class and it's clear she's going to be late." I can hear the wipers thumping feverishly, back and forth, rain hammering down on the roof, the glare of lights from all directions. "We're stationary at traffic lights and she's urging them to change, hands banging the wheel. I tell her to chill, but she ignores me then lets out a gasp, like she's been winded. She's staring in the mirror, terror in her eyes, and floors the pedal. It's a red light at a busy crossroads and there are blinding headlights to our right bearing down on us and the deafening blast of air-horns and then…bang."

"Good lord."

"I wake up in hospital. They said I climbed out of the wreckage in a daze, but otherwise unscathed. I don't remember anything else. It's a miracle we survived at all, but Clare…" I take another drink even though I know I shouldn't, "…Clare suffered multiple fractures, legs, arms, ribs, punctured lung and catastrophic head injuries. There's a machine keeping her body alive, but her brain…"

"I'm very sorry to hear that."

The kitchen clock continues its circuit, a lone voice in the aural void, marking the inexorable march of time. I note it's already nine-thirty.

"I should be going."

"Not yet." It sounds like an instruction, but it's just Edmund. "I need to ask you something."

"Ask me what?"

"You displayed an extraordinary intuition regarding the ancient history of my troubled family…"

"I told you, it was just…" he holds up a calming hand and I fall silent.

"…I know. I believe you imagined it. I'm just nonplussed, that's all. No one gives two hoots about the damn cottage or what happened afterwards, apart from poor old George of course, but something about the sorry saga has touched you and that touches me. We have something else in common too. We both lost someone precious on the same day."

"Coincidence."

"I'm the last one to believe in fate, miracles, or divine intervention, so I'm inclined to agree with you. Nevertheless, and for whatever reason, here we are."

"What was your question?"

"Come and live here."

It's the last thing I expect, and I'm not prepared for it.

"That's not a question."

He sighs deeply. "Will you consider leaving my cottage and coming to live here?"

"Why?"

"Because I'm asking you."

"That's not an answer! Anyway, it's not your cottage." I had intended to raise the issue, but because the evening hadn't gone to plan, it had slipped my mind. It's also useful in diverting him from his wild proposition.

"What are you talking about?"

"It's not your cottage. It's owned by some property company."

"Balderdash!" he says gruffly. "Where did you get this nonsense?"

"The agent."

I can see Edmund getting wound up, a growing look of outrage forming on his face, but the fact is, he provoked me with his ridiculous suggestion and his alcohol is fuelling my response.

"Snooping! I knew it!"

"I was *not* snooping!" I shoot back. "I merely rang the agent to ask him if he had a number for Jackie Thomas."

"Who's he?"

"*She* was the previous tenant at Farrier's Cottage."

"Never heard of her."

"No of course you haven't. You would never have heard of me if I hadn't come *snooping* around, as you put it."

"Why did you want her number?"

I hesitate to answer this one. I'm not sure if I want to tell Edmund about the graffiti as I don't know how he'll react and anyway, I want to deal with it myself. I'm also embarrassed to mention it, for some irrational reason.

"Doesn't matter. But I told Jeremy…"

"Who?"

"Jeremy, the agent."

"Never heard of him."

"Exactly!"

"I'm not with you."

"Just listen!" He's startled by my outburst but he's driving me mad, so I must do something to calm us both down. Edmund puts on a face like a recalcitrant child and folds his arms. I continue slowly and calmly, fighting the soporific effects of the wine. "I mentioned in passing I had met the landlord, Edmund Fitzgerald, and he said he'd never met you and that the cottage was owned by some company."

"There's some mistake."

"There certainly is."

"Eleanor owned the cottage, not me, but it amounts to the same thing. Financial advisor told us to put it in her name about forty years ago. Tax reasons. I had a good income and she didn't, so we put it in her name to save a bit of tax."

"You've seen no rent for forty years?"

He shrugs. "No."

"And you haven't noticed anything awry since she died?"

He waves a hand in the air. "Eleanor dealt with it all. She handled all financial matters. I don't know what she did with the money, and I don't care," he says defiantly. "She's gone and nothing matters anymore."

I try to rationalise what he's saying. Edmund has been living in a bubble of his own making since Eleanor died, unable to function on anything other than the most primitive level, as if waiting for his own time to join her.

"What of her affairs?"

"I don't understand."

"Her accounts, investments, things: clothes, jewellery, possessions?"

"They're still here," he says meekly, as if the awful truth is just beginning to dawn on him. "Plus, a big pile of unopened mail."

"Have you told anyone Eleanor has died?" He gives me a mournful look and slowly shakes his head. "Oh, Edmund. What am I going to do with you?" He has no answer to that, so I get to my feet. "I'll make us some coffee."

***

The clock strikes ten as the coffee pot comes to the boil. Edmund has been uncharacteristically subdued and for the first time, looks vulnerable and lonely. I pour two cups, the crockery chipped and cracked. He's been thinking.

"You see, that's why I want you to come and live here."

"What? To clean the kitchen and sort out your personal affairs?" It sounds unduly harsh but I'm still a little agitated despite the effects of the wine. His eyes light up.

"Would you like a brandy?"

"No!" I say a little too quickly. "Thank you, but I've had quite enough to drink for one evening."

He nods sagely.

"You're right, and no, I don't want you to take Marian's place. I want you to take Eleanor's."

I feel a nervous chill and suddenly wish I had accepted the offer of brandy. I've never been proposed to before, had never imagined how it might come about nor what I might say when it did. Even if I had, way down the list of possibilities would be an eighty-five-year-old widowed peer of the realm. I need him to clarify before it gets embarrassing.

"What on earth are you saying Edmund?"

"I'm dying Kate, and I don't want to die alone. I would finish myself off now if I had the courage, but I don't. I have nothing to live for and nothing to look forward to other than being reunited with Eleanor."

"You don't do God, but you're preparing for the afterlife?"

"Nothing to do with him, it's all in here," he says, patting his chest. "The only thing I have that makes each day remotely tolerable is the thought of being with her."

"You must have loved her a lot."

"Yes, I did. I still do, but I'm lonely. More than anything I need a companion, and on a practical level, someone who can get everything in order, help me plan for the grand exit, and ultimately, hold my hand as I slip away."

"Are you sick?"

"I beg your pardon?" He suddenly looks offended. "I may be feeble in many ways but I'm perfectly compos mentis."

"That's not what I meant. I mean, do you have a terminal condition?"

"Not that I'm aware of."

"Are you on medication?"

"The odd aspirin."

"Then you could go on for a long while yet."

"But I don't want to."

"Well barring sticking a finger in a plug socket or throwing yourself down the stairs, it's pretty much out of your control."

"Which is why I need help to sort things out, before I lose my marbles and leave one unholy mess behind."

"Why do you care? You'll be dead."

"Allow me some self-respect, please. As the last Fitzgerald to walk the earth, I won't be the one to let the side down."

It would be a reasonable and understandable premise for most people. Anyone with a semblance of pride in their family history, especially with no means of perpetuating it, would wish to leave a positive legacy. Somehow, it doesn't fit with Edmund. I have no choice but to come out with it.

"Are you asking me to marry you?"

He looks aghast. "Heavens no!" he exclaims. "Why on earth would you want to do that?" I was asking myself the same question. "I assure you my intentions are totally honourable."

"Just wanted to clear that up."

"Good lord. I'm sorry if I gave you that impression."

"It's fine, but what you're asking is not that much different. People will talk, you know."

"Let them! None of their damn business."

I'm suddenly reminded of the visit from DI Stride. "The police came back."

"Yes, they came back here too."

"They know I've been here a couple of times. They probably know I'm here now."

"Let them! Imbeciles, suggesting I bumped off Hawley just because he bore a grudge. I told them he'd threatened me many times over the years. It's a miracle they didn't find me face down in the mere."

"And they're fishing for a link between George and his intimidating behaviour towards me..."

"Are they indeed?"

"...insinuating you and I are, well..."

"What?"

"...more than friends."

"Fools!"

I would have spared both Edmund's and my own embarrassment by not mentioning the graffiti, but somehow its now apposite. "Someone painted the word 'Whore' on my front door."

"They did what? That's outrageous. Who did?"

"Well, it could have been George, or it could have been someone else who wants me out of the cottage. Someone who knows I've been here, jumped to conclusions and wants to punish me. The same person or persons told the police about the row at the Parish Council."

"Cowards!" proclaims his Lordship. I have a fleeting vision of a dashing young nobleman drawing his sword in defence of a lady's honour.

"I'm led to believe Jackie Thomas suffered similar treatment. That's why I was trying to contact her. She may have known who it was."

"And does she?"

"I had to write her a letter. It will take time to get a reply if I get one at all."

"That damned cottage," he mutters, "been nothing but trouble all my life."

"Did you never think of giving it to old George, just to shut him up."

"Eleanor and I discussed it from time to time, but I refused to give in to threats and intimidation. If Hawley had exhibited one ounce of civility towards me, I might have considered it, but his obsession, and that of his father before him, drove him to the edge of insanity. He was not someone to be reasoned with."

"Well, neither Mrs Hawley nor her son are going to pick up where George left off."

"How do you know?"

"I went to see her, to offer my condolences. Turns out she was a victim too." The clock chimes eleven and catches both our attention. "I must be going."

"What about my suggestion?"

"I shall need time to think about it Edmund. It's a big decision for me and it's come out of the blue. I hope you don't mind."

"Of course not. Take as long as you like. I'll try not to trash the kitchen in the meantime," he says with a mischievous glint in his eye.

***

I can't sleep, thinking about Edmund's suggestion whilst listening for another attack on my front door. If his invitation was a forgery and not some severe lapse of memory, then whoever did it probably saw me leave the cottage and perhaps saw me return. If Edmund had written it and simply forgotten, then he also forgot who delivered it, and given his fallout with Marian, it's couldn't have been her. I checked the invitation again and there was nothing to suggest it didn't come from him, but I can't compare the handwriting to the previous one because I threw it out. It's possible Edmund contrived to get me there to see the mess he was in, garner some sympathy and then spring his proposal on me, but unless I've seriously misjudged his character, he's not one for subterfuge.

His proposal is perplexing and as far as I can see, fraught with difficulty. I feel sorry for him, an old man desperate not spend his last years alone, but that's something many people have to bear. It has its attractions. It might be stimulating to live in a grand house and spend time with him, talking about his past and the origins of the family, but I'm hardly qualified to review and advise on financial or legal matters any more than I am to offer support when, inevitably, he succumbs to illness. I accept such an arrangement would be nobody's business but ours, but I can't escape the conclusion it would be regarded with cynicism at least, and at worst contempt. *Whore!* The barb has more substance when I'm living at his Lordship's pleasure. It's just not possible, and next time I see Edmund, I shall explain why. I left him my phone number so he could call me, but I neglected to take a note of his, so I either must wait or go back and see him in person.

CHAPTER 13

The bells are ringing joyously at St John the Baptist this afternoon, so I slip on my coat and wander off in the direction of the church. It's a wedding and I'm delighted to see people dressed in their finery, joyful and exuberant on the happiest day of a young couple's lives. I keep a reasonable distance because I'm not suitably dressed, never mind invited. *Snooping again.*

Tiffany Gibbs is standing arm in arm with an extremely tall, thin young man. She looks beautiful and elegant in her long white dress, clutching her posy and beaming through her veil. Alongside is her sister Melanie in purple and next to her Mr and Mrs Gibbs, smiling with pride. On the opposite side is another middle-aged couple I assume to be the groom's parents. Everyone in the crowd is holding a phone aloft, recording the proceedings, each planning their own digital clip of happiness going viral on social media.

"Lovely," says a voice next to me. It's Mrs Hawley, properly turned out in heavy overcoat and woolly hat, despite the warm weather. "I do like a good wedding," she continues. "Don't you Mavis?"

"Yes I do," says her companion, an elderly lady in similar garb who then cackles and puts her hand on Mrs Hawley's arm. "It's like saying me vows all over again." Mrs Hawley cackles with her.

"Hello Mrs Hawley. Are you well?" I venture.

"Oh, hello dear. Mavis, this is the lady in Farrier's Cottage."

"Kate," I say to avoid any difficulty. Mavis nods her head demurely but seems disinclined to speak. "Who's the groom?"

"That'll be Steve Marshall," says Mrs Hawley. "He lives in Bradwell, but they're planning to buy a house in Oakdale, so I hear. He's a painter, you know."

It hits a nerve, and I can't resist conflating two facts even though I know it's absurd. Someone with a paintbrush violated both my door and my honour, in order to intimidate me and potentially, drive me away. The young couple want to live in the village, Farrier's would make a perfect starter home, and he's good with paint. Stride asked if I knew him. I do now.

We're standing in an elevated position looking over the heads of the well-wishers. The groom is smiling and looking in our general direction at what or whom I can't tell but I smile back instinctively, enjoying the moment with them. He's twenty metres away, but his gaze is fixed, and I look around without thinking but discover there's no one behind us. He says something to his bride out of the corner of his mouth and she switches her gaze on me too. They look happy and benign but there's an inscrutable aspect to their expression; people who know something you don't, but won't say, preferring to stay aloof and enjoy another's discomfort. I'm instantly discomforted.

"Well, ladies. I must get back. Nice to meet you, Mavis." Mavis offers a polite but vaguely condescending nod.

"Bye bye my dear," says Mrs Hawley.

I turn away and almost collide with John Lee, who seems to have materialised out of thin air.

"Kate!" His black long-sleeved clergy shirt and white collar are pure vicar from the waist up, the faded jeans and scuffed leather boots down below, a curious contradiction. He looks over my shoulder, eyes on the happy couple, long hair wafting in the breeze. "Another one bites the dust."

"Sorry?"

"Weddings. Those two will never be happier than they are today, and that's the way it should be, but it's all downhill from here." I'm not sure whether to laugh or challenge his cynicism. I try a bit of both.

"That's a bit harsh for someone who's just married them in the eyes of God. I hope that wasn't part of your sermon."

"God no!" he says putting hands on hips. "Wouldn't spoil the party for anything."

"Aren't you still on duty?"

"No. They're done with me. They're going off to gorge themselves and get bladdered down at The Crown. I had an invite but told them I had a prior engagement. Come and have a coffee."

He turns away and wanders down the path before I can answer and I have to run to catch up.

"Bit cynical for a vicar, isn't it?"

"What? Imagining their long-planned nuptials to be a waste of time? It's a simple fact. The divorce rate is well over forty percent and rising, so their chances of making dotage together are near as dammit fifty-fifty."

"That's no reason for not getting married though. I don't think anyone goes into marriage expecting it to be anything other than permanent. Who would do that?"

We reach the wooden arch over the wrought iron gates, and he turns right, striding out purposefully away from the mere. "Why indeed. It's just something people do. A box in life that needs to be ticked. The next box is kids and the one after that, divorce most likely." I wonder if this is just sardonic humour or if he harbours a bitterness born of his own experience. "That's what happened to me," he says, as if reading my mind.

"Yes, Sara told me."

He stops suddenly.

"Sara told you what?" He looks serious, threatening almost, and I shrug to make light of it.

"She told me she was Mrs Lee number two, and the kids were from Mrs Lee number one."

"She told you I had kids?" he says, frowning, and I shift my weight to one leg and put my hands on hips; the body language of defiance. *Why does every conversation I have in this village turn into an inquisition?*

"I met them. At your church last Sunday."

"Oh," he says, and carries on without hint of explanation or apology. "Amber and I worked hard and played hard. Our parties were legendary, attended by a massive circle of appalling, so-called friends who brayed and boasted of their vulgar wealth. We gave hedonism a bad name. Getting married was all part of it. We didn't want the party to end," he says wistfully. He turns into a gate in front of an Edwardian villa that bears a sign; *The Vicarage.* I stop at the gate.

"Won't Sara mind? She's probably making Sunday lunch."

"Ha! Firstly, she doesn't cook and secondly, she's down at The Crown playing piano, entertaining the wedding party."

This is not good. I'm suspicious my every move is monitored, and word is bound to get out the Whore of Oakdale has visited the trendy vicar when his wife is elsewhere. I shouldn't feel uncomfortable, but I do.

"John, I think I'll pass on the coffee if you don't mind…" but he's already opened the door and gone inside. I find him in the kitchen pulling open cupboard doors and assembling ingredients. "John…?"

"I heard you."

"I think I should get back."

"What about a sherry instead?" he asks, plucking two schooners from a cupboard and retrieving a bottle from the fridge.

"Not on my own."

"I'll join you."

"Oh, I thought…"

He stops and looks at me. "You thought what?"

"Nothing."

He sighs and hangs his head theatrically. "What did she tell you?"

"Nothing."

"She told you about AA, didn't she?"

"She mentioned it."

"And you assumed we were both recovered alcoholics."

"What else am I supposed to think? Anyway, it's not a crime."

"Sara was, …is, an alcoholic. I was just there providing moral and spiritual support to all as and when required. She required it, and a lot more besides."

"I'm sorry."

He screws the top back on the bottle looking subdued. "As long as they don't invite her to join in the toast, she'll be okay. Trouble is, once she starts, she can't stop. Doesn't happen very often but..."

"I'm sure she'll be fine," I offer with no evidence to support it. "I should go."

"Wait!" he says, coming closer until he's much too close. "I wanted to say something, which is the reason I needed to get you alone. I know you've not had a good reception here in Oakdale, what with loads of gossip and the business with George and that horrible graffiti." I'm nervous about him getting me alone, and what he's going to say next. I've already formed the view the trendy vicar Reverend John Lee and his wife are not who they seem to be, but despite initial impressions, I owe them the benefit of the doubt, so I wait for him to continue. "What I'm trying to say is, be very careful of Edmund Fitzgerald." It doesn't go down well, and I take a step back.

"Why?"

He takes a step towards me and gives me a patronising look. I stifle the urge to slap him but only because he's a man of the cloth. "His family has a dark history, and a reputation passed down through generations. You don't inherit all that wealth and privilege without inheriting the baggage that goes with it."

"Is that so? And how would you know?"

"I've had a run-in with him."

"A run-in?" I emphasise the words because the phrase is melodramatic and absurd.

"A disagreement shall we say."

"When? He never goes to church."

"But his wife did. Lady Fitzgerald was a devout Christian. She was very active in the church, much to his Lordship's dismay. She made her views about him very clear, and I think, paid the ultimate price."

"What are you saying? Edmund loved his wife!"

The patronising look is back and it's profoundly annoying. "Is that what he told you? Then ask him about Jennifer, next time you see him," he says, pointing a finger. He's trying to throw me with facts, real or imagined, that might reveal how close I've become to Edmund Fitzgerald, his words clearly designed to provoke a reaction. I could say that I know all about 'Jennifer', but apart from Ethel mentioning the name, it isn't true and would be a risky strategy. It's time to leave.

"Bye John. Have a good day." I turn away, but he's caught hold of a wrist and tugs me back towards him.

"I'm trying to help you!" he says with a hiss, his eyes fierce and intense.

"Let go of my arm," I say calmly, but I can hear blood thumping in my ears and I'm genuinely afraid of this man, vicar or not. I stare at him until he slowly loosens his grip.

"Sorry. I didn't mean to…"

"Yes, you did. You know exactly what you're doing, and it won't work." *Why am I saying this?* I turn my back on him and take a few steps.

"I know who you are!" he shouts after me "and I know why you're here!" I want to keep walking, but I'm confused. Against all instincts my body turns me around to face him.

"You know nothing. You may be blessed with divine guidance and have a hot line to the heavenly father, but to me, you're just a bloke in jeans who's as screwed up as everyone else around here." He reaches out to the worktop as if for support. I walk out of the house, pulling my coat around me.

CHAPTER 14

My phone is displaying an unknown number. I usually ignore them, assuming they're cold-callers or scammers, and I figure if someone I don't know really wants me, they'll leave a message. But something makes me take this one.

"Kate Duvall."

"Miss Duvall. This is Freda Thomas. You wrote to my daughter Jackie." I sit up at my desk, pleased to get such a quick response.

"I did Mrs Thomas. Thanks so much for calling me."

"Are you a reporter?" The question is unexpected. It's direct, asked without qualification. I sense suspicion and feel a prickle of unease.

"Not really."

"Not really?"

"I'm a writer, but that's not why I wanted to get in touch."

"Then why do you want to contact her and how did you get this address?" I don't want to mention the post office giving it to me, but I don't want to lie.

"I live in Farrier's Cottage in Oakdale." No response. "Where Jackie used to live?" No response. "In the Dales."

"I know where it is!" she snaps. I have no idea how old Mrs Thomas is, but if she's of similar age to my mum she may suffer from the same lapses of memory and concentration that sometimes provoke anger. "How did you get this address?" Mrs Thomas is losing patience, having to repeat the question, and before I have time to respond she continues. "Why do you want to contact Jackie?"

"I was told your daughter was the previous tenant and I simply wanted to ask her about her time here. I had a few queries, and I thought she might be able to help me."

"I don't know what sort of game you're playing Miss Duvall, but I think it's in very poor taste."

"I assure you Mrs Thomas, there's no game."

"Who told you she lived there?"

"Lots of people. She was well known."

"And did these people tell you she was hounded out of her home?" She's getting more agitated by the second, and I wish now I hadn't troubled her, but at least I have confirmation that my experience is not unique and whilst unpleasant, probably not personal.

"I understand she may have been subjected to some form of intimidation that made her want to leave." The line goes quiet, but a faint hiss tells me she's still there. "Mrs Thomas?"

"Do I take it you have experienced something similar?"

"Yes, I have."

"My daughter called me in January. She was in tears." Mrs Thomas sniffs, tears of her own. "It wasn't the first time she'd called me in a distressed state, but this was much worse. She said there were dark forces at work. I told her to come home immediately, get away from there and those ghastly people. She packed up and left the next day."

"I'm sorry about that. How is she now?" I ask without conviction or optimism. The drumming in my ears has started again and involuntarily, I stop breathing.

"Get away from there Miss Duvall. Before it's too late."

"What happened? Tell me what happened." There's a numbing silence between us, the heartbeat pounding in my head.

"She was driving home to us, and she was in an accident." The rain, the thump-thump of wipers, the blinding lights and the deafening blast of horns followed by explosion, crushing impact, blackness, and silence; silence apart from the peep-peep of the life support machine. I don't have to ask because I know what's coming next. "She was killed."

The tragedy is somehow worse than my own and I want to embrace the poor woman and comfort her in her grief, but all I can think of is Clare and the incessant peep keeping her alive.

"I'm so sorry. I didn't know."

"They said it was an accident, but I will never accept it. Someone, or something was responsible." I risk prolonging her agony, but I sense Mrs Thomas wants to unburden herself to anybody who might listen. In the absence of convincing evidence, her pleas would be ignored and dismissed. A mother's intuition counts for nothing.

"Did she mention any names? People who may have upset her."

"There was an old man, but she never spoke his name. He behaved in a threatening manner towards her. He said the cottage belonged to him and she should leave."

"I think I know who you mean."

"She said the vicar and his wife helped her a lot, especially the wife."

"Sara?"

"Yes, Sara."

"Anyone else?"

"Yes. Worst of all were her landlords, a rich elderly couple who lived in a Manor house." I feel a chill. This is the last thing I want to hear.

"You mean Lord and Lady Fitzgerald?"

"Yes. I would strongly advise you to have nothing to do with them." *Be very careful, said John Lee.*

"Lady Fitzgerald died in February, Mrs Thomas. Before I moved in."

"Did she indeed? Forgive me if I don't shed any tears. And what of her husband?" I can't tell her I've had dinner there, I like him, and he's asked me to move in with him. It would be even more incomprehensible to her as it is to me.

"He's eighty-five, I believe, so not long for this world," I say, the disingenuous comment pricking my conscience, but I'm only repeating his own words.

"He's a monster. Leave Oakdale, Miss Duvall. For your own good."

***

The Crown is busy. People of all ages from small children to grandparents, families treating themselves to Sunday lunch and walkers in outdoor gear with their dogs.

I sit at the bar nursing a gin and tonic. I needed a drink, I needed to get out of the cottage, and I needed to interact with the world outside, meet some people I haven't met and perhaps, some who have no idea who I am. It's risky; the Whore of Oakdale sitting on a bar stool drumming up business is not a good look, but it's a risk worth taking. I've had a chat with nineteen-year-old Emma serving behind the bar and mercifully, she seems oblivious to village gossip, hailing as she does from nearby Thurston.

"I'm off to Thailand as soon as I can save the fare. Vietnam, Laos, Cambodia, then over to Oz for a bit and back to Bristol for Uni." She's brimming with excitement and optimism for the future which, at least for the next few years, is mapped out in her mind. The ten years between us seems like a lifetime. I wonder what crossroads Emma will encounter along the way and the path she'll take. No matter how clear you are about where you're going, life will throw obstacles at you. "Do you live in the village?" she asks, and I'm thrilled she seems not to know I live in the accursed cottage known as Farrier's.

"I have a cottage in the High Street, next to the Old Forge."

"Cool," she says. "I couldn't afford anything around here."

"It's just a rental."

"Even so. This time next year I'll be in a dingy flat share with a bunch of other students," she chuckles in irony, but I can tell she's looking forward to the adventure. "Not staying long them?"

"Not sure. I thought an escape to the country would be nice but, it's not working out as I'd hoped."

"I'd love to live in London."

"It has its attractions." No one took any notice of me, threatened me or called me a prostitute. I had friends nearby and family who were much closer than they are now, a boyfriend who kept me company and amused me when he wasn't being an arse and a sister who was alive and well. A lot has happened since I decided a life change was in order. "But I'd much rather be here. It feels more like home." *Why say that?* Emma attends to a customer then returns and wipes the bar.

"Would you like another one of those?"

I should decline. I've had nothing to eat, but I can't face eating a Sunday roast by myself, and today, bar snacks are not on the menu. "Go on then." I think of Jackie Thomas, that fateful day she ran away from Oakdale, the parallels with my own incident with Clare, and the death of Eleanor Forbes Fitzgerald, allegedly one of Jackie's tormentors. I briefly consider the notion all three are connected. *That's the alcohol, Kate. 'There are dark forces at work',* Jackie Thomas had told her mother the day before she died. Nothing I've experienced so far supports that assertion; however unpleasant it may have been for me. But then, one of our mutual tormentors has since been murdered. "Did you know that chap who was murdered?" I ask Emma as she brings my refill.

"George? No not really. I remember him coming in here and being a grump, but I never much talked to him. Alan knows better than me, don't you?" she says to a thirty something chap at the till.

"What's that?"

"That bloke George who got killed. He came in here a lot."

"Yeah, mostly weekends. He was here the night he… you know."

"What time did he leave?" I hear myself asking. Alan looks bemused and uncertain.

"You a copper?"

"No."

"I already told them…"

"I'm not police, just a local who's shocked someone in the village was murdered. It's all a bit too close to home." I sip my gin and stare at him expectantly.

"Well, he had several pints, and then about eleven he had a row with another bloke…"

"Do you know who?" I can't believe I'm asking, but I must sound as if I'm entitled to know because he doesn't hesitate. He's told the police the same thing and others will have witnessed it, so it's hardly privileged information.

"Yeah. Big Steve the painter."

"Steve Marshall?"

"Yeah. He was here yesterday. Him and Tiff had their wedding reception."

"Do you know what they were arguing about?"

"I never heard it myself, but someone else said George muttered something about Tiffany, and Steve got the hump and was going to deck him. Arthur and Barry calmed him down and Steve walked away. George had another pint before I threw him out around eleven thirty."

"Arthur? Arthur Needham?"

"Yeah."

"And who's Barry?" *Why does every conversation in this village turn into an inquisition, Kate?*

"Barry Wilson. He's got a dairy farm. I told the police all this."

"I'm not police, Alan." I say soberly, fearing I may nevertheless have slurred my words. *Drunken whore comes on to barman.*

"No."

"Can I ask you something else?" Emma and Alan stand to attention. "Do you know Lord Fitzgerald?" They both shake their heads.

"Heard of him," says Alan, "but that's all."

"Didn't know we had a lord around here," says Emma.

"The Fitzgeralds used to own this pub, back in the nineteenth century." It's useless information, the gin's making me garrulous.

"That right? Part of a chain now. Dale Inns, private equity backed," he says with a touch of gravitas. It's the faint whiff of flirtation, aimed at one or both of us. Mark was the same, charm making way for swagger.

I ask them if they knew Jackie Thomas but draw a blank, and as the pub empties and the staff reset the tables for the evening session, I head for home, names ringing in my ears. Steve Marshall and Arthur Needham, I already knew; Barry the dairy farmer and Alan the barman I didn't, but all witness to a dispute between George and Steve that may have had deadly repercussions. I don't know why it need bother me, the police are on the case and in due course the murderer will be found, but I don't expect the attacks on me to stop. Jackie Thomas was here six months before she was driven out 'by dark forces' and never lived to tell the tale. John Lee is right about something. I need to be careful, of everyone.

CHAPTER 15

I do some research online. I find Farrier's Cottage on the Land Registry and for a small fee, download a single page document that tells me the owner is Belles Fleurs Investments Limited, registered in Jersey. I find it listed at the Jersey Financial Services Commission but unlike Companies House, directors' names are not divulged. It's possible Edmund is a director or shareholder in Belles Fleurs and de facto owner of the cottage, but if so, he has either forgotten, which is hard to believe, or Eleanor sold it without his knowledge, which is even less plausible. He appears woefully ill informed about his own financial situation, so anything is possible, but even if he is connected to Belles Fleurs, there is no reason to lie about it or keep it a secret from me. It remains a mystery and not one worth pursuing unless I agree to Edmund's request that I help organise his affairs.

***

"Belles Fleurs? Never heard of it," comes the predictable reply from his Lordship. "Have you been snooping?" he continues, twinkle in his eye.

"You're the one who asked me to be your PA!"

"So you've agreed?"

"No I haven't. I just thought it was an easy one to clear up. The information is in the public domain so hardly confidential."

"Well, it's not good enough!" he booms.

"What isn't?" I continue to be exasperated by Edmund's non-sequiturs.

"That some company in Jersey owns my cottage and I don't know about it."

"Eleanor's cottage."

"Alright, alright. It's the same thing."

"She was an individual. If she wanted to sell the cottage and not tell you about it, then it's her right to do so." It sounds harsh. I understand a man of Edmund's generation and standing might find it difficult to accept his wife did something without his knowledge or consent. I wait for the explosion of rage, but he's not angry, just confused.

"Yes of course. I'm just astonished she didn't mention it. I wouldn't have objected you know. As far as I'm concerned Eleanor could do no wrong, but it's totally out of character. Do you know when it was sold?"

"No. But it must have been a while ago. At least before the letting agent was involved because he didn't know anything about it."

"Why would she do such a thing? It's been in the family for generations."

"Maybe she did it to end the feud with George Hawley once and for all and to rid the Fitzgeralds of the curse of Farrier's?"

"No, it's not possible. If Eleanor sold it just to shut George up, she would have told him and me and that would have been the end of it."

"But where's the money?"

"What money?"

"The proceeds of the sale. It must have been a reasonable sum."

"Oh yes. You see? That's why I need your help."

"Edmund…"

"I can't do this myself. I'm helpless."

"No you're not. You just think you are. Take your time and step by step you'll get everything sorted out."

"I haven't got time!"

"You keep saying that, but you tell me you're not ill and you're not on serious medication, that is, if you exclude the champagne." I wink at him, and he looks affronted, then bursts out laughing.

"Wonderful idea! It's coming up for twelve."

"No Edmund. Not today. I must get back. I have work to do."

"You have work to do here." I throw him a look of reproach and he raises both hands up in defence. "Alright. But just help me find out when Farrier's was sold and track down the money. That's all I ask." It sounds like the thin end of a very large wedge, but having now brought it to his attention, I can hardly refuse. I let out a sigh, just so he's in no doubt I'm indulging him. I'll find a solicitor to do the legwork and it will buy me more time to think. But there's something else I wanted to share with him, for no other reason than it's on my mind and still festering.

"Do you remember my mentioning Jackie Thomas?" He looks vague so I remind him. "The lady who rented Farrier's before me."

"Of course."

"George and others made her life a misery. That's the reason she left."

"How do you know that?"

"I told you I wrote to her."

"Did you? Yes, I remember." He clearly doesn't but it's no matter.

"Her mother called me. By her own account Jackie was so traumatised, she left without warning." I pause to make sure he's listening. "In January."

"I don't understand the relevance."

"Jackie was driving back to her parents in London when she died in a car crash."

"Good lord! That's..."

"Quite a coincidence."

Edmund reaches out for a chair and lowers himself into it. Despite professing never to have known Jackie, news of her death has had a profound effect on him.

"That damned cottage," he says, thumping a fist on the table. "All that conflict and bitterness, a century of feuding. It was cursed from the day Jacob and Julian went to war, and all over a game of cards." He casts me a look of concern and becomes agitated. "You must get out of there. You must come and stay here." It isn't the reaction I expected. I didn't mean to conflate the tragedy of Jackie's demise with my becoming his personal assistant, I just wanted to jog his memory and see if he had any antipathy towards her. There's no trace of a monster. Mercifully, I don't have time to answer as we're interrupted by the doorbell clanging loudly in the hall.

Edmund looks startled and goes off mumbling "Who the devil..?" under his breath. I hear a familiar voice, the officious timbre and tone unmistakeable My heart sinks. The last thing I want is to be here when the police call. Edmund reappears followed by Stride and his flunkeys. He should be surprised, but much to my annoyance, he's not. I wonder if they have been following me.

"Miss Duvall."

"Inspector."

DC Gerrard casts an eye around the room as if primed for some threat or hoping to strike lucky and find a blood-stained murder weapon lying somewhere. WPC Jenkins brings up the rear and stays by the door, her expression an irritating mixture of arrogance and satisfaction. Stride strolls around the island towards me.

"I'm pleased to find you here. Kills two birds."

I wish I hadn't come. My presence will fuel suspicion Edmund and I have something other than a platonic relationship. Worse, it might feed WPC Jenkins' salacious fantasies.

"What can I do for you Stride?" says Edmund, disinclined to show any respect for officialdom.

"We're still investigating the murder of George Hawley."

"Pleased to hear it," says Edmund. "Found the murder weapon?"

"No, but we're fairly certain Mr Hawley was killed by a single blow to the head with a hard object, hammer or similar. There was no water in his lungs which strongly suggests he was killed and then his body dumped in the mere to make it look like he'd drowned."

"Or more likely, to make sure," I suggest. "You would have to be fairly stupid to think a blow from a hammer wouldn't be spotted easily by forensics."

"Very impressive Miss Duvall."

"That's the power of TV."

"Perhaps you'd care to apply for a job?"

"Thanks for the offer, but I'm not going to be attracted to an organisation where, by all accounts, misogyny and prejudice are rife. What do you think, Jenkins?" The smirk evaporates and her face begins to twitch. Stride ignores the jibe. Gerard's poisonous look suggests I've hit the mark. I bet he'd like to train me, personally.

"I regret to inform you it's now become a double murder enquiry."

"What?" says Edmund.

"Do you know of someone by the name of Jeremy Jones?"

"Never heard of him."

"I do," I say, the drums starting all over again. "What's happened?"

"He was found dead in his car. Multiple stab wounds."

"Oh God!"

"Who is this chap?" demands Edmund. I feel faintly nauseous and take a deep breath. I note Gerard and Jenkins watching me closely.

"He's the letting agent for Farrier's Cottage. The one you say belongs to you," says Stride.

"Farrier's? No, no, no. It once belonged to me, but we sold it sometime ago."

"Do you remember when?"

Edmund makes a show of thinking. "Memory's not what it was. My late wife dealt with it. She was the administrative brains. I'm sure I can find out."

"If you would, your Lordship. That might be helpful."

"I don't see how. You don't think it has anything to do with George Hawley?"

"We don't think anything at the moment. We're just making preliminary enquiries. The cottage is a common factor."

"I'll contact my solicitor, once I remember who it is."

"Thank you, your Lordship. I understand you told Miss Duvall here that you were the owner?"

"A simple misunderstanding. I said I *was* the owner, as in 'used to be' the owner."

"We've already cleared that up, Inspector," I say. "It was Jeremy who told me the freehold was owned by an investment company."

"I see. When did you last speak to Mr Jones?" I swallow deeply and try to kick my memory into gear, then remember my phone and flick through the calls.

"Last week."

"And what was the nature of the call?" I know it's foolish and dangerous to withhold evidence from the police or mislead them, but they have no way of knowing what I know, unless I tell them. Jeremy was, of course, returning my call, but for some reason, I don't want to mention Jackie Thomas.

"It was just a courtesy call, to find out if I had settled in and was happy with the cottage." I know I sound nervous. I'm genuinely shocked at the news, but I'm also shocked by my own lie. I feel sick; my phone could betray me. The previous entry is the call from me to him. I'll have to delete it. *Are you crazy Kate? What the hell are you doing? Stride will ask to see the phone. You'll refuse because it's private and he has no right, he'll be instantly suspicious, he'll arrest and caution you and get a warrant and discover you lied. That's how it works, isn't it?* I haven't done anything, but already, I've put myself in the frame. Thankfully, he doesn't ask me to prove it. He can't, not without a caution.

"And during this conversation, you just happened to mention his Lordship?"

"I told him I'd met the landlord and that confused him. I then discovered I was wrong. It's no matter."

"But you've remained friendly?"

"Who has?"

"You and Lord Fitzgerald. Isn't that why you're here?" I try to control my anger at the impertinence. But I know the insinuation is deliberate. A provocation. It's what they do. I smile sweetly to let him know I know.

"Why I'm here is none of your business Inspector, but I shall tell you anyway. I'm here for an interview. Lord Fitzgerald has offered me a job as his PA." Stride spins around to look at Edmund who's grinning mischievously.

"I need help to tidy up my affairs. Miss Duvall's administrative skills will be invaluable."

"I see," says Stride.

"Her first task will be to discover exactly when my wife and I disposed of Farrier's Cottage." Edmund looks so pleased with himself, I want to slap him again, but the fact is I fell into a trap of my own making. My thoughts return quickly to Jeremy Jones.

"Did Jeremy have a family?"

"Wife and one child."

"How awful for them."

"If anything occurs to either of you, please call us. Good luck in your new job. We'll let ourselves out."

We wait until we hear the front door close before I say, "I need that drink." Edmunds rubs his hands together and retrieves a bottle and two glasses. Instinctively, I check the hallway to make sure they've gone.

"I know they're annoying but there's nothing to worry about," he says wrestling with the foil. "Rum old business about Jones though, even if I didn't know the chap."

"It's terrible. Another death connected to Farrier's."

He pours the champagne and I stare at the bubbles racing to the surface, thoughts in a whirl. Both John Lee and Freda Thomas warned me to be careful of Edmund, but apart from his initial outburst when we first met, I've come to regard him as a charming if eccentric old gentleman. Feelings are mixed about Eleanor, and I have no way of judging, except that, if I were to agree to unravel the Fitzgerald's financial affairs, a lot may become clear.

"Thank you for agreeing to help me," he says raising his glass. "I know you were reluctant, but I must get organised for an orderly exit."

"There you go again. If I'm going to help, we shall have no more talk of that. It's my only condition."

"Agreed."

"And I'll stay in the cottage for the time being thank you."

"No, I'm not happy about that. The place is cursed."

"That's my decision. Take it or leave it."

"Agreed," he says grudgingly, and consoles himself with a mouthful of Veuve. It feels odd sipping a drink meant for celebration when someone I know has been murdered. *It's to calm your nerves, Kate.*

"Now, I have to go home and do some of my own work. I'll be back tomorrow morning around ten and make a start on Eleanor's mail. Cheers."

***

I wake with a start. Echoes of a noise. The bedside light is on, and my laptop screen is black. I must have dropped off while working. I press a key and the screen lights up. It's gone two-thirty. I was woken by a noise I heard in slumber, and I listen intently for a moment, but there's only silence. I close the laptop and switch off the light hoping to go straight back to sleep, but I'm wide awake now, staring at the ceiling. I consider going downstairs to check the doors and windows are locked, but I know they are. It's the last thing I do every night.

I listen for sound from outside the front door, paintbrush on wood, footsteps, maybe even whispers, but there's nothing. Whatever noise woke me, it was not surreptitious, it was short and sharp and high pitched, neither wind, nor wind induced. It was the cry of an animal, a fox or an owl or a cat and then it comes again, distant, muffled, two anguished syllables.

"Jacob!"

The skin on my face tightens as I suck in breath and hold it, the familiar drumbeat building. I'm sure of what I heard and equally sure it's an illusion, an unwitting impersonation of a human by a dumb animal misinterpreted by a tired mind.

"Jacob!"

I let out a whimper. There's no mistake. It's a woman's voice and it's coming from downstairs. Someone is in the house. It's dark and it's the middle of the night, when imagination and fear supplant rational thought. The sound would be mildly puzzling in the light of day, but here and now it makes my flesh crawl, and I want to pull the covers over my head to make myself disappear. I wait for repetition, but seconds turn into minutes and silence prevails.

"Jacob!" A cry for help, followed by a loud bang, the sound of rolling thunder, heavy footsteps pounding up the stairs at speed, getting louder, coming closer… The bedroom door crashes open and I jerk upwards, letting out an almighty scream at the monster that's come to cut me and stab me and strangle me and bludgeon me to death in a bloody orgy of violence.

But there's nothing.

Nothing but the drumbeat in the head, the heaving chest, and the desperate search for oxygen to fill the lungs. I sit, body shaking, wet with sweat, lips trembling, staring at the open door. That's no illusion. The cottage is quiet again, and I wait for a signal but there is none. I must turn on the lights, I must get up and walk around. I must check, prove it was a bad dream, prove what it was, in order to prove what it wasn't. *The door flew open, that's no dream!*

A trembling hand extends to the switch on the bedside light and in the yellow glow of the dim bulb, the rational world comes back into focus. I slide out from under the duvet, fearful of a cadaverous hand grabbing an ankle as my feet touch the floor. I find slippers and dressing gown, and look around for a weapon, anything that might offer defence, protection, or at least, boost a flagging confidence.

There is nothing.

I step through the open door into the short corridor and onto the landing, slow and steady, stealthy as a stalking cat, hearing attuned for anything anomalous. I wait a few seconds, peek around the baluster down the stairs and into the darkness below.

There is nothing.

I reach for the light switch, fearful the monster will react, charge around in a frenzy, rear up and resume its attack. The click of the switch is loud, the light dazzling.

There is nothing.

One step at a time, hand on the rail, the fourth step down, as always, squeaking like a familiar friend, descending to the sitting room, where everything is quiet in the gloom. Another light switch and it's day for night. Everything is in place. No overturned chairs, lamps, ripped cushions, or evidence of intrusion, everything as I had left it. Apart from the red paint on the mirror over the fireplace, dripping like blood onto the mantelpiece.

WHORE

CHAPTER 16

I'm an hour late, but Edmund is there waiting on the porch, smiling broadly. I couldn't warn him because I don't have his number, but he seems unperturbed, having little concept of time other than when it's time to open a bottle.

I couldn't go back to bed after my ordeal. I checked all windows and doors for evidence of entry, but everything was secure. If I believed in ghosts, I'd blame a poltergeist for the bedroom door, but I suspect painting a vicious term of abuse on a mirror and then clearing paint pot and brush away, is beyond the scope of your average evil spirit. The thought someone entered my house is marginally more chilling, as were the plaintive cries calling out the name of a long dead resident. Furthermore, there was no forced entry, which means the intruder had a key and locked the door on the way out.

I placed a chair against the front door and took a hot shower, then dressed, made some strong coffee and sat down to consider the possibilities. The back door is secured by a mortice lock and barrel bolts top and bottom, ruling out entry without force, even with a key. The front door has a five-lever mortice lock and rim latch, each operable from either side of the door provided the snib isn't down, which it wasn't. *Note to self.* Assuming someone used keys to let themselves in through the front door, they would have plenty of time to paint the graffiti, let themselves out and leave me to find it the next morning.

But the intruder wanted more, wanted to terrify me with chilling sound effects before running up the stairs and kicking in the bedroom door. Then, in my state of terror and confusion, they made their escape. I thought about this a lot, and it didn't make sense. It would be a high-risk strategy, reliant on my being paralysed with fear and hiding under the bedclothes. Otherwise, I might catch sight of them, be armed with club or knife, or taken a picture on my phone before chasing them out. I think back to the moment the door flew open and I don't recall any other movement, not even a shadow. The perpetrator may have been intent on instilling fear but was not motivated to physical attack, otherwise, why leave so abruptly and why bother with the paint? The two actions simply don't go together.

I waited until the paint had dried before scraping it off with a razor blade. The letters bore a resemblance to the ones daubed on my front door, particularly the 'E' which was fashioned from an 'I' plus three horizontals, rather than an 'L' and two, suggesting it was written in the same hand. I called an emergency locksmith in Bradwell who arrived within the hour and replaced both rim latch and mortice lock on the front door. He also fitted barrel bolts top and bottom like those on the back.

By ten o'clock I had stopped shaking and fortified with toast and coffee, assessed the position. Apart from George Hawley's verbal aggression, I had been subjected to two physical attacks, the second far worse than the first. I shall never know if Jackie Thomas experienced the same unless she confided in her mother, but I'm loath to ask her and cause further distress. Jackie was here six months, and I've been here only one, but already I've been frightened out of my wits by someone who wants me out. I can pack up and move back to London but that's giving in and against all instincts. I would forever be haunted by this place if I don't find out who and why. If I accept Edmund's offer to live in the Manor, it amounts to the same thing and I'll be giving credence to the vile accusations of my tormentors. If I stay, I must accept the next attack will be more extreme than the last and in the light of last night's escalation, it does not bode well.

Jackie Thomas, former tenant, killed in an accident, but whose mother alleges foul play; George Hawley, murdered, Jeremy Jones, murdered. Eleanor Fitzgerald died too, although apparently through natural causes. My sister Clare, on life support following an accident after visiting this cottage. All deaths linked to Farrier's. It leaves me with a chill, feeling isolated and alone.

"I thought you had changed your mind," he says, standing aside to let me through.

"I'm sorry I'm late, Edmund. Something came up." I'm not going to tell him what happened. Two seemingly unconnected people have warned me about his Lordship and although it doesn't ring true, I've decided to be wary. I feel a trace of regret as Edmund clearly trusts me enough to open up his financial affairs to me, a relative stranger, but then, that's his decision. If I told him I had been threatened again, he would insist I came to live at the Manor and I'm not ready to do that.

"Well, if you were resident here, you would never be late, would you?"

"We've been through that Edmund. I don't think it's a good idea."

"I think it's a splendid idea."

"I know you do. You've said so. Please understand, I'm not ready to give up my independence just yet. I don't think helping you get your affairs in order will take a long time and I'm sorry, but I'm neither qualified nor ready to take on the role of full-time carer."

"I'm not doolally yet!" he says with mock outrage.

"You keep telling me you'll be dead soon."

"Well maybe now you're here I'll have reason to live?"

I don't know how to take that and I'm reluctant to get into deep debate about what he means. I want to believe he's being complimentary, but I don't know him well enough. I fear he's trying to put pressure on me by suggesting if he's left alone, his health will suffer, and I bear responsibility not to let that happen. It's worrying because the longer I spend here, the more needy he's likely to become. I just hope that I can clarify his financial position, and he'll be able to see a future of some sort, rather than the nihilistic view he has at present. In the meantime, I need to keep him at bay.

"Let's be clear Edmund, I'm not Eleanor and I'm not taking Eleanor's role. I'm here to shed some light, that's all."

"And a brighter light there can be none," he gushes, and I roll my eyes in exasperation. If he goes on like this and has no thirst for life, I may yet help him on his way. "The study's through there."

He leads me into an oak panelled room. French windows open onto the rear garden affording expansive views across the Dales. Floor to ceiling shelves like those in the drawing room cover most of two walls and are not only laden with books but also files and piles of papers. An antique desk is stacked high with loose paper and unopened mail. The only equipment in sight is a leather captain's chair, angle-poise desk lamp and telephone/fax machine.

"I take it she didn't use a computer."

"Heavens, no. We were too old for that. She used that phone contraption now and then but I've no idea how it works."

"I'll figure it out." I brought my laptop in case I needed to do some research, but for now, it appears a major tidy up is in order. "Did you get probate?"

"I'm not sure."

"Did you apply for it?" He shrugs, which rather answers the question. "Have you been in touch with anyone since Eleanor's death? Solicitors? Bank?" He looks blank. "Government? Pensions?"

"You see, that's why I need your help!"

I try my best not to show any frustration or laugh out loud. It would humiliate him, and he's right, he needs help. If he'd always relied on Eleanor to deal with the rest of the world on their behalf, and the rest of the world thinks Eleanor is alive and well, then goodness knows how much more complicated it's become since she died. And it's only getting worse by the day. I have no expertise, but some experience. Last year, Clare and I jointly administered the estate of our grandmother because my father's condition was deteriorating, and he was not in a fit state. Granny Duvall's estate however, comprised a bungalow in Beaconsfield, a bank account and a few thousand in premium bonds. I fully expect the Fitzgerald estate to be immeasurably more complex. I ask the next question with some trepidation.

"Do you have a death certificate?"

"Yes!" he says in triumph, waving a hand at the pile of papers on the desk. "It'll be in there somewhere."

"I'll find it." I slip off my coat and he rushes to help. "I'll hang it up in the hall and then make some tea."

He trots off and I survey the piles of paper on the desk, deciding it's best to open all the mail to find out if anything is urgent and in need of reply. I glance around the room, take in the scale of the task and a wave of depression hits me. It may just be delayed reaction to last night's trauma, but I feel it's more than that. I arrived in Oakdale a month ago, full of optimism and enthusiasm for the prospect of a new life in an idyllic setting, yet feel as if I've stepped into a parallel universe. On the surface, most things look familiar, but every day, something happens to suggest they're not and I dread to think what I might find buried in the lives of Eleanor and Edmund Fitzgerald, the last Lord of Oakdale. *What on earth am I doing here?*

CHAPTER 17

Summer sunlight reflects in the wake of a paddling duck, the ripples sparkling as they roll inexorably towards the bank. Further down the mere where the surface is unbroken, the church of St John the Baptist, flanked by ancient oak and beech, stands mirrored in the shimmering water. I'm sitting on a bench that was, according to its brass plaque, kindly donated by Mrs Margaret Hodgson way back in 1984 in memory of her husband Neville, *'a pillar of the community'*. I try to imagine Neville Hodgson sitting here today, taking in the view from his very own bench, contemplating the meaning of life, and wonder what made him a 'pillar'. I suspect the likes of Arthur Needham, Chairman of the Parish Council, might be in line for recognition of that sort, but I haven't had a chance to form an opinion. I doubt whether Edmund will be remembered fondly once he's gone. Popular opinion on the Fitzgeralds generally and his Lordship in particular, seems to range from scorn to outright hostility. I fail to understand this as I've seen nothing in Edmund's character to justify it although I expect I might find a clue as I delve deeper into his history.

I've taken a break from the Manor for a day or two while I deal with some of my own work commitments, but I've made a decent start, despite Edmund's attempts to assist. He spent a large part of the first day hovering, looking over my shoulder, expecting me at any moment to shout 'Eureka' and hold aloft a single sheet of paper that would make everything clear.

"Go away, Edmund."

"But you're bound to have questions. I thought we could do this together."

"No, I can't do this or think straight when you're standing over me like that."

"I'll be quiet."

"No, go away! Leave me to wade through all these documents, make some notes and then we can have a question and answer session at the end of the day."

"Would you like some more tea?"

"GO AWAY!"

It seemed unduly harsh at the time, but he took no offence, merely scuttled off into the garden and clipped some of his shrubs. I declined lunch and made myself tea in the afternoon when he went for his nap. I wrapped up the first session at four o'clock, resisted the offer of Veuve 2012 and bid him good day, determined to keep him at arm's length at least for the duration of the assignment.

"Come for dinner," he said on Friday.

"Thank you but no. I want us to maintain a strictly professional relationship until such times as I have reported to you in full your state of affairs."

"And when will that be?"

"I can't say. A couple of weeks perhaps." He grunted at that, and tried to ply me with drink again, but I remained resolute.

"How much is this costing me?" he asked, his curt manner making me bristle until I realised my insistence on a professional relationship implied remuneration for services rendered.

"I don't know," I said. "We didn't discuss rates and I can't give you an estimate of time." I was playing with him. I had no intention of giving him a bill. "We'll have to see."

"You realise I may be broke?"

"I'll take that chance."

I bade him good evening and went home. I'm content in the cottage and mentally prepared for another attack, secure in the knowledge that now, no one can get in without a sledgehammer.

A pair of swans cruising majestically over the village catch my eye and I gaze skywards, squinting, as momentarily they eclipse the sun.

"Beautiful afternoon," says Sara Lee. "May I join you?"

"Of course."

She sits down beside me and pulls out a packet of cigarettes. I must look interested, as she tentatively offers me the pack.

"No thanks. Not for me. I didn't know you were a smoker."

"Ah, there's a lot you don't know," she says winking. She lights up and takes a deep draw before remembering her manners. "You don't mind, do you?"

"Not at all." It's not true of course, I'd rather she didn't. It's just something we say rather than make a fuss, but I hate the stench of cigarette smoke, even outdoors.

"You have to have at least one vice. I gave up all the others. What's yours?"

"Champagne, I suppose."

"Now there's an expensive habit." She chuckles, puts her head back and blows a cloud of white smoke into the air. "Didn't see you on Sunday."

"No. To be honest, I'm not really a churchgoer."

"I used to say that, before I met John."

"Did he convert you?"

She considers the question before answering. "Yes and no. I fancied him, despite the dog collar. It rather added to the intrigue, wondering what it would be like to spread my legs for a vicar." She catches my eye. "Are you shocked?"

"No." I try to laugh it off. She blows more smoke and this time I can smell something else.

"I wasn't sure if he would pray to God before or after sex, and whether he'd talk dirty. Wanted to find out." It's brandy, which explains why she's being so candid, but her and her husband's sexual predilections are not something I can engage in, even out of politeness. She's happy to answer her own question. "Turns out, all of the above!"

"How was the wedding reception?" I say, keen to change the subject. She screws up her face.

"Proletarian." This is not the same Sara I spoke to before. This Sara is a loose cannon. "All they wanted was Chas and

Dave and the Wind Beneath My Wings." I must look a bit lost, and she laughs again. "You're too young."

"So, what brought you to Oakdale?"

"God did. He had a vacancy here and John fancied it, so I tagged along. Three years we've been here. Seems longer." She finishes her cigarette and stubs it out on the concrete under the bench. She's had a drink and it's made her true feelings difficult to hide. If I want to know more about all the strange goings on in Oakdale, there may not be a better time.

"How well did you know Jackie Thomas?"

"Why do you ask?"

"You said she suffered intimidation like me, because she lived in the cottage. I wondered whether you knew her personally." She lights another cigarette before she answers.

"I don't want to make a big thing of it. For your sake."

"For my sake?"

"People react to different things in different ways. Jackie was a gentle soul and struggled to cope with the threats. They were mild at first, just the occasional aside, the odd snide comment. You know the sort. But it was the drip, drip and then the graffiti on the door. It freaked her out."

"Can't say I was very happy about it."

"No, but you're far more grounded."

"How do you know?"

"I found Jackie praying one day, in church. Crying her eyes out. She had only been once or twice before but this time she was a wreck. I put my arms around her and gave her a hug and told her God loved her and lots of people loved her and she shouldn't worry about some maniac intent on making her life a misery." She turns to face me. "You don't seem particularly bothered about the abuse and you aren't going to go running to God or the Church for help. You're certainly not a wreck." I think about the terror I felt three nights ago and consider taking issue with her.

"Did it get worse?"

"The abuse?" She nods, takes a draw, and blows a white, carcinogenic cloud into the air. "Noises in the night, threatening letters, dead crow on the doorstep. Every time something happened, she'd call me, and I'd go running down there to try and comfort her. She even stayed with us a couple of nights after her place was broken into, and it took all her courage to go back."

"Someone broke in? While she was there?"

"No. She'd been up at the Manor and when she got back that night, she discovered someone had broken in and painted 'Whore' on the sitting room mirror." I don't know whether I'm shocked or comforted to learn I'm not the only one to have experienced it, but in Jackie's case the finger of blame would point squarely at George Hawley. It's hard to believe someone else would know in detail about that assault and choose to replicate it after George's death, which suggests it wasn't George in the first place. Despite all that, it's not the thought of the break-in that's bothering me most. It's that Jackie had been to the Manor.

"She knew Edmund Fitzgerald?"

Sara looks at me as if I'm a child. "Oh yeah. She spent a lot of time up there." A wave of nausea hits me in the gut. Edmund categorically denied ever knowing her, but Sara's revelation somehow rings true. "His Lordship needed someone to help him. Lady Eleanor was becoming progressively erratic, and he couldn't cope with looking after her and dealing with the Manor. Jackie was a kind of PA for a while."

"For a while?"

"Until he went berserk. Threatened her. Told her to get out of his house and never come back."

"This was after the break-in?" She nods and sucks hard on her cigarette, grimacing at the effect of noxious gases before blowing it away.

"It was the last straw, to find someone she trusted and, she thought, befriended, turning on her like that. She called me and she sounded desperate, suicidal almost. I rushed down there, and she clung to me and wouldn't let go. I stayed with her all night." She leaves the statement hanging in the air like another poisonous exhalation swirling around in my addled brain, daring me to reach the obvious conclusion. "One thing led to another. It wasn't my idea, but what could I do? She needed someone and I was there." She steps on her cigarette butt. "How well did I know Jackie? Very well, it turns out." I don't trust myself to speak, but I want to know more.

"And then what?"

She shrugs. "Two days later, she was gone."

I need clarification, it's important. "When you say 'gone'…"

"Disappeared." I wait for the denouement, the tragic final chapter of Jackie Thomas's life as told by her lover Sara Lee, but there's no more. Instead, I feel her hand on mine, cold and soft, and it startles me. "Don't leave without telling me, Kate." Her eyes are unblinking, intense, and seductive. I draw my hand away and gather my senses.

"Course not!" I want to defuse the tension and send the right message. If Mrs Lee number two has a thing for me, she'll have to work harder than that. She may know Jackie is dead and doesn't want to say it in case it sends me into a state of panic. She may think I'm grounded but still need to be protected, for her sake or mine. I don't know which it is, but while she's still prepared to talk, I'm prepared to listen.

"John tried to warn me about Lord Fitzgerald. Is it because of Jackie?"

"John had his own problems with His Lordship," she says, sidestepping the question.

"How about Lady Eleanor?" I know the answer because John told me, but it would be interesting to hear her side.

"She was devoted to the Church, much to her husband's dismay. I think she fancied John; a good-looking woman in her twilight years stuck with a miserable, irascible old sod. No wonder she found solace in a church led by a dashing young vicar. You could see it in her eyes whenever they met."

"Goodness. Was it that obvious?"

"It was to me. He wasn't interested of course, she was old enough to be his mother, but he couldn't bring himself to tell her straight up, so he had to play along." I can't imagine what she means but I suspect she's about to tell me. "Complimenting her hair or perfume, going wild about the ghastly home-made muffins she kept bringing before binning them, telling a risqué joke that made her giggle like a coquette and she wishing she were thirty years younger. You know the sort of banter. Drove her wild with lust and probably gave him a kick too."

I'm beyond astonished, not so much by the subject matter but that the vicar's wife is being so candid. I've caught the whiff of flirtation every time I've been around John Lee. I'm many years younger than him so it's not unusual, even coming from a man of the cloth. It's not the first time it's happened to me. Girls get used to it and mostly it's harmless, unless you're the flirt's other half, when it takes on a different dimension. Sara probably succumbed to his charms in the same way, so she knows her husband well and can smell it a mile off. There's more than alcohol at work here.

"And when she was on her death bed, she demanded John be there holding one hand, as God's representative you understand, while His Lordship held the other, seething with rage. When she passed, he exploded, berating John for manipulating and deceiving her for his own perverted pleasure and accusing him of having an affair. It was awful."

"And that's why they don't speak?"

"Not unless they have to. Trouble is, Fitzgerald owns the large plot in the graveyard where all his ancestors are buried. Bought it in 1655 for three pounds ten shillings, but the deal is the Lord of the Manor must maintain it. It was less of an issue when Lady Eleanor was alive, but since then they're constantly at each other's throats about when and how. The last time he was there was when he buried Eleanor and he wouldn't even let John take the service."

"I think I get the picture."

"Has he said anything to you?" It sounds an innocuous question, so she gets an innocuous answer.

"Only that he's not religious." I'm not sure she believes me, but I'm not sure of anything now. I'm dreading going back to the Manor armed with the knowledge I now have, true or false. Edmund is certainly absent minded and disorganised, and I've caught a glimpse of the foul temper, but he never once said anything disparaging about Eleanor, neither has he mentioned John by name. *Charlatans and hypocrites*. No more critical than your average atheist.

"Don't let him suck you in like he did Jackie." Her concern appears heartfelt, and I'm touched, even though my instinct is to argue with her and defend Edmund. I don't want to tell her I am, effectively, his new PA; she'll likely find that out for herself in due course, but at least I can be vigilant for any change in his behaviour, and unlike Jackie, I'll be mentally prepared.

"I won't."

Sara Lee gives me a weak smile and squeezes my hand again. It feels benign and unthreatening compared to being touched by John and I'm intrigued by my own reaction. She's as good as admitted she slept with Jackie, so this has to be part of the game, but it would have far more sinister connotations if she were a man. I try another angle. "Did you hear about Jeremy Jones?" She looks genuinely puzzled. "Estate agent in Bradwell."

"God yes! Was that the chap who was murdered in his car?" I nod vigorously. "Must say I've wanted to kill an estate agent on more than one occasion." It's meant to be a joke but given the circumstances it's in terribly poor taste. She sees my expression. "God, sorry. That was uncalled for."

"I knew him."

"Really? How?"

"He's the letting agent for Farrier's. He knew Jackie too."

Sara lets out her breath slowly. "Wow. That damned cottage has a lot to answer for."

"That's what Edmund said." I curse myself for using his first name, but she doesn't appear to have noticed.

"You and he discussed it?"

"The police arrived when I was there and told us about Jeremy."

"They don't think Fitzgerald had anything to do with it?"

"Who knows what they think. But George Hawley and Jeremy Jones are both linked to a cottage owned by Edmund Fitzgerald and they've both been murdered." I've left it wide open for her to mention the death of Jackie Thomas and the fact that the cottage was sold long ago, but she still bears a look of shock.

"Kate! For God's sake be careful." She grabs my hand again and this time so tightly I would struggle to release it, then digs into her bag and thrusts a card at me with the number of The Vicarage and two mobiles. "If you're frightened or need anything, anything at all, you must call me; any time of day or night."

CHAPTER 18

I'm in N&N's getting a newspaper and a few provisions when I bump into Arthur Needham. He's at the counter buying a lottery ticket.

"Feeling lucky this week?" Arthur turns slowly and gives me a bemused look. I'm grinning broadly, crossed fingers in the air. He's slow on the uptake, but eventually his face softens.

"Oh, hello. It's Kate, isn't it?"

"Well remembered."

"Nirvaan here always promises he's fixed it so my numbers come up and I fall for it every time. Never trust a foreigner," he says winking at me, and I cringe. I can't believe he's not joking, but even so, it's shocking to hear a blatant racial slur. It may have been acceptable in his day but it's totally unacceptable now and I flash a look of alarm at Nirvaan who's leaning forward on the counter with a severe expression on his face.

"It's not my fault you gullible old bastard. Anyway, I'm not a bloody foreigner. I'm from Bradford!"

I've stumbled into a vicious argument, unsure how it will end.

"What do you call Yorkshire if not foreign?"

"God's own country, that's what it is. Now, two quid old man and be off with you!"

Arthur's face lights up with a huge smile and hands over a coin. "You're frightening the customers." He slips his ticket into the inside pocket of his tweed jacket and turns to me. "Have a good day Kate," he says, gently squeezing my arm, then heads for the door, stick in hand.

"What time at The Crown?" says Nirvaan to Arthur's back.

"Seven. Don't be late!"

"Yes boss." He sees my bewildered expression. "Pub quiz. We're on the same team."

"You were just joking."

"Arthur and I are always winding each other up. You didn't think...?" he says, then laughs at my embarrassment.

"I confess, you had me fooled for a moment."

"Did you manage to get hold of Jackie?" he says while scanning my items. I don't want to tell him about her death. He couldn't have known when he gave me her address and clearly Sara didn't either. I'm not going to be a source of gossip in Oakdale.

"No, I'm afraid not. But thank you anyway."

"My pleasure."

***

I spot Arthur Needham tottering slowly up the High Street in the opposite direction to my cottage and run to catch him up.

"I understand you and Nirvaan are good friends."

"Yes, we play in the same quiz team. We trade insults on a regular basis," he says, still grinning at the exchange.

"So I see."

"You can only do it with friends of course. These days everyone takes things too seriously. I wonder if mankind is losing its sense of humour. That would be terrible."

I have no answer to that. My generation behaves differently from his and no doubt the next will be different again. One thing we have in common is that we all think we know best.

"Do you mind if I ask you a question?"

"Fire away."

Before I can say anything, a car horn interrupts, and a scruffy white pickup draws alongside, window rolled down.

"What time tonight Arthur?" says the driver.

"Seven, or better still, six thirty if you want to get a couple in first."

The pickup is old, covered in mud and fairly battered, typical for a working truck in the countryside, but what stands out amongst the scrapes is a dent in the front wing smeared with streaks of blue paint.

The driver waves and drives off leaving a cloud of grey smoke.

"Barry Wilson, local farmer," says Arthur. I remember the name. It's relevant.

"Pub quiz?" Arthur nods and we walk on. "I wanted to ask you about George Hawley."

"Unfortunate business that. A sorry end to a sorry saga."

"You mean the cottage?"

"Yes, but not just that. George was, shall we say not terribly popular. In fact, he seemed to go out of his way to make himself unpopular. There aren't many grieving for his loss, which is a shame. He always laid claim to that cottage, just as his father had, but years and years went by when it was never mentioned. It was something he grumbled about in the pub after a drink or two, that was all. It was only about three years ago when it all blew up again and he started to become more vociferous and dare I say, aggressive."

"Do you know why?"

"Not really. The place had been empty for about thirty years. Fitzgerald wouldn't sell it in case it fell into Hawley's hands and no local would rent it because they thought it was haunted."

"Haunted?"

"That's what people still think, and it was George who put it about. I don't buy into that mumbo-jumbo myself, but legend has it that it was the scene of a grisly murder."

"Gosh. When?"

"Don't know exactly. 1890 or thereabouts."

I stop walking and he turns to look at me. "1892," I say absently, "following the bust-up between the Hawleys and the Fitzgeralds." The words come out without thinking.

"You seem very well-informed Miss Duvall." He's reverted to formality. It's either a mark of respect or a means of maintaining a distance.

"Kate."

"Kate." He points his stick towards West Street. "I live down there. Come and have some tea."

***

The Needham residence is tucked away along a private drive. It's a ranch-style bungalow with a triple garage set in wooded grounds, block paving to the front and landscaped gardens either side. Its understated elegance oozes affluence; a far cry from Edmund's decrepit old Manor.

Marjorie Needham greets me warmly and shows me into the conservatory. The back garden is blooming with flower beds; hydrangea, roses, cosmos, and allium providing a riot of colour. They run either side of an immaculate lawn, parallel stripes leading the eye to an impressive view across the dales.

"Who's the gardener?" I ask in full admiration of someone's efforts.

"We both are, but we're not as young as we once were, so we have a bit of help from young Marcus Wilson, a farmer's son."

"Would that be Barry?"

"Yes, that's right. Do you know him?"

"No, we just saw him in the High Street. Your garden is beautiful. I haven't done anything to the cottage yet. The back yard is overrun with weeds; poppies and all sorts coming out of the cobbles. Don't seem to have time."

"Are you planning to stay in Oakdale for long?"

In normal circumstances, it would be a perfectly reasonable question, but in light of recent events, it carries a certain ambiguity.

"Not sure, is the honest answer."

"I can ask Marcus to pop over if you like?"

"Thank you."

Marjorie disappears into the kitchen and Arthur hobbles over to a wing chair gesturing me to sit opposite.

"I take it you've met Edmund?"

"Yes, I have. Do you know him well?"

"We go back years, decades almost. Marjorie and I used to see the Fitzgeralds a lot. They were very active in and around the village and we often played bridge. I used to regard him as a good friend."

"Used to?"

"Edmund went a bit funny in his old age. I suppose we all change as we get old and doddery, but we fell out over something trivial and then Eleanor got ill, and we hardly saw them after that. In fact, the last time I saw Edmund was at Eleanor's funeral and we barely spoke a word. Very sad."

"May I ask why you fell out?"

He waves a hand dismissively. "Something came up at the Parish Council. Hawley complained 'his' cottage wasn't being maintained and there was no doubt it had been allowed to fall into disrepair; thatch covered in moss, paint peeling off the windows, ivy eating into the stonework. No wonder, since no one lived there for years, and Edmund wasn't minded to spend money on an empty property. It was certainly an eyesore, in a prime spot in the High Street and the Council felt it had to do something. So I wrote to Edmund and Eleanor, respectfully requesting they tidy it up or else dispose of it so that someone else could have a go."

I can see Edmund's study and the antique silver letter opener Eleanor uses to open the letter from the Chairman of Parish Council and erstwhile friend, Arthur Needham, and I can hear her cultured accent, her words shaky, enfeebled by impending illness as she reads aloud its contents to an increasingly irate Lord of the Manor, Edmund Fitzgerald. I take up the story.

"Edmund goes berserk. He lambasts you and your duplicity, that damn gigolo of a priest, the drug-addled lesbian masquerading as his wife, and everyone else on the Parish Council for meddling in his affairs and launching an unwarranted attack on the integrity of his family. Even worse you've done it at the behest of that maniac Hawley who everyone knows is deranged, has contributed nothing to the village and been trouble for as long as anyone can remember, just like his father and grandfather before him. He and Lady Fitzgerald will attend to Farrier's Cottage at a time of their choosing and not a moment before and if George Hawley so much as raises the matter again he will have Edmund himself to answer to."

I'm distracted by movement in the garden. A squirrel hops and skips across the lawn and darts up a sycamore, carrying a spherical object in its mouth.

"Arthur. Arthur!" says Marjorie Needham, trying to get her husband's attention as she lays a tray on the bamboo-framed coffee table. "Would you like me to pour?" But Arthur appears to be in a trance.

"I'll do it Mrs Needham, thank you." She tuts at him, shaking her head and wanders off. He comes out of his stupor.

"How do you know this. Did Edmund tell you?"

"I'm just guessing," I say, pouring the tea, trying to appear nonchalant. I don't know why that scenario came to mind, but knowing what I do about the characters involved, it has a certain logic to it.

"That's impressive guesswork Kate. It's all come back to me now. I remember it well. Edmund wrote the Council a blistering riposte that you have just repeated almost verbatim." I wasn't going to mention my association with Edmund, but I judge Arthur Needham to be a man of honour and integrity. I have to offer some plausible explanation if he is not going to be suspicious of me. To my shame, I can fabricate one easily.

"I've been doing some work for Lord Fitzgerald, tidying up his files and papers and helping him get his affairs in order. He seems a bit lost without Lady Eleanor. Amongst his hundreds of documents, I remember a letter to the Parish Council like the one I've just described, handwritten original, block letters. I suppose it must have been sent by fax." I remember no such letter, but it's there in my mind. I've not only related its contents accurately, I've also been specific in my description of the handwriting.

Arthur nods. "It was indeed."

"I didn't realise the significance."

"Well, it marked a schism in our friendship which has never healed. Soon after, the Fitzgeralds relented and sold the cottage to a property investment company that spent a reasonable amount making it habitable and then began to rent it out."

"Yes, he told me that," I say, because it's simpler than the truth. *Kate Duvall, when did deceit trip off your tongue so easily?* "But if you knew that, then George must have known it too."

"Everybody knew it. It was no secret. We saw the painters and decorators go in and the roof rethatched and then the 'To Let' sign went up. In no time it came down again, but it was over a year before a young woman like yourself moved in."

"Was that Jackie Thomas?"

"Yes, I think that was her name."

"So why did George continue his feud with Edmund when he knew the cottage had been sold?"

"It was of no relevance to George. The feud, as you put it, was against the family, in the person of Edmund Fitzgerald, last Lord of Oakdale. George demanded the Fitzgeralds pay him the sum they received for the sale of a cottage which he believed was rightfully his. He was desperate to get resolution before either he or the Fitzgeralds died, because there was no heir, and this was his last chance."

"But then he was murdered."

"It's all too tragic for words. I assume that was why you wanted to know about George, know why he was so unpleasant towards you? It wasn't aimed at you; it was aimed at Edmund."

"I don't see how being beastly to the tenant would bother Edmund once he'd sold it. Why would he care?"

"He wouldn't, directly. But George was determined no one would live there until the Hawleys got it back, by any means. When that happened, he would finally have vanquished the Fitzgeralds."

"But now that's not possible."

"No, it's over."

I feel I can trust Arthur Needham; he reminds me of Edmund, and I can see why they would once be friends. He appears measured, has no difficulty with recollection and has none of Edmund's intemperate nature. But I wrestle with conflicting thoughts of what and how much to say. He thinks the feud is over, but I know it isn't and I need to know why.

"I have been subjected to threat and intimidation since George was found dead. I've met Mrs Hawley and I'm satisfied it's not her or anyone from her family. George's claim on the cottage died with him. So, who's doing it?"

"I don't know Kate, I'm sorry."

"Maybe the place really is haunted?" I try to make light of it. Normally, I would share Arthur's attitude towards 'mumbo-jumbo', but, like Jackie Thomas, my experience has been all too real. The difference is she, directly or indirectly, died shortly after. "Maybe it needs to be exorcised? Do you think it's worth asking Reverend Lee?" I'm fishing for a reaction, I know, but Arthur won't be drawn.

"If you feel strongly enough. Are you the religious type?"

"No, I'm just being flippant." But I'm still fishing. "Who was the vicar before John and Sara moved here?"

"Chap called Michael Fenton. He was here a good number of years. Decent chap, or so we thought, until we received complaints."

"Complaints?"

"Improper behaviour towards under-age girls. He denied it of course and nothing was proven, but he was quietly removed by the diocese and sent to another parish. Caused a lot of fuss at the time."

I glance at my watch. "I must be going; I've taken up too much of your time." He shows me out and I thank him for his help.

"Anytime, Kate. Perhaps you'd care to join the Parish Council? We do have a vacancy."

"I'll think about it," I say. We both know it's unlikely, but I appreciate the gesture. A final thought occurs to me.

"Who made the accusations against Reverend Fenton?"

"A young woman called Melanie Gibbs."

CHAPTER 19

I pay little attention to the white van parked in the High Street near my cottage until I see the name painted on the back and sides. *Steve Marshall, Painter & Decorator*. I think back to the wedding and the way he and Tiffany were staring at me and it still makes me think, given everything that's happened. There's someone in the driving seat and I walk past pretending not to notice, but then stop and go back.

Steve is on his phone, flicking the screen with his thumb, oblivious to my presence, even as I stand there looking at him through the side window. He looks up with a start, sees me and the window slides down. I'm nice as pie.

"Hi Steve! I'm Kate and I live in that thatched cottage," I say, pointing down the street." He knows fine well who I am and where I live but makes a show of turning his head to look. "I need an expert to paint my front door. Would you be interested?"

He clears his throat. "Yeah, alright. Do you wanna show me?"

He gets out of the van and follows me to the cottage. The square white patch I painted on the dark green door is an abomination, never mind what's underneath. I wait for him to ask the obvious question, but he sidesteps it.

"I suppose you want it all green?"

"Or all white, what do you think?"

"Green's traditional."

Six foot six towers over me and I have to tilt my head back to look at him. "That would be lovely. Would you need to strip it off?" He blinks and swallows, then rubs a hand over the surface in various spots.

"Rub down and primer should be alright, then two topcoats. Good as new. Next week okay?"

"Perfect."

"Hundred do you?"

"Fine." I briefly wonder how he and Tiffany manage both vertical and horizontal. "I thought you'd be on honeymoon."

"Put it off 'til January. Going to Dubai."

"Lovely." I can hear Sara Lee scoffing. "Lucky for you and lucky for me!" I giggle. He looks satisfyingly uncomfortable.

"Nice cottage," he says looking up at the thatch.

"Yes, it is."

"Me and Tiff are well jealous."

"I'm very happy here."

"Haunted you know."

"Really? Just as well I don't believe in that stuff."

"Neither do I."

"Did you know that chap George?" I know he does because of the altercation in the pub.

"Hawley? Not really. Never had anything to do with him. Bit of a nutcase by all accounts."

"His family lived here, way back."

"That right?"

"In the 19th century. Hey! Maybe there's a body buried in the back garden?" I raise eyebrows to simulate shock, but he takes no notice. I want him to know I'm not afraid of ghosts, nor fazed by graffiti or criminals who break into my house.

"Wouldn't surprise me. Them Hawleys were all crazy."

"What makes you say that?"

"Tommy Gibbs was at school with their boy Si and they both did a stint in the army. Tommy said Si was a bit of a psycho. Psycho Si is what they called him."

"Tommy. Is that Tiffany's dad?"

"Yeah."

"What made him a psycho?"

"They were in the Falklands. I don't know all the details, but Tommy says he'll never forget it." I suspect he wouldn't hesitate to tell me if he knew anything. Men like to discuss nasty and distressing stuff with a woman just to provoke a reaction. It feeds their ego. But I'm more interested to know what caused the argument in The Crown between him and George.

"Well, I don't wish to speak ill of the dead, but I had an unhappy experience with George. He was quite unpleasant towards me, and I don't know why because I didn't do anything."

"If you ask me, he got what was coming."

"What do you mean?"

"We were in The Crown and he was drunk and mouthing off and I just lost it. Told him to shut up or else I'd take him outside." His body twitches as if he's back there in the Crown, flexing his muscles, ready to have a go.

"Gosh."

"You don't go saying those things about a lady and expect to get away with it."

"Especially not when she's your fiancée."

"What?"

"I assume you're talking about Tiffany."

He looks at his watch. "Better be off."

***

"Is that your handwriting?" I had said, thrusting Edmund's last invitation to dinner under his nose. He'd put on his glasses and squinted at it.

"Yes."

"So, you did invite me after all."

"Must have done."

"Who delivered it?"

"Don't know," he'd said shaking his head. It hardly matters now, but at least eliminates the conspiracy theory; the notion that someone was playing games. It didn't explain why Edmund forgot so soon afterwards nor can remember how it got to me. Until I found the evidence.

I'm sitting at his desk. The piles of paper have gone, most of it junk and now in the bin, the rest organised neatly so I can brief him on what I've discovered so far. I went to Bradwell Register Office and obtained certified copies of the death certificate so I could write to various organisations telling them of Eleanor's death. I believed initially, courtesy of online research, that probate was not necessary, as everything appeared to be in joint names. The exception was Farrier's cottage which was sold three years ago and should no longer be relevant, but there's more.

The evidence is to be found in their medical files. There are many documents regarding Eleanor's condition. Her death certificate states the cause as 'cerebrovascular accident' or stroke, in plain language. She had her first one five years ago and although relatively mild she would suffer two more serious ones before finally succumbing. Her illness is what prompted the sale of the cottage. According to correspondence with the estate agent, both she and Edmund decided it would make life simpler for them both if it was disposed of before her death.

Edmund's medical history is here too. His memory loss became apparent after Eleanor's first stroke, but probably began years earlier. He was tested for Alzheimer's, but his memory lapses were ultimately diagnosed as transient global amnesia. I looked it up and it didn't fit. It might explain why Edmund forgot about inviting me to dinner, forgot about selling the cottage, or forgot ever meeting Jackie Thomas. But such lapses are usually temporary, and the sufferer normally remembers events sometime later, which in Edmund's case was not true. Furthermore, it's not a chronic condition and sufferers rarely experience more than two episodes.

I'm reading a letter from the estate agent attached to a copy of the sale particulars for the cottage and it's also worrying. The sale was handled by none other than Jeremy Jones and although all the correspondence is addressed to Eleanor Forbes Fitzgerald, there are several references to Edmund. I understand why Edmund might have forgotten Jeremy but not why Jeremy would deny ever knowing Edmund. I find letters and invoices from solicitors Franklyn Jones acting for Eleanor and discover the partner handling the conveyancing was Felicity Jones. A brief online search brings up stories of the hideous murder of a local estate agent and the agony suffered by his wife, Felicity. Another connection.

I guess Stride and his team will have done similar research during their enquiries, so I'm not about to call them and disclose what I've found. Despite the connections between the parties, they don't have any obvious significance for me and don't explain why someone is still trying to frighten me out of the cottage. I can see Edmund out of the corner of my eye, tiptoeing into the study. He's carrying a silver tray with teapot, cups and saucers and a plate of cakes.

"Is it safe to come in?"

"Yes."

"I don't wish to disturb you in your work." I swing the captain's chair around to face him. He's wearing an annoying grin.

"I'm almost done for the day. I was just about to call you and give you an update. Pull up a chair."

"Marvellous!"

"Everyone who needs to know about Eleanor has been told and most have sent an acknowledgement. The bank has changed the name on your accounts to you alone and cancelled her cards."

"How much do I have?"

"About ten thousand in your current account and just over twenty in savings."

"Keep me going for a while."

"You will have to pay back the pensions people."

"Why?"

"You've been receiving her pension since February."

"If you say so."

"You have your own state pension plus an occupational pension from Lloyds of London. In total, your income is about twenty-five thousand. Enough for most retired widowers to live on, provided they live in a small property and don't have expensive tastes."

Edmund grunts. "I live in a sprawling, decrepit, old, listed building that's far too big for me and costs a fortune to run."

"And have a penchant for fine wine."

"Man has to have a little pleasure."

"Yes, I've seen some of the invoices and I wondered how on earth you managed on such a modest income."

"And are you able to tell me how I managed?" he says, bridling at the criticism as he pours the tea and hands me a muffin.

"Maybe. Your available funds are dwindling fast, but twenty five years ago, Eleanor was bequeathed a sum of two million pounds from her aunt, Jemima Forbes Larsen, she of the shipping dynasty."

"Was she? I don't remember," is the predictable response.

"Your financial advisor at the time recommended she invest it in a broad range of stocks, shares, cash and gilts covering all sectors of the world economy. The investment was wrapped up in multiple funds managed exclusively by a firm called Hollis Warburton."

"Rings a bell," he says. I'm unconvinced.

"Unlike your other assets, the funds are in her sole name, so you will need probate to get them transferred to you. I'll get straight on that tomorrow. The latest reports from Hollis Warburton show average investment growth of 11%."

"Really? I suppose that's good."

"Very good. Eleanor liquidated some of it from time to time, presumably to pay for major repairs to the house, not to mention your wine bill."

"I say!" he says, looking affronted.

"Just a joke, Edmund. But to be clear, the last valuation is around eighteen million."

"Good lord! I never knew."

"You probably did at one time. Maybe you just forgot."

"I'm hardly going to forget sums like that."

"Maybe Eleanor kept it from you. Didn't want to bother you with it. Maybe she forgot about it herself. If you have more money than you need or can reasonably spend, it loses any significance, especially if you have no one to leave it to."

"Well, I certainly don't need it."

"There is a twist."

"What's that?"

"The last documents I can find from Hollis Warburton are three years old."

"Maybe they're filed somewhere else?"

"Nothing is filed Edmund. It's just lying around in boxes. The point is, without up-to-date documents, I can't be sure where it is, or even if it still exists."

"It must do! Where would it have gone?" He then frowns and scratches his chin. "But what am I going to do with eighteen million?"

"It's a terrible dilemma," I say with a sigh, ladling on the irony. It seems to be lost on him.

"You have it!" he says, suddenly animated.

It hits me like a hammer blow. *Whore!*

"No! I mean...no Edmund you can't do that."

"Why ever not?"

"For the same reason I didn't want to move in here. People will think..."

"To hell with what people think!" He's angry now. I dismissed his suggestion too quickly, an emotional reaction to everything that's happened. "You can't live life worrying about what other people think of you," he bellows. "As long as you're not hurting them, why would you pander to their petty prejudices? It's envy, that's what it is." I've lit the Fitzgerald powder keg and can only wait for it to burn itself out. "I have had this all my life. Other people questioning my legitimacy for no other reason than I appear to have more than they do, and they want some of it because they think they are more deserving. Well, they can all go to hell! I didn't choose to be who I am and I'm not going to feel guilty about it. I have no interest in wealth and no one to leave it to. When I die, the vultures will descend and pick at my bones, and I sincerely hope it poisons them!"

He stomps over to the French window, staring out over the grounds of Oakdale Manor, his back towards me. I could have been more gracious, but his rant was not aimed at me, merely a manifestation of the bitterness that's built up over a long life that's now coming to a close and the frustration that frailty brings.

"You have no will?" I ask, partly to break the silence.

"What would be the point?" He sounds weary and defeated. The fire is still smouldering.

"It will go to the state. Is that what you want?"

"Then I shall leave you everything."

"No, Edmund."

He spins around and glares at me, the fire reignited. "Then you are no longer any use to me!" he shouts, pointing a trembling finger. "Get out of my sight and never return!"

CHAPTER 20

Connections. Teasing and tormenting, sharing a secret known by all but me. Nothing would surprise me now. I was offered an estate of potentially twenty million pounds, including the house, for no other reason than I was in the right place at the right time. Right, that is, provided one does not regard the inheritance of huge wealth desirable, in which case I was in the wrong place at the wrong time. It could be either. Connections.

Arthur Needham, erstwhile friend of the Fitzgeralds until circumstances forced them apart. The very same Arthur Needham who, as former financial advisor to Eleanor recommended investing her inheritance with Hollis Warburton, delivering a fortune to a man who never knew it existed, and now that he does, doesn't want it. I made mention of Eleanor's financial advisor but not his name and Edmund was not moved to identify him or even ask. Another memory lapse or another petty prejudice? I don't know when Arthur retired, but he will know how well the funds performed while he was still involved, and no doubt made a tidy commission along the way. The Needhams' impressive residence is testament to that.

Arthur didn't mention that connection to me either, but why would he? Professional etiquette? Envy? Jealousy? Petty prejudice? I can't imagine what drives the actions of such a disparate group of individuals. Connections, real and imagined.

On this misty, damp June morning I again study the granite headstone of Lord Julian Fitzgerald, the inscription mournful and benign. Edmund showed me his portrait hanging on the wall by the oak staircase. He's standing in a corridor of the Lords, resplendent in ermine, golden mace over one shoulder, chin up in arrogant pose, every inch the man whose wealth and status were God given and sacrosanct, yet beneath my feet, he's nothing more than a rotting corpse returned to earth like all those around him.

Pall bearers are emerging from St John the Baptist carrying the coffin of George Hawley to the opposite end of the graveyard to be buried next to his father Albert, and his father Jacob. A meagre gathering of mourners trudge behind, heads down, all in black. Mrs Hawley in front, supported by a tall, heavy-set man, the legendary Psycho Si, presumably. Arthur and Marjorie Needham are there, possibly in an official capacity, one or two others I don't recognise, but precious few, testament to George's reputation.

I don't know why I came. Perhaps to tell George there were no hard feelings? If he'd lived longer, and carried on with his threats and abuse, I may have judged him like all the others did, a sad, bitter old man, whose life was ruined by obsession, dedicated to righting a wrong, seeking justice but ultimately failing. I can't help feeling some sympathy for him, if, as legend has it, Julian behaved as scandalously as it's believed. But no one alive was there and no one alive knows the truth and whatever version of the story may still be told, it can never take the place of the truth.

"Miserable day for a burial," says DI Stride. I haven't noticed he's sidled up next to me. He's staring up at the trees as crows circle ominously. "Didn't expect to find you here."

"Paying my respects."

"As I said, didn't expect to find you here."

"I didn't murder George," I say without looking at him.

"No. I don't think you did." *You don't think?*

"And I didn't murder Jeremy Jones either."

"No, I don't think you did that either."

"Glad we cleared that up."

"Miss Duvall, do you know of a woman by the name of Jackie Thomas?"

He knows I do, so hesitation would be fatal, at least as far as my reputation is concerned. "Yes. She rented the cottage before me and like me, she suffered abuse and intimidation. When it became too much for her, she left."

"And do you know where she is now?" *He already knows this too.*

"She's dead."

"Why did you not say this before?" They've been to Thurwell Jones estate agents in Bradwell, talked to the other partner and the staff and of course been given access to Jeremy's files. They followed the same trail as me, albeit for different reasons and got the same result.

"All I wanted was some advice, to compare notes with someone who'd experienced the same thing as me and try to pre-empt further attacks. What relevance is it?"

"Everything's relevant."

"How would I know that?"

"What else did Jones say apart from telling you Jackie Thomas was dead?" It may be a trick, or they may just be stupidly making the assumption. Jeremy didn't know she had died, or surely, he would have said. *Jackie's number is unobtainable,* he'd said. But Stride got his information from Jeremy's office, so Jeremy must have known. Two months ago, before I set foot in Oakdale, I was naïve; given to trust everyone until they proved unworthy. Now I revert to convention. Everyone must earn it, including the late Jeremy Jones and DI Stride.

"He said a strange thing." I pause, to make him focus on what's coming.

"Go on."

"He said he didn't know Edmund Fitzgerald."

"Well, that's not impossible. Even estate agents can't know everyone."

"Jeremy Jones sold the cottage for the Fitzgeralds, and his wife did the conveyancing."

***

There's no wake going on in The Crown. Not even George's closest relatives are raising a glass in his memory, but given what Mrs Hawley told me, that's no surprise. Psycho Si has probably driven back to York, like everyone else, getting back to normal as soon as possible. But I need a drink.

The Whore of Oakdale is pleased to find her barstool unoccupied, so I take my place and contemplate today's connections over a gin and tonic. I'm now certain Jeremy Jones knew all about Jackie Thomas. I can understand him not wanting to mention to any prospective tenant the death of their predecessor, whatever the circumstances. The merest suggestion of threats to a tenant with or without rumours the place is haunted, would make it virtually unlettable. But to be asked a direct question and lie about it, stretches the reputation of even the most cavalier estate agent to breaking point. No one else in the village knew what happened to Jackie, only that she left suddenly, and it would be of no interest to local police until they discovered it during their enquiries.

And I still can't fathom why he lied about Edmund. Both Mr and Mrs Jones's roles in the sale of the cottage and his subsequent role as managing agent would be well documented. They could not hope to keep it secret from the police even if there were any reason to do so. The only assumption I can make is that he wanted to keep it from me. The question is why?

A thick-set man of about sixty approaches the bar and orders a pint. I recognise Tommy Gibbs, the man with Ma Gibbs and his two daughters that day in church. He's wearing a dark suit and black tie, as if he's been to a funeral. It only ever takes a sip to make me fearless.

"Mr Gibbs?" He turns his head and he's scowling, which I take to be his natural expression. "I thought I recognised you from church. I'm Kate. I know your wife and daughters and I also met your son-in-law the other day."

"Alright," he mumbles, clearly not one for pleasantries.

"Were you at George's funeral? I didn't see you there."

His pint arrives. He hands over a note and drains a quarter of his glass in one gulp. "Didn't see you there neither," he says without looking at me.

"I was at the back. Staying out of the way. Just wanted to pay my respects." He has nothing to add so I press on regardless. "Was he a friend of yours?"

"George Hawley had no friends."

"I find that very sad." Another gulp and it's half gone. "His family must be distraught."

"Doubt it." It's the standard response but I really want to know about Simon.

"Was that his son?"

"That was him." He takes another gulp. One to go. "He's just as bad. I only went to make sure he behaved himself."

"Steve said you were in the army together."

"That was a long time ago." *Blood from a stone.* He drains his glass and waves it at the barman. I need to get straight to the point.

"And that Simon was, er, volatile."

"He was a bloody psycho." The alcohol has kicked in and Tommy Gibbs is opening up. He hands over some coins and takes a drink, more slowly this time. Another push is needed.

"I understand you both served in the Falklands."

"I served. He was just there to butcher as many Argies as he could. Four of them, hands up, shot 'em dead. No prisoners, that was his style. Hand to hand with a knife was what he liked best. Kept stabbin' even after they were dead. Psycho."

"Goodness. He's not still like that?"

"Leopards and spots. That's all I'm sayin'. Never forget it I won't. The look in his eyes. Saw it again today. He hasn't changed." Tommy Gibbs takes another sip. It looks like he's going to be here for a while, and I've heard enough.

"Well, nice talking to you."

He turns towards me as I slide off the stool.

"I hear Steve's painting your door." It's no secret, but I can't imagine all of Steve's clients getting a mention in the Gibbs family. And there's something vaguely mocking in his tone that I don't like.

"Yes, he is. It was vandalised."

"So I heard." He's playing with me, implying he knows something I don't, just like Steve and Tiffany at the church. "It'll happen again. Always does. Until you're out of there."

"I have no intention of leaving. I'm getting extra security on the front door. Cameras and lights." I invented the last bit on the spur of the moment; a reaction to a veiled threat. But it makes sense.

"Stay away from red." He winks and returns to his pint.

I leave before he sees any tears.

***

There's a bike leaning against the fence, its owner coming out through the gate just as I arrive home.

"Hello?"

He's about seventeen, scruffy tee-shirt, jeans, and trainers. "Hi. Just put something through your door."

"What is it?"

"Dunno. Envelope from his Lordship."

"I'm Kate," I say expecting he'll reciprocate, but he's a typical teenager, surly and uncommunicative.

"Yeah, I know."

"What's your name?"

"Marcus."

"Are you the one who does gardening for Mr and Mrs Needham?"

"Lord Fitzgerald too."

"Really? Nice to meet you, Marcus." He shifts uncomfortably in the saddle. "Did you by any chance deliver me an envelope from Edmund a week or so ago?"

"Yeah. I run all his messages." He steps on the pedals and sprints down the High Street. The mystery of the last invitation has been solved; Edmund wrote it, Marcus delivered it and Edmund forgot all about it, not that it matters anymore. I've been summarily dismissed from the service of His Lordship, yet it appears he's deigned to write to me again.

I unlock the door and pick a brown envelope from the mat. I'm primed for a single sheet of hand-written, block lettered vitriol, confirming termination of employment. Instead, it's the familiar white card. *Come to dinner Friday 7pm. Edmund.* I shake my head in frustration and dial his number. It rings about twenty times before he answers.

"Fitzgerald."

"It's Kate."

"Hello Kate!" He's bright and breezy. Not at all like the last time we spoke. "Did you get my invitation?"

"Yes, but…"

"You're otherwise engaged."

"No, but…"

"Marvellous. I'll see you on Friday. I've got another task for you I'd like to discuss."

"Edmund, I got the distinct impression you weren't happy with me."

"Nonsense! Whatever gave you that idea? I look forward to seeing you. Come at six and I'll tell you all about it. The deli is sending over boeuf bourguignon and sticky toffee pudding. You will come, won't you?"

"Yes, I'll come," I say, weary but relieved there has been no lasting damage to our friendship. I should know by now Edmund is prone to violent outbursts and he's probably forgotten all about it, but it also means I will have to bring up the subject of his will again. I resolve to manage the issue more sympathetically next time.

Whatever new task Edmund has in mind, I haven't finished the one I started. I managed to inform all interested parties and agencies of Eleanor's death and collate a schedule of assets, so Edmund knows broadly how much he's worth, but I haven't been able to track down the funds Eleanor received from the sale of the cottage nor verify the status of her multi-million-pound investments. I also want to probe his erstwhile friendship with Arthur Needham and find out who Jennifer is, or was, preferably without having to ask. I'm worried it may be another bone of contention. I have no reason to trust

Reverend Lee, and I'm not convinced by Sara's explanation for the rift between him and Edmund. I have to get to the bottom of it myself.

CHAPTER 21

Mum is feeling the strain. I meant to call her every two or three days but with so much going on here, it slips my mind. She doesn't want me to anyway, says there's nothing I can do.

"What about domiciliary care?"

"What's that?"

"Home help."

"You father won't be having that, and I don't like the idea myself. Have a stranger come into the house and interfere?"

"So you can have some respite, mum. You can't do all this yourself."

"Yes I can. My only worry is if something happens to me, then who's going to look after him?"

"I will."

"Oh, darling, if only that were possible. I'd love to have you here with us, but we both know that's not going to happen."

"Why not?"

"You've got a new life and there's no going back, is there?"

"Suppose not."

"Are you happy dear?"

It breaks my heart. The most important thing to her is that her children are happy. "Yes mum." There's no other answer. "I'll do some research on care homes. See what the costs are."

"You do that Kate. God bless."

***

"I want you to write a history of the Fitzgeralds. You could call it *The Last Lord of Oakdale,* documenting Sir Gerald's origins in Ireland, his subsequent ennoblement, the rise and fall of the Fitzgerald dynasty through the ages. You know, hereditary peers, landed gentry, lead mines, industrialists, wealth, power, hedonism, the sorry saga of the dastardly

Julian and the feud with the Hawleys, the entire, no holds barred, warts and all, epic. A veritable ripping yarn! What do you think?"

We're in the study and the drinks tray is already there on the desk, charged with bottle and glasses. He reaches for the champagne and starts to attack the foil.

"Wait Edmund. Can we conclude our business first? I need to keep a clear head."

He snorts and puts the bottle down. "Alright, but make it quick. I'm parched."

"Why would you want to do that?"

"It's six o'clock. Sun's over the yard arm."

"No, I don't mean the champagne, I mean write a history of the Fitzgeralds."

"Because I'm the last in line. Don't you see? There's no one left to carry the burden of history. No one to pass on all the gory details. No successors. I need to leave something behind. It's my legacy and my duty."

I honestly don't know what to think. His reasoning has some logic and if it gives his final years more meaning then I'm all in favour of that. But I don't know how to articulate the deep sense of disquietude I feel. I may be a writer by profession and I'm no idiot, but I am neither qualified as a historian nor intellectual enough to pen anything more substantial than a one-page magazine article or a trashy novel. It wouldn't be so bad if Edmund were not so excited about it and I'm loath to burst his bubble. Given his volatility, the consequences don't bear thinking about.

"Well?"

"I think it's a brilliant idea, Edmund."

"Good!"

"In all respects but one."

"What's that?"

"Why me?"

"Why not?"

"I'm not a historian."

"You can read, can't you?"

"Yes, but..."

"And you can write?"

"Yes, but..."

"Then that's settled."

"I wouldn't know where to start."

He extends both arms, gesturing around the study. "Everything you need is here. Books, chronicles, diaries, letters, pictures. The entire saga is right here in front of your eyes. All it needs is researching, transcribing, editing, and presenting in some cohesive form." He taps his forehead with one finger. "And you also have me, a lifetime of memories and recollections, anecdotes passed down through generations." I briefly consider relying on Edmund's memory and almost burst out laughing, but it's far too serious for that. "Please say you'll do it?"

"Are you sure you'd not be better off with a professional biographer? It's not as if you can't afford one."

"Certainly not. Haven't got time for that."

"What do you mean?"

"Where am I going to get one of those from? Might take months to find someone suitable. I'd have to interview them, get to know them, then they wouldn't be able to start immediately and before you know it, I've dropped off my perch and never get to see the damn thing published."

I wag a finger of reproach. "I warned you not to say that again."

"Say what?"

"About you dying. It's tiresome."

"Look, my point is this. You've already demonstrated an intuitive knowledge of the family, I like you, I trust you, you're here and you're now. Who better?"

I'm touched and to be truthful, I'd be very interested to pore over the Fitzgerald archives and read about four hundred years of colourful family history. It's the scale of it that concerns me, but there's no way I can refuse. It would upset him too much. I can only try. "Okay. I'll give it a go."

"Marvellous!" he says, clapping his hands together. "So you'll be moving in."

"No!"

"But you must."

"Why?"

"Because it's a full-time job, that's why, and time is of the essence."

"I won't tell you again."

"Kate, my dear. Let's be realistic about this. Even if you dedicate every waking hour to this task, it's going to take a year or two. With the best will in the world, you can't expect me to hang on much longer than that."

"You want me to give up my career as well?"

"I'll pay you handsomely."

"We've been through that."

"It's a perfectly respectable arrangement. I would demand the same of anybody. There are not many who'd turn down such a lucrative assignment."

I'm annoyed with myself on two counts. Firstly, that he's managed to wear me down so easily and secondly, I'm tempted to ask how lucrative. It's vulgar to talk about money, especially between friends and I'm struggling to visualise the transition from friend to business associate, but that is the nature of what Edmund is asking.

"If I leave the cottage, give up all my clients and my novels and it all goes horribly wrong, I'll have no home and no income."

"Five hundred thousand and fifty percent of the royalties." He's been thinking about this. He's dropped the ridiculous notion of leaving everything to me and come up with a figure that will give me a generous income for several years, plus a share of the spoils if, for some unexpected reason, anyone out there wants to publish it. It's still a large sum of money, certainly more than I've ever seen before and I have to agree with him. Who in my position would turn down the opportunity on offer?

"What if you drop dead before it's published?"

"Then you get one hundred percent of the royalties."

"That's not what I mean!" I must learn to control my frustration with Edmund, or we won't last five minutes together. I take a deep breath. "I need security. You need to make a will."

"I told you…"

"No, Edmund. I don't want your money. All I want is that you make a will that includes provision for the agreed remuneration with the condition I publish a book about your family within, say, five years of your death."

"Agreed!"

"You can leave the rest to charity, or some other worthy cause."

"Agreed!"

"And you also need to make a living will in case you go doolally before I finish."

"Agreed!"

"And I'm going to stay in the cottage for the next three months until we're sure this arrangement is going to work."

"Why three months?"

"At least."

"But you're not safe there!"

"I'm not afraid of ghosts and I'll not be hounded out of my own home. Anyway, I need time to wind down my other commitments."

"I'm not sure about that. I shall worry."

"Take it or leave it."

"Agreed!" He thrusts out a hand and I go to shake it, but he turns it over and kisses the back. "May I now open a bottle to celebrate?"

***

The dinner has gone down well, and I've resisted the temptation for constant refills, worried my liver will eventually go on strike. Living here with Edmund and his wine cellar is an occupational hazard I didn't consider when I agreed to his ambitious plan. I shall have to formulate strict rules and be sure to follow them.

Edmund has no such compunction. He downed most of the Veuve and virtually the entire bottle of Bordeaux Superieur with little help from me. Curiously, his memory seems to perform better when he's had a drink so it's the best time to ask questions. Alcohol appears to have little effect on him other than to make him even more garrulous, so if I am to touch on sensitive issues, of which I am sure there will be many, then now's the time to do it and test the water.

"I bumped into Arthur Needham. He seems like a nice chap." Edmund pulls a face. "He said you used to be friends."

"Judas!"

"I don't understand."

"They all let you down eventually. Sooner or later, they show their true colours. Become a…disappointment."

"Is this about the cottage?"

He looks confused for a moment. "That was the proverbial straw. After everything that happened, everything I did for him, everything I forgave him for, that was how he repaid me."

There's obviously more to this than meets the eye. A letter from the Chairman of the Parish Council to Oakdale's most affluent residents, politely requesting they give a village eyesore a lick of paint is not likely to provoke a violent reaction or destroy decades of friendship. I thought it odd when Arthur told me and now Edmund has confirmed it, I'm no clearer.

"I saw from Eleanor's investment papers that Arthur was your financial advisor."

"I don't wish to talk about it."

"But he may be helpful in finding out what happened to her funds."

"Find out some other way, I don't want him involved."

"Edmund?"

"I said…" He gives me a steely look and refills his glass.

"This is not going to work, is it?"

"What isn't?

"You said 'no holds barred', 'warts and all'. What's the point of my trying to piece together the history of the Fitzgeralds if you're going to refuse to answer any questions?"

His lip is quivering. He knows I'm right and the full implications of his grandiose scheme are becoming clear. He manages to keep his anger in check, but only just.

"There are some things that will not be spoken of," he says calmly, but through gritted teeth.

"Why?"

"Because they're too painful!" He pounds the table with a fist, but it's half-hearted, like a wounded animal. I give him a minute to compose himself and decide to press on.

"Don't you think it might help if you got it all out? When you discuss or write down painful memories, you often get a different perspective. Hidden away in your mind, they fester. They're uncontrollable."

He considers me carefully. "Good lord. I can now add 'shrink' to your list of talents." It sounds like sarcasm but may just be a grudging compliment.

"I'm not skilled in psychoanalysis either, it's just common sense."

Edmund twirls the stem of the glass in his fingers. He's thinking, building up the courage to speak and his sullen expression says it all. I'm braced for a tantrum.

"Eleanor and Arthur had an affair. There, I've said it and I must say I don't feel any better for it."

I wasn't prepared, and I can see now why he was reluctant to explain. "Oh. I'm sorry Edmund."

"Sorry you asked or sorry they had an affair?"

Edmund's grand project was bound to dig up skeletons; he probably knows where most of them are regarding his ancestors, especially Julian, but he's bound to have some of his own. No history would be authentic or have integrity without disclosing them and I can't be afraid of asking difficult questions. If Edmund wants a sugar-coated biography of the Fitzgeralds, he will need to get someone else. I must decide. Either call a halt here and now and forget the whole thing, or turn over a few rocks and be damned at what lies beneath. I'm persuaded by the former, but I'm not in control.

"Sorry it still upsets you. But I want to know everything. When, why, how, who knew, who knows, who doesn't, what were the consequences. Chapter and verse. Leave anything out and I'll know."

"How will you know? How will you know if I simply spin you a yarn and make it go away?"

"Because you're not capable of duplicity. It's not in your nature and because the truth will out. Somewhere in that study lies the evidence and as long as you want me to research and write this epic tome of yours, I'll uncover it, so you may as well tell me now and save a lot of time. But if I find you have been dishonourable or duplicitous towards me, I'll walk away without hesitation."

CHAPTER 22

Steve Marshall has been here all morning; scrubbing, scraping, sanding, and hammering at my front door, the noise making it impossible to work. Instead, I went out into the back yard and pulled some weeds from between the cobbles. It hardly seems worth bothering if I'm moving into the Manor, but I decided it was prudent to continue renting the cottage even if I won't be there much, if at all. Edmund is making a generous monthly payment on account for my services, so I can easily afford it.

His unpredictability is part of the rationale. It's all very well spending a few hours with him in the evening, enjoying fine food and wine, but living there 24/7 is another thing altogether. Who knows how tolerable that will be for either of us, especially if, as I fully expect, I uncover something controversial or upsetting? The cottage will provide a bolthole if I need temporary respite from the Fitzgerald temper and in extremis, a place of refuge if we have an irrevocable falling out.

"I'm off now Kate," Steve calls out from the front door. I go and inspect as he clears away his things. "All prepped and primed, plus one topcoat. I'll come back tomorrow and finish off if that's okay with you?"

"Looking good."

"And if you want anything else doing, give me a call." He hands me his card. "Just in case I forget."

"How's married life? Does Tiffany miss her family?"

"Misses her mum's cooking. Has to do it all herself now." He laughs. "Otherwise, couldn't wait to get away."

"What about her sister?"

"Mel? Gets a room to herself so she's happy, and they were always squabbling anyway."

"I thought they were close."

"They were once. But that was before."

"I'm not with you." He twirls a paint scraper in his hand, looks down at the ground, then scratches his chin. "Sorry. It's none of my business."

"No, no. It's okay, everyone knows." *Everyone but me.* "I started off dating Mel but fell for her sister instead."

"Oh, dear. I can see why that might cause a bit of friction."

"You're not wrong there. It was a bit tricky for a while, then she said she got over it, but I think she's still bitter."

"Hell hath no fury."

"What?"

"It's an old saying. Hell hath no fury like a woman scorned."

"Is that right?" Steve hasn't a clue what I'm talking about but it's not worth pursuing. "Anyway, she swings the other way, does our Mel."

"She's a lesbian?" My directness causes big Steve to look shocked and furtive at the same time.

"You didn't get this from me, but yeah, she's one of them. I know she is."

"Nothing wrong with that," I say.

"No, no. Nothing wrong with that. Not unless you're Tommy Gibbs' daughter."

"Tommy doesn't approve?"

"No way. You just have to mention it and he goes apeshit."

"Who's going to mention it? Presumably Mel's told her parents how she feels."

Steve shakes his head. "Tommy won't accept it. Her mum's not that bothered but she's caught in the middle. And then there's the bloody vicar's wife."

"Sara?"

"Stickin' her nose in. Encouraging her."

I feel awkward and I hate gossip, but I'm beginning to think even the gossip is relevant. What started off as innocent chit-chat has opened another can of worms. Ordinarily, I would make an excuse and end the conversation, but Steve seems quite willing to talk about it, and instinct tells me this is important.

"In what way?"

"You know. Tellin' her it's fine and she needs to be herself and live life the way she wants to live it."

"Sounds like she was just doing what the vicar's wife should do. Being supportive and sympathetic to the emotional needs of the parishioners."

"She was a hell of a lot more than that!" I think I know what's coming, but I want him to tell me without my asking. "Mel bragged to Tiff about it. They had this row about me, and Mel told her she was going to dump me anyway because she wasn't interested in men anymore. More or less said she'd slept with Sara Lee."

"More or less?"

"Everyone knows she's a dyke." He looks suddenly panicky. "Here, you're not…?"

"No."

"…phew. Thought I'd put my size twelves right in it."

"Nor am I homophobic."

"Me neither! Doesn't bother me," he says and I stifle the urge to laugh at him.

"But did Mel actually say she had?"

"Not as such. But I bet you she has."

"What makes you so sure?"

"Wouldn't be the first time."

Connections. I sense another is about to be made.

"Did you know Jackie Thomas?"

"That girl who was here before you?"

"That's her." He looks shifty. "Did she receive support and encouragement from the vicar's wife too?" He doesn't answer, just swallows. "You repainted her door just like you repainted it for me." It isn't a question because I already know. I just don't know why I know. "Didn't you?"

"Yeah. I was going to say but I didn't want to freak you out."

"Thanks. That's very considerate, but I'm not one to freak out about this or anything else. I'm just a bit cross, and when

I find out who's responsible, they'll find out just how cross." He nods his head vigorously.

"Right," he says. "Best be off." He picks up his tool bag and paintbrush storage box.

"See you tomorrow?"

"Yeah," he says without looking back.

"Steve?" It stops him in his tracks. "Do you know what happened to Jackie?"

He makes a show of looking bemused and shakes his head. "Went back to London, I heard."

He says he doesn't know but offers an explanation anyway. I don't believe him. "Just wondered."

***

I thought long and hard.

I would feel terrible if I caused any further distress, but instead of filling in the blanks, more have appeared. There are key facts I need to know and there's no one reliable source. Despite warnings from the vicar and his wife, I'm still convinced Edmund is harmless, it's his memory I need to be wary of. His recollections come and go and that alone means he can't be relied upon to reveal the truth. On the matter of Eleanor's affair with Arthur, he agreed, albeit under duress, to reveal the circumstances. It was clearly painful for him at first but as I anticipated, he was philosophical about it and I hope felt some sort of release. I took the opportunity that night to drag it out of him, worried that were I to raise the subject the next day, he would have forgotten what he'd said and then have a tantrum. Bizarrely, once prompted, his memory returned.

It was a long time ago. The Needhams and the Fitzgeralds were good friends. They socialised, played bridge, went on the occasional holiday together, and shared a passion for classical music, art, good food and fine wine. Neither couple had children, so neither had the distraction of families nor the need to conduct or tolerate one-sided conversations about them. The overriding distinction between them was wealth and privilege. According to Edmund, he was always vaguely embarrassed by his privileged background and sought never to exploit his position nor flaunt his wealth. The fact that the Fitzgeralds' wealth was squandered by his grandfather Julian, leaving them virtually penniless was never mentioned. The retention of the Manor was little consolation given the monstrous costs of maintaining it, and there was little or no income from the cottage due to its sordid reputation and the interminable feud with three generations of Hawleys. But Edmund's father had forged a solid career for himself in maritime insurance, one which his son would ultimately follow, and his income, though modest, was sufficient to keep his family's head above water.

Eleanor had no such compunctions. Financially secure through her family connections to the Larsen Group, she revelled in the title Lady Fitzgerald, often to the chagrin of her best friend Marjorie. Paradoxically, the Needhams were much better off, Arthur's career in personal finance and Marjorie's as a district nurse afforded them a comfortable lifestyle without having the burden of maintaining a centuries-old Manor house. Consequently, the Fitzgeralds had had little need of Arthur's professional advice until Eleanor received the inheritance from her aunt and it seemed the obvious thing to do to call upon Arthur's skills and invest the funds for the long term. Inevitably, the nature of their relationship changed as Arthur's role took on a new significance and as Eleanor watched the value of her funds increase dramatically, she became ever closer to her financial advisor.

"I made her a Lady," Edmund had said, "but he made her rich, and she couldn't decide which she preferred. In the end she thought she could have both. It wasn't the first time, so I shouldn't have been surprised."

"Eleanor had another affair?"

"The first one was in the mid-seventies, five years after we were married. An old school friend with an E-Type Jaguar, a cravat, and a house in the Dordogne. She promised it wouldn't happen again, but then after that she seduced a young gardener who agreed to satisfy her Ladyship's desires in lieu of pay."

"Gosh! Edmund, you don't need to continue if you don't want to."

He'd ignored me.

"I acquiesced because I loved her. Whatever made her happy made me happy, and I took a perverse pride in knowing other men found *my* wife as attractive and vivacious as I. For Eleanor, I don't think it was so much the sex, I think it was the ungodly thrill of immorality, the insatiable desire to be wicked allied to the terror of being caught. Yet when at last she tired of them, she made sure I would find out. It gave her an excuse to finish with them and reminded me to avow my undying devotion. But there were others I didn't know. She visited her sister in London three or four times a year, but I'm certain each time it was just a cover for a secret assignation. And of course, my best friend Arthur Needham."

"And when did that end?"

"Marjorie put a stop to it. It was New Year's Eve, the millennium celebrations. We had a black-tie dinner here with the Needhams and several others. As you can imagine, by the time the bells struck, a lot of drink had been taken, a lot of nonsense spoken, and Eleanor felt emboldened enough to snog Arthur in full view of everyone. Marjorie objected, there was a stand-up row, and Eleanor was provoked into revealing intimate details of Arthur's anatomy."

"Oh my God! Didn't Marjorie know already?"

"She knew. We discussed it, but like me, she was content not to rock the boat, provided it was infrequent and kept behind closed doors. Eleanor spilling the beans in public was the last straw."

"You discussed it with Marjorie?" I had been feverishly taking notes but finding it impossible to keep up.

"Oh yes. What's good for the goose…"

"What? You and Marjorie?"

"More of a fling really. We were never suited."

The thought of the Fitzgeralds and Needhams as swingers made me reach for what was left of the 2016 Chateau Latour, desperate for something to calm my heart's imminent fibrillation.

"I hesitate to ask. Were there any others?"

"Just one, that I know of. Eleanor had always been active in the Church. She derived a perverse pleasure from being ungodly in real life and deeply pious in church, safe in the knowledge God would forgive her. For one or two years, she had an affair with the vicar, chap by the name of Fenton."

"Michael Fenton."

"How did you know that?"

"I asked Arthur who was the vicar before John Lee."

"Ah yes. I forgot to mention Gigolo John."

"Surely they didn't…?"

"She'd already had two strokes, the second one quite serious, and saw him as her final conquest. He played up to it, returned her flirtatiousness in equal measure, the creep. Fenton was a creep too. Must run in the Church."

I spotted an opportunity for corroboration, so took it.

"Why did Fenton leave? Was it because of Eleanor?"

"No. He was accused of abusing teenagers. Chap called Gibbs made a complaint about one of his daughters. Forget her name. Never proven, but Fenton was moved on, so there must have been some substance to it."

"And John Lee took his place."

"And brought his ghastly wife with him."

There had been so much material there, I was tempted to call a halt, but I wanted to try one more time on a different subject. Edmund's memory seemed flawless when it came to relating Eleanor's affairs and berating Arthur Needham, and I wondered whether his amnesia was random or selective. It was time for an experiment.

"What did Jackie Thomas do for you and Eleanor?" I fully expected a blank look and repeat of his claim not to know her.

"I asked her to do what you did."

It was as if a light came on. It could be Edmund finally confessing something he'd originally wanted to keep secret, now regarding it unimportant in the light of revelations about his married life. Or he may simply have remembered. Forgotten he forgot. Either way, he didn't hesitate to reply and made no attempt to explain his previous claim to ignorance.

"You mean the admin?"

"Yes. Eleanor's behaviour was becoming increasingly erratic, and she was frail. We thought she would be able to help us. Like you, she suggested we made wills, but never got around to it. She simply disappeared."

***

Which is why I thought long and hard.

I dialled Freda Thomas's number, got her husband, and introduced myself. There was a pause before Freda came on the line.

"Miss Duvall. What can I do for you?" Terse, tense, defensive.

"Please call me Kate, Mrs Thomas."

"Alright, Kate."

"I think I can help you."

"In what way? What can you possibly do to help us now?"

"Jackie told you dark forces were at work, and you said you believed her death wasn't an accident."

"Directly or indirectly, her death was caused by others."

Long and hard.

"I believe she was murdered, Mrs Thomas." I can hear only the faint hiss of background noise. I give her time. I give her ten seconds and then another ten. "Are you still there?"

"Why are you telling me this?" Broken, and suspicious.

"Two other people have been murdered in Oakdale and I think they're connected to Jackie."

"Then you should go to the police and tell them."

"I have no evidence."

"Then what good is that?"

"I have no evidence and nor do you. But it doesn't change what you believe or how you feel." I give her another ten. "What did Jackie do for a living?"

"She was a solicitor."

"And was she freelance, or did she work for a firm?"

"Both. She had her own clients but also worked as consultant to a small firm in Bradwell."

"Do you remember the name?"

"No, but if you give me time, I'm sure I can find out. My memory is not what it was."

"I understand. Why did she move to Oakdale?"

"She worked for a large London firm and frankly, found it difficult to cope. The pressure of it all filled her with anxiety, and she was close to having a breakdown. She had to get away from all that madness in the city so when she saw a job for a part-time solicitor in a country practice, she decided to take it."

"I'm sorry. I can empathise. I did something similar, but neither of us could have known what was in store."

"Franklyn something," she says suddenly.

"Franklyn Jones?"

"Yes, that was it. They said they could also find her a place to live as it was very difficult around there." It fitted. Felicity Jones, partner in the firm Jackie was about to join and who carried out the conveyancing, married to estate agent Jeremy, managing agent for the owners.

"Farrier's Cottage."

"Yes, she loved it there until the threats started."

"Was she explicit?"

"I…" She stumbles. I know what she's going to say, and it must be heart-breaking, but I need to know. "It was vile and obscene."

"Did someone paint 'Whore' on the front door?"

"Yes."

"And break in?"

"Yes. During the night. She was completely terrified. Someone demented, stomping around in the house shouting for Jacob. She locked herself in the bedroom until everything went quiet, but she was too afraid to leave. In desperation she called the vicar's wife, who rushed to her aid but when she eventually went downstairs…" The woman is sobbing, unable to continue, so I do it for her.

"She found the same word painted on the mirror."

"Oh Kate! You have no idea the danger you're in. You must get away from there."

It's sound advice, but I'm thinking of something else. This is all wrong. Jackie's experience sounds virtually identical to mine but not quite how Sara Lee explained it. She said Jackie had been at the Manor when it happened, and only found the break in when she got home. That much is inconsistent, but there's something far more important.

"If Jackie had locked herself in her bedroom, how did Sara get in?"

"She had a key."

The drumbeat starts again, accompanied by a tingle at the base of my neck.

"Why? Why would she have a key?"

Freda Thomas is not sure why I'm asking such an obvious question. "Well, because they were friends. Sara offered to keep a spare in case she ever got locked out and Jackie felt comforted that Sara was looking out for her." It's vaguely plausible, but there's more to it than that. "And she gave Jackie one for The Vicarage in case she needed a place of sanctuary and she and her husband were out. Sara was very good to her."

I desperately want to ask Jackie's mum whether she knew her daughter was a lesbian, but I can't risk it. It's entirely possible she does and considers it of no importance, but if she doesn't, it could come as a massive shock and that's something she doesn't need right now. Even if she does, Freda Thomas does not sound like the kind of person who would condone her daughter having a relationship with the vicar's wife. I suspect Jackie was not gay, or at least not until she met

Sara Lee, but the mere fact Freda knows they were very close raises another question.

"Have you spoken to her?"

"Who? Sara?"

"Does she know Jackie died?"

"Yes of course. She called me to offer her condolences."

I rub a hand over my eyes. I had thought long and hard, worrying about causing Freda Thomas unnecessary distress with my questions and its rebounding on me. I'm getting tied up in knots, unable to rationalise conflicting facts, to the extent any are facts at all and not just misguided opinion. Every question begets another and drags me deeper into the morass, but I'm not finished with Freda Thomas. She has more to offer and there's no going back now.

"May I ask you something else?"

"Alright."

"Last time we spoke, you were very scathing about Lord and Lady Fitzgerald."

"With good reason."

"Can you explain?"

"All I know is they asked Jackie to get their affairs in order. Lady Fitzgerald was ill, nearing the end of her life and he wanted to plan his own exit, so to speak."

"Not an unreasonable request."

"But in the course of her work, she uncovered some things they didn't know about each other. You know, dirty secrets."

"What kind…?"

"I don't know. Jackie would never betray a client's confidence. She was very professional."

"Of course."

"But they went mad at her, told her she was a liar, that she was trying to manipulate them, exploit their age and poor health for her own personal gain. They threatened her, told her never to repeat her lies and complained to her superiors."

"Who was that?"

"I don't know. A woman."

"Felicity Jones?"

"I don't know, sorry."

"That's okay Mrs Thomas. One last thing. Can you tell me the date Jackie died?"

"I'll never forget. It was the 15th of January."

"And where did it happen?"

"About ten miles from Oakdale. Her car went off the road and into a ditch."

"Thank you. I'm sorry if I've upset you."

"What are you going to do, Kate?"

"I'm going to find out who was responsible for Jackie's death."

CHAPTER 23

I decide an audience with the Almighty is overdue. St John's is well attended this Sunday and many familiar faces are there: the Needhams, the Gibbs, including the Marshall newlyweds, Ethel Hawley, and her friend Mavis, and others whom I recognise but whose names I don't know. Reverend Lee pontificates on the question of truth, quoting several passages from the bible in which truth appears to be a recurring theme. I'm struck by the irony; the truth is in short supply here in Oakdale and I wonder whether John Lee realises that too and feels the need to remind everyone.

The church empties quickly, and as everyone drifts off into the sunshine, I manage to intercept Arthur and Marjorie Needham.

"Lovely service."

"Yes indeed," says Arthur.

"Are you settling into village life?" asks Marjorie.

"Yes, I have a charming cottage in a charming village and people couldn't be more friendly."

"Good!" says Arthur. "That's what we like to hear."

"Arthur, there's something I wanted to ask you. I need your advice. On a sensitive matter."

"Alright, what's it about?" I make a show of looking embarrassed and strain every sinew to avoid looking at Marjorie. "Is this something to do with Edmund?"

I nod nervously. "It's just that I know way back you were their financial advisor and I'm trying to tie up some loose ends."

Marjorie stiffens and Arthur's smile fades rapidly.

"I'm afraid I can't help you my dear. It was a long time ago and it wouldn't be appropriate. I'm sorry."

Marjorie takes his arm and without another word they saunter off down the path. I curse myself for being stupid. The mere mention of Edmund's name in front of Marjorie was bound to raise hackles; I should have waited until Arthur was alone. I'll try again another time and if he still refuses to talk, I'll just have to wait for probate and contact Hollis Warburton directly.

I step back into the church as the stragglers leave, waiting for the opportunity to throw a few more pebbles into Oakdale's murky waters.

"We'll make a Christian of you yet Kate," says Reverend Lee, looking more ebullient than usual, a far cry from our tense encounter in The Vicarage. Maybe vicars get a rush of adrenalin from performing in the pulpit and take a while to come down from the high.

"I never doubted I was a Christian. Doesn't mean I have to attend church."

"But you came anyway, and I'm very pleased."

I see Sara coming down the aisle, clutching a green cloth bag containing today's collection.

"I wanted to talk to Sara, actually."

"Do I hear my name being mentioned?" She holds up the bag smiling broadly. "One eighty-eight and five Euros. Not bad, I suppose."

"Makes you wonder how the Church got so wealthy," I ask. John Lee ignores the dig.

"Kate wants to ask you something."

"Both of you actually."

"Shoot," says Sara.

"I don't suppose you have a forwarding address for Jackie?"

"Jackie Thomas?" says John, knowing full well who I mean.

"Why do you want that?" asks Sara without confirming one way or the other.

She can't hide it. It's in her voice. Unless she and the vicar have an open marriage and he already knows of her relationship with Jackie, then she's beginning to regret confiding her wickedly delicious little secret to me. This is the first time I've mentioned Jackie's name with both of them present and I want to see who's going to react. I have no sympathy. I don't trust them and I want them to think I don't know what happened to her.

"I found a couple of personal things in a cupboard that must have belonged to her and wanted to return them."

"Oh? What kind of things?" says Sara.

"Personal."

Sara casts her husband a nervous look but he's looking down at the floor, hands on hips. He eventually catches Sara's eye and speaks first.

"Kate. There's something you need to know."

"What?"

"Not here. Why don't you come up to the house tomorrow evening and you and I can have a chat over a drink." I glance back and forth between them. I don't want to be alone with John Lee and I'm surprised he's mentioning drink in front of his wife given her stint at AA. Sara gets it.

"All three of us can have a chat. Six o'clock?"

***

There's a petite blonde woman in jeans and tee-shirt waiting by my gate, flicking at her phone. I don't recognise her until I get close, and she looks up.

"Hi Kate. Miss Duvall," says WPC Jenkins looking nervous and as if she's about to curtsey.

"Hi, er, constable. What happened to the uniform?"

"Off duty. And it's Sue."

"Hi Sue, nice to meet you." I stretch out a hand and she takes it limply. "Do you want to come in?"

"Is that okay?"

"Of course. Fancy a drink?"

I retrieve a bottle of Prosecco from the fridge, two flutes from the cupboard, and take her out to the back yard. The plastic patio table and two chairs have seen better days, but I wiped them down yesterday and they do the job.

"So this is not an official visit?" I say, wrestling with the cork, suddenly wishing Edmund were here. He'd have it out in seconds.

"No."

"Do your colleagues know?"

She shrugs. "Don't care. I can do what I like in my spare time. They do." The cork yields with a loud pop and I pour the fizzing wine. "Cheers."

"What's it like working for the Dales force?"

"Pretty much as you'd expect. You summed it up the other day. Arrogant, boorish men, strutting around, enjoying the trappings of power. Making sexist comments, brushing up against you, grabbing your tits and patting your bum. Misogynist, racist, homophobes."

"That good, eh?"

"Not all of them. But it's no place if you're woman, black or gay."

"Then why do you do it?"

"I'm leaving. Handed in my notice."

"And you've come to tell me there's a vacancy?"

"No!" she says missing the joke. "There's something you need to know." Twice within the hour someone has said that and I'm unimpressed with both. It had better be good. "There was another girl in this cottage before you. Her name was Jackie Thomas."

"Yes, I've heard the name mentioned." WPC Sue Jenkins is getting nothing out of me. For all I know she's here fishing on behalf of her racist, misogynist pals. She's no more to be trusted than anyone else. *There's something you need to know - beware Greeks bearing gifts.*

"I know you've had some trouble. Graffiti painted on the door and that stuff with George Hawley. It was meant to get you out. Well, she had the same."

"I know." I need to move this along a bit or else we'll be here all afternoon. "Other people have told me I'm not the first to experience it."

"Jackie contacted Dales police and made a complaint. I know because I took the call, and I came out to see her. She was in a terrible state. I tried to be sympathetic; promised to file a detailed report and said we'd investigate." She sips at her drink trying to compose herself.

"And?"

"It's not down to me, is it? Gerrard said we had more important things to do and didn't have time for minor stuff like that, so I took it up with Stride and he pretty much said the same thing. Gerrard then made life very difficult for me, going behind his back. Treated me like a child and gave me all the crap jobs like filing, watching car park CCTV and dealing with missing dogs and cats. Bloody men."

"I'm sorry."

"So, nothing happened and then there was a break-in." I sense this is getting interesting. I didn't know Jackie had reported it to the police.

"The cottage was broken into?" *You're getting worryingly good at deceit, Kate Duvall.*

"She called me in a panic, and I came over but there was no evidence of forced entry, and nothing was taken. Just some abuse painted on the mirror. I made a full report, but it got buried. Gerrard's view was she did it herself to get attention."

"But you believed her."

"Yes. But I couldn't do anything."

"Why are you telling me this?" I know exactly what's coming but I'm not sure why.

"Because she's dead." The alcohol and the guilt and the heightened emotions that go with it are about to overflow. I forage around in my jeans and pull out a wrinkled but clean handkerchief. She takes it without question and dabs her eyes. She's not fishing, and I'm tempted to lower my guard but decide against it. Stride and I discussed Jackie on the day of George's funeral, so he knows it's not news to me. He just hasn't liaised with his junior officer. I skip the display of shock and ignorance and take the role of inquisitor instead.

"Tell me what happened."

Sue Jenkins takes a deep breath and composes herself.

"She left two days later but was killed in a car accident on the way back to London. We got an alert from South Peaks force because they found this address in the car. They thought there'd been a collision because there was a dent and some white paint streaks on the rear end, but there were no witnesses. She ended upside down in a ditch full of water." The notion there might have been a collision is news to me, and given everything that's happened, another depressingly familiar nugget of information. I don't need to push her further because the flood gates are already open.

"Stride and Gerrard kept their heads down. Refused to accept there was any connection and told me to button it. They didn't want to admit they should have done something sooner. But I'm pretty certain she was killed. Murdered by someone connected to this cottage."

"Why are you telling me this?"

"I'm telling you because you're in danger! I'm telling you because I don't want the same thing to happen again." The tears are smudging her mascara, staining her puffy eyelids black. "If only I'd done something, then this wouldn't have happened."

"It's not your fault. You couldn't have known." She may have come to unburden herself and, belatedly, try to salve her conscience, but there's more to it than that. "What does Stride think now we've had two murders on top of a suspicious death?"

"He and Gerrard now believe there is a connection."

"But they weren't about to warn me."

"That's just it! Their priority isn't your safety, it's covering their own arses, otherwise they would have told you about it; warned you so you could have taken extra care before things get out of hand. Instead, they're just watching and waiting for something to turn up, something else to happen."

"Using me as bait."

She nods and blows her nose on my handkerchief. She doesn't know I've also had intruders and I see nothing to be gained from telling her now. But I'm curious about something else. Stride asked me to find out when the cottage was sold. I know the conveyancing was done by Felicity Jones and my instinct was not to bother her in the wake of Jeremy's murder, but Stride hasn't chased me for the information, which means either he already knows, or he doesn't think it's important. I decide to go fishing.

"Your boss asked me to find out when the cottage was sold, but I haven't been able to yet. His Lordship's records are in a terrible state, and I didn't want to hassle Felicity Jones… you know… after what happened to her husband."

"That was really bad. Multiple stab wounds. Pathologist says cause of death was a single cut to the throat but whoever did it kept stabbing him in the chest. Bloody maniac."

Tommy Gibbs' description of Psycho Si comes immediately to mind.

"Does Stride think it had anything to do with the cottage?"

"Can't rule it out, but we're still looking into his other business dealings. He knew a lot of rich and powerful folk in and around the Dales. He may just have upset one of them. But don't worry about the date the cottage was sold. He got it from the Jersey Registry."

"That'll be Belles Fleurs Investments, I assume."

"Yeah. How did you know that?"

"I saw their name on a document amongst Edmund's files. I looked them up but didn't get very far."

"That's Jersey for you. Tax haven. A lot of info isn't available to the public, but they have to respond to police enquiries."

"Who are they?"

"Listed as a property company, but they only have the one."

"This one?"

"And a load of financial assets on their balance sheet. Quoted and unquoted investments." She says this with a nod and a wink. WPC Sue Jenkins has recovered her composure. She's enjoying this, she's got it off her chest and is now happily divulging police information. Mentally, she's switched sides. I take the opportunity.

"How much?"

"About thirty million."

"Who owns it?"

"Sole shareholder is a chap by the name of Arthur Needham."

Time to show genuine surprise. "Chairman of the Parish Council?"

"Yep."

"That's a weird coincidence."

"He's a director, and his wife is secretary. There's one other director; a local man called Barry Wilson. He and Needham both have a military background."

Another connection. Arthur Needham, Tommy Gibbs, Psycho Si and Barry Wilson, soldiers all. I'm reminded of my chat with Alan in the pub. Arthur and Barry breaking up a fight between George Hawley and Steve Marshall the night George was murdered. I'd assumed it was over Tiffany, but Steve had acted strangely when I mentioned it and I thought nothing more. Alan the barman said the police knew about it. They probably interviewed everyone involved.

"I've heard his name mentioned. The guy who repaired my front door, Steve Marshall, told me he had a row with George Hawley in the pub the night he was killed, and Arthur and Barry broke it up."

"That's right. We interviewed Marshall as a suspect but ruled him out because he had an alibi."

"What was the row about? Between Steve and George."

Sue Jenkins has some colour in her cheeks and looks vaguely embarrassed. "Don't you know?" Her lascivious grin betrays a deliciously guilty secret, and she's happy to reveal it. "It was about you."

***

I thanked WPC Sue Jenkins profusely for telling me about Jackie Thomas and warning me, not just about Farrier's Cottage, but also of the questionable tactics of her male colleagues. I told her I thought she was very brave, and I hoped she would be happy and successful in her new career, whatever that might be. Before I gave her a big hug and sent her on her tearful way I asked, in passing, the colour of Jackie's car. Blue, she said.

A few more stones were turned over during our discussion and I know they all fit somewhere, but at the moment, I just have to add them to the mix. Steve Marshall told the police George had accused him of defacing my front door. Steve had already repaired it once when Jackie lived there and George had questioned how he'd been paid, suggesting he'd done it again just so he could *'get into her knickers'* too. I know George would have taken any opportunity to smear my character, but picking on big Steve was bound to cause trouble. I'd like to think Steve had jumped to my defence, but I didn't know him at the time and I doubt he knew much about me. None of this precluded him doing exactly as George alleged, but I got no sense that Steve had designs on me, only that he coveted the cottage. Strangely, there were no other witnesses to the altercation itself, only the dust-up that followed.

I've been wondering what tomorrow's appointment with the Lees will reveal, so I have a long soak in the bath and afterwards, lie in bed, thinking. Regrettably, I can't rely on Edmund to provide any answers. Memory issues aside, his antipathy towards Arthur Needham means he can't know Arthur is behind the company that bought the cottage. Eleanor's cottage or not, he would never countenance its sale to a company controlled by his deceased wife's lover. If I told him, he would probably go berserk and that would have unconscionable consequences. It occurs to me Jackie Thomas may have got this far, her revelation tipping Edmund and Eleanor over the edge, as Freda alleges. I still haven't tracked down the funds but provided I can be confident full value was received for the property, it may prove perfectly benign, an arm's length transaction done for the right reasons: to rid the Fitzgeralds of the curse of Farrier's whilst ensuring it didn't fall into the hands of the Hawleys. The obvious way to do this is to trace it back through solicitors Franklyn Jones and it should be possible for them to retrieve the file without unduly upsetting Mrs Jones. In those circumstances, and assuming everything is in order, Edmund need never know, and I can get on with my work.

I am intrigued by the relationship between Arthur Needham and Barry Wilson. They're friends, former army comrades and in respect of Belles Fleurs Investments, business partners. Wilson isn't a shareholder, and Belles Fleurs probably had enough financial clout to purchase the cottage outright, but somehow they're in it together. The fact they bought it through a Jersey based company strongly suggests they wanted their ownership to remain secret. *Title to the property is a matter of public record...* Arthur had told an irate George Hawley at the Parish Council meeting, and he was right; anyone could find out Belles Fleurs Investments was the freeholder, but not who owned the company itself. I think back to my discussion with Arthur. He was very open about the rift between him and Edmund but blamed it on the letter he'd written regarding the state of the cottage. I would hardly have expected him to confess his affair with Eleanor, that it had anything to do with their falling out, or his role in secretly purchasing the cottage through Belles Fleurs, but I told him I was tidying up Edmund's financial affairs and he never once mentioned his role as Eleanor's financial advisor, something I was bound to discover at some stage. And when I did mention it in the churchyard, it was clearly very sensitive.

Sue Jenkins' revelation that the police now think Jackie's car was in a collision and her death not only suspicious, but also connected to the murders of George Hawley and Jeremy Jones, has my mind racing. The police seem content that I endure the same level of intimidation and threat if it helps them solve their case without revealing their ineptitude. I saw Stride at George's funeral and he said nothing about my taking extra precautions. Admittedly, they don't know I've reached the stage of a break-in because I haven't reported it. They might reasonably judge I am some way off being murdered. *Charming.*

The Lees also know something, and now I'm trying to contact Jackie Thomas, are motivated to reveal it. I just hope it's not another vague warning about Edmund and the malign spirits that reside within Farrier's.

I shall go back to the Manor tomorrow and pursue Franklyn Jones for details of the money transfer for the cottage. Then I can continue my work documenting the history of the Fitzgerald dynasty.

***

A scratching sound wakes me. It's distant, downstairs. A key turning in a lock. I'm bolt upright, listening, adrenalin pulsing. It comes again and again then stops. I leap out of bed and peek through the curtains, just in time to see the back of a shadowy figure disappearing, unable to tell whether its man, woman, large or small. I race downstairs, heart thumping, and stare at the front door. It's secure. The intruder with the key now knows the locks have been changed. Whoever it is, will have to be more inventive in future.

A clang of metal on metal. My heart stops. It sounded like a muted bell and it's upstairs. The boiler is off so it's not plumbing. I'm frozen to the spot, ears straining, eyes dancing in the gloom, breathing shallow to avoid making any noise of my own. A clang of metal on metal. My breath comes in fits and starts and I'm suddenly icy cold.

"Jacob!"

It's a woman distressed. I've heard it before and I'm sure.

"Jacob!" It's accompanied by a whimper, but its mine and I clasp a hand over my mouth. Rolling thunder, feet pounding the staircase, the creak of floorboards on the landing and the bang of the bedroom door colliding with the wall.

Then silence.

CHAPTER 24

I'm alone in Edmund's study, surrounded by piles of letters. We had another disagreement. I found a locked drawer which he said contained Eleanor's personal papers.

"I need to see what's in there."

"That's Eleanor's private stuff."

"Well, they may well have been once, but Eleanor has left them behind." It was the most sensitive I could be in the circumstances. "They may contain something important."

"I shouldn't think so."

"So you know what's in there?"

"Of course not! It's private."

We bandied this around while I tugged at the drawer until I lost patience. "I can't do this with one arm tied behind my back. If you want the unexpurgated saga of Oakdale's most famous family, plus an orderly exit from this mortal coil, I have to be sure I've seen all documentation, personal or private. Everything I do and see will be kept in strictest confidence, so either you trust me or get someone else!"

"Of course I trust you."

"Then open the drawer."

"I don't have a key."

"You must have one somewhere." He shook his head. "Do you have any tools?"

"I suppose. In the shed."

"Show me."

I'm a little on edge, it must be said. The terrifying noises I heard last night were the same as I heard during the break-in. On that occasion, I thought they were the work of the intruder, but clearly not. I'm not ready to succumb to the notion Farrier's is haunted, but I have no other explanation. Edmund is no more or less exasperating because of it, it's just that my tolerance threshold is lower.

He took me out through the kitchen door and across the yard where there's a dilapidated brick-built outhouse with a slate roof.

"I keep garden tools in here," he said undoing a padlock and stepping aside, "but I'm sure there are some hand-tools near the bench." I found a couple of rusty screwdrivers and took them with me back to the study.

"I'll try to be careful but there's going to be some damage."

"Go ahead," he said standing over me. I gave him a look that said all he needed to know, and he wandered off, muttering under his breath. The desk was well made and there was barely a gap to get the blade of a screwdriver in, but eventually, the lock surrendered along with a small piece of mahogany veneer.

They go back fifty years, tied in bundles with ribbons in various colours. Love letters, each lover a different colour. I count nine, the postmarks spanning the decades, the dates on some bundles from the 1980s overlapping, eventually fizzling out just before the millennium. I pick a few at random and scan them quickly, fooling myself that it's less of an intrusion just to skim the surface, but I get the sense and Edmund's more right than he knows; they're intensely personal and I can feel my neck growing hot. I tell myself it's all relevant to the story but can't in all conscience read them at Eleanor's desk in Edmund's house. I use the printer-scanner I brought from the cottage and set about digitising each one, cataloguing and storing them on my laptop. I shall read them in my own time and space.

There's also a brown leather-bound file with 'Coutts' embossed on the front. Bank statements bearing the name of Lady Eleanor Forbes Fitzgerald, dated between 1972 when the account was opened and 2002, when it was eventually closed. I flick backwards through the pages, until I find a CHAPS payment of two million pounds to Hollis Warburton, after which there was only a trickle of activity. Two months earlier a receipt of over two million pounds arrives from

Freshman Baker, a name I recognise from other correspondence. Aunt Jemima's bequest. Most of the other transactions are unintelligible, bearing only cheque numbers and paying-in slip references, but form a regular pattern in terms of timing and amounts paid and received.

In the drawer beneath, I find cheque books stubs, neatly bundled in years, and look up a few items on the statement at random. One that catches my eye simply bears the initial 'J' and appears regularly between 1980 when the amount was five hundred pounds, rising progressively to fifteen hundred by 1982 when it abruptly stops. Edmund might be able to shed light on it but in the absence of any documentation, I would only be speculating.

I am worried about Eleanor's letters. I made a great show of demanding access to her private files, but perversely, I'm now determined to keep them secret from Edmund. I insisted I should know everything so I could write a complete and candid family history but have very quickly encountered a major hurdle; there are some things too painful to disclose, at least while he's alive. The drawer is now broken so they can't be hidden and despite being an honourable gentleman, Edmund would not be human if he could resist taking a look when I'm gone. I mentally park the problem in the 'too difficult for now' category and stuff the bundles into an ancient box file marked 'Tenant Farms 1900-1910' which is stacked in the far corner with a dozen others, covered in dust.

After lunch, I call Franklyn Jones and ask for Felicity. "She's on compassionate leave," says receptionist Kelly to my relief. "Would you like Mr Franklyn?" I explain to David Franklyn that I'm acting as PA to Lord Edmund Fitzgerald and what exactly I'm trying to establish in respect of the disposal of Farrier's Cottage. An hour later, I email Franklyn a letter of introduction signed by Edmund, a certified copy of Eleanor's death certificate, two utility bills addressed to Oakdale Manor and an old letter from Felicity Jones to Eleanor regarding the sale.

By the end of the day, I've had a reply from Franklyn's assistant. The sale of Farrier's Cottage was completed on 10th December 2017, the completion statement showing net proceeds of just over three hundred and seventy-five thousand pounds, satisfied by a promissory note issued by Belles Fleurs Investments Limited to Lady E.F. Fitzgerald.

There was no cash. The property was transferred to Belles Fleurs and a loan note issued in return. Attached is a copy of a Belles Fleurs board minute authorising the transaction and signed by its directors: A. Needham and E. Fitzgerald.

***

I don't regard this as a social occasion and I don't expect it to take long, so I haven't dressed up. The Lees are pretty casual at the best of times, so I figure jeans and short-sleeved blouse will suffice but I've slung a cashmere cardigan over my shoulder in case it's cool walking back. John answers the door looking less effusive than on Sunday, and I fear I'm in for a re-run of his bizarre outburst last time I was in his house.

"I wondered whether you'd come."

"You invited me, so here I am."

Sara is in the kitchen, seated on a stool at the breakfast bar, nursing a tall glass containing a colourless liquid with ice and lemon. *Doesn't mean it's a gin and tonic, Kate.* She embraces me and I present a cheek instinctively, but she's quick and her lips catch the corner of my mouth. They're damp and I do my best not to flinch at the sensation or react to the taste of tonic.

"You're looking lovely," she says, hands still on my waist, our lips inches apart. There's no smell of alcohol on her breath.

"Drink?" asks John. Either he hasn't noticed or he's inured to his wife's flirting.

"Water's fine," I say, disengaging from her grip and she sashays back to her perch. He busies himself at the sink and hands me a glass.

"Chateauneuf-du-Tap," he says with a flourish, not for the first time, I suspect. "Come through to the sitting room."

It's tidy, modestly furnished courtesy of the diocese and seen better days. John takes a wing chair and I, the sofa opposite, with Sara at the other end. Pincer movement.

"What's this about?"

"You asked for Jackie's address?"

"It's no big deal. A simple yes or no would suffice. Do you have it?"

"No."

I glance at Sara who has tucked her legs underneath and looks casual and sultry, regarding me intensely. "Well, then. Thanks for a lovely evening." I move to stand up.

"Wait," he says. "You don't understand. We're trying to help you. Why do you always behave like someone who doesn't want to be helped."

"Rubbish! I'm not going to cry like a girlie just because some old bloke was nasty to me and my door got vandalised."

"That's not what I mean."

"What then?"

"Edmund Fitzgerald."

"Here we go again." I knew this would come up and I lay on the weariness. He sits forward and gives me his best, self-righteous, patronising look.

"Jackie worked for the Fitzgeralds. Both of them."

"I know. Sara told me. He told me as well."

"He admitted it?"

"I asked him. He said she was doing some work tidying up his financial affairs, then suddenly disappeared. That's why he asked me to take over." It's not quite true but would be had Edmund not forgotten about it in the first place.

"And did he tell you why she disappeared?"

"He doesn't know."

"Oh yes he does. She discovered something awful about him and when she confronted him, he went berserk, threatened her, and threw her out. You'll have already seen what a temper he has."

I ignore his last comment. "What did she find that was so awful?"

"The noble lord had a dirty little secret he kept from his wife for over forty years. Did you ask him about Jennifer?"

"No."

"Well ask him."

"I'm tired of this John. You obviously know already so why don't you tell me, then I'll ask him and provided he doesn't threaten me or throw me out, I'll compare notes and decide which of you is telling the truth."

"This is the truth, so help me God." I want to laugh at the absurdity of Reverend Gigolo John, but I am interested in finding out who Jennifer is. I've already assumed she's the 'J' who features on Eleanor's bank statements and I hope he's not about to disappoint me.

"Jennifer Young lived in Farrier's Cottage in the late seventies. She was a twenty-seven-year-old widow with a four-year-old daughter. Her husband was killed in a farm accident and after his death she found it impossible to find work. She couldn't pay the rent, feared she would be evicted, and her daughter taken into care. She was also being harassed by Albert Hawley and his son George, in the same way the Hawleys had harassed everyone who rented that cottage, including peddling the myth it was haunted."

"Poor woman." I mean it. It sounds like it was worse for her than both Jackie and me, especially with a child to support. Somehow, John doesn't see my concern as genuine.

"Poor woman indeed. She threw herself on the mercy of Lord and Lady Fitzgerald and begged them not to evict her."

"How do you know this?"

"Later," he says, dismissing the question. He doesn't want to interrupt his dramatic flow. "They were sympathetic, especially Edmund, and he gave her six months to find work, during which time they'd waive the rent."

"Good for them, I'd say."

"Remember, the cottage had been unoccupied for many years. The Hawleys had made sure of that, so any rent they received was a bonus. It was hardly philanthropy."

"What did he get in return?"

"A nice warm feeling," he says, and waits for a reaction that doesn't come before almost leaping out of his chair. "What do you think?" he barks, as if I'm to blame. John Lee has a curious temperament for a vicar. Sara says nothing. She's heard this all before and has nothing to add. "While Lady Eleanor is cavorting around with her toy-boys, her husband is finding solace in the bosom of young Jennifer."

"How do you know this about Eleanor?"

"She told me. In fact, she boasted of her conquests," he says huffily.

"And you take that as gospel."

"I have corroborating evidence," he says, missing the jibe. He may be making this up. Arthur Needham is hardly going to confess, even to the vicar and I doubt his predecessor Reverend Fenton revealed all. "Everyone is happy until Jennifer gets her timing wrong and finds she's pregnant."

"By Edmund?"

"Who else?"

"You tell me."

"There was no one else."

"How do you know? How do you know she wasn't on the game? One of the Hawleys' dirty tricks was to paint 'Whore' on the front door. Maybe she did the only thing she could. The only thing desperate women can do."

"Because he did a deal. If she left the village, he'd pay her for five years to keep her quiet. He must have been sure he was the father."

"Or generous. Maybe he loved her?"

"Bollocks!"

"Is that an ecclesiastical term?"

"She would have brought shame on the Fitzgeralds," he says, ignoring me. "The last thing he wanted was a bastard child when they were still trying for one of their own."

I saw the payments to 'J' in ever increasing amounts, so his story is consistent with that. I also know the payments came from Eleanor's account, one that was locked away from Edmund's view, so it's possible it was all Eleanor's doing and Edmund knew nothing about it. If so, it directly contradicts the view there was a cover up by Edmund and suggests Eleanor knew of it all along. I know the payments continued for almost three years and then stopped but not why. I'm sure Reverend John is going to tell me.

"Is that it?"

"He paid her for almost three years, then killed her."

"What?"

"It was treated as suicide, but it wasn't. Edmund Fitzgerald killed her."

"I don't believe it. What evidence do you have?"

"He had her killed because she asked for too much money."

"That's not evidence, and anyway, first you say, 'he killed her' then it's, 'had her killed'. Which is it?"

"It's the same thing." John Lee has reached the climax of his story. He sits back in his chair, resolute. But I'm not finished. It's a tragic story, if true, but I'm a long way off believing Gigolo John, man of God or not. He hasn't offered any justification for his claims and has no first-hand knowledge because he's only been here three years. There may be an element of truth in it, but the more lurid details he either made up or got from someone else.

"What happened to the kids?"

"Split up and adopted."

"By?"

"Social services at first, then foster parents."

"How do you know all this?"

"Eleanor told me when she knew she was dying."

"Why would she do that?"

"Absolution."

"Rubbish! You said it was Edmund's secret. How did it get out?"

"Jackie uncovered it, found out about Jennifer and what Edmund did to her. She thought Eleanor knew but it almost finished her off. She couldn't go to her grave without confessing her part in it all. She was a religious woman, for all her faults."

"Convenient she can't speak for herself."

"Ethel Hawley, she'll confirm it."

"George's wife?"

"Widow," he says, as if making a point. "She knew Jennifer."

"You probably think Edmund had George killed too?" John shrugs it off. "You do, don't you?"

"There's more, and this is the real reason we wanted to warn you. You're following in Jackie's footsteps. You're heading down the same path, fulfilling the same role, doing the same work, will come to the same conclusions, and when you do, you'll be in mortal danger. There's evil in the house of Fitzgerald, there always has been, and it will only end when the last Lord of Oakdale is finally laid to rest. You must get away while you can." Gigolo John's portentous tone would be laughable if the subject matter were not so serious. I don't believe Edmund is a danger to me any more than he was a danger to Jackie, Jennifer, George, or anyone else. But I'm not ready to challenge John Lee's increasingly paranoid delusions.

"You said there was more. Is that it?"

He casts a glance at Sara, and I follow the exchange of looks. It's the trump card and they're not certain whether to play it or keep it for another time.

"We're sorry to have to inform you Jackie passed away."

I've been waiting for this. They denied knowing what happened to her before and no one else I've spoken to, other than Sue Jenkins and the police, seems to know either. I make them wait, as if trying to rationalise a shocking revelation.

"How?"

"She was killed in a car crash."

"When?"

"January. The day she left the cottage."

"And you think Edmund is responsible for that too?" He offers that shrug again. Sara says nothing. It's his gig. He's presented the facts, such as they are, to achieve only one aim; to get me to leave Farrier's. Time to disappoint.

"I already know about Jackie." His face drops. "She left notes behind, and I've spoken to her mother, so I know how she died. I know about the payments to Jennifer, and I know about Eleanor's multiple affairs. I know the history behind Farrier's Cottage, and I know of its sale to a Jersey based investment company. I have quantified Edmund's considerable assets and I'm helping him rationalise his affairs and draw up a will so he can, in his own words, depart this world in an orderly fashion and meet up with his beloved Eleanor in the next, something I'm sure you and your God will be happy to facilitate when the time comes. Edmund Fitzgerald is a good-hearted man who suffers from acute memory lapses, otherwise known as dissociative amnesia. He is prone to an occasional aggressive outburst, but that's a consequence of his advanced age and increasingly confused state, not from any inherently violent tendencies. Thank you for your concerns which, I'm sure, are well meant, but in my view totally misplaced." I've made my speech. I stand, ready to go.

"Then we can't help you," he says. "You're either a deluded young fool, brainwashed by an evil old man or more likely, bought off with the promise of great wealth after he's gone." *Whore!* I turn to leave, but there's one more thing to clear up.

"You claim to know who I am, John. Who am I, John?"

The Reverend John Lee gets slowly to his feet and makes the sign of the cross. I stare into his dark eyes and feel a chill.

"You won't succeed. God is on my side."

CHAPTER 25

The lights are on in Ethel Hawley's cottage and there's a shiny new BMW parked outside her gate. I think twice about knocking in case it's the police as I don't want to explain why I'm here, but I examine the car and can see nothing to suggest it's anything other than private. The door is opened quickly by a tall, well-built man, aged around sixty. He wears a frown but it's curiosity, not aggression and I've seen him before. Psycho Si is visiting his mum.

"Hi!" His expression doesn't change, nor does he open his mouth. "I'm Kate. You must be Simon," I say thrusting a hand in his direction, smiling broadly to cover up my anxiety, but he ignores it. "I'm sorry to bother you. I was just passing and thought I'd call on your Mum to make sure she was alright. But I see she's got you here, so I'll come back another time." He opens the door wider and steps back.

"Come in."

"I don't want to trouble you."

"She could do with the company."

"Who's that Simon?" says a voice from behind and Ethel Hawley appears. "Oh hello, Kate. Simon, this is the young lady I was telling you about. Come in and have a cup of tea." Ethel turns on the spot and heads for the kitchen. There's no going back. I step over the threshold and into the living room catching a whiff of male cologne as I slide by his ample torso.

"Have a seat, Kate." He holds out a fleshy hand that envelopes my own but he's gentle and sits opposite me in George's armchair. "Mum said you came round. That's very kind of you. In the circumstances."

"I never got to know your father properly."

"You didn't want to. Anyway, it's over now. All for the best. Me and him fell out years ago."

"Over the cottage?"

"That was part of it. He was obsessed with it just like Grandad and I wasn't going to be the same. He couldn't accept it, so I left. Joined the army to get away from him."

"I met one of your ex-army colleagues the other day," I say brightly, but he doesn't look particularly impressed. "Tommy Gibbs." He nods slowly in acknowledgement. Ethel comes back with a tray.

"Here, mum. I'll take that. You sit down."

"No need to fuss. I can manage." She pours the tea and cuts a slice of fruitcake. "Kate lives in Farrier's," she says.

"I know mum."

"Where she belongs."

"I know mum."

"I wanted to ask you about that Mrs Hawley. Last time I was here you mentioned a lady called Jennifer who lived there in the late seventies?"

"Yes, dear. I remember Jennifer, poor love. Her husband got himself killed. Tractor turned over, very sad."

"And she had a little girl?"

"Yes, don't remember her name though."

"How long was she in Farrier's?"

"Don't know. Maybe a year or two. You remember her don't you Simon?" Simon nods in agreement.

"She was a good-looking woman. Older than me. I had a bit of a crush," he says sheepishly, and for a moment I imagine Psycho Si has a heart after all. "Dad actually encouraged me. Thought if he could get a Hawley in there, he might find some way of getting the cottage back."

"Were you and Jennifer…er, together?"

"God no! I was only sixteen."

"Yes, sorry." For a second, I wondered if he might be the father of her child and not Edmund. I was so engrossed in alternative conspiracy theories I strayed into Psycho Si's personal relationships.

"But then his Lordship stepped in, so to speak."

"Just like before," says Ethel, shaking her head. "History repeating itself."

"Do you mean like Lord Julian?"

"Yes, you'd know all about that." Ethel Hawley keeps making these asides as if we share an obvious frame of mind. It's not sinister, just a little bewildering. "George went mad, and it pretty much killed Albert. He was sick anyway, but that was what finished him off. Knowing a Fitzgerald was behaving like that all over again."

"I understand Jennifer had a child by Lord Edmund."

"Well, what was she supposed to do, poor girl? What is any girl supposed to do when her whole life depends on a rich bloke like his Lordship?"

"Did you ever see the baby?"

"No, she moved away before it was born. Lady Eleanor found out about it and next minute, Jennifer disappears, just like the rest of them." Ethel puts her cup and saucer down and leans over to grab my hand. "You will be careful, Kate. Don't want you disappearing as well. Not now you're finally here."

Ethel Hawley's version of events matches John Lee's except for what Eleanor knew about Edmund's child. I saw the payments from Eleanor's private account which proves she knew. I suspect she whitewashed her role to cosy up to the trendy young vicar and justify her own actions, but while there's no doubt Edmund and Jennifer had an affair, there's no evidence he knew she was pregnant. Only Edmund and his erratic memory can be counted on for that.

"I don't plan to disappear Mrs Hawley," I say, but it sounds hollow. I'm sure neither Jennifer Young nor Jackie Thomas had planned to disappear either. But I'm weirdly relaxed in the company of Ethel Hawley and her allegedly psychopathic son. As usual, there's more than meets the eye and I can't rely on others for the truth. "Your husband wanted me to leave the cottage in the same way he wanted Jackie and Jennifer to leave, but even after he died, the threats have continued." I see Simon bristle and I know I'm taking a big risk, but it's not outrage at any implied accusation, it's outrage at the notion itself.

"There's some sick folk around here, that's for sure. If you get any more trouble, you just let me know." He pulls out his wallet and hands me a business card. *Simon Hawley, CEO, Rampant Security Systems.*

"That's very kind."

"Not at all. My old man was a twisted sod and I'm sorry he made life difficult for you. It's the least I can do to make amends." He looks at Ethel and takes her hand. "As far as we're concerned, you can stay in that cottage as long as you like. You've earned it. But if anyone upsets you or tries to get you to leave, tell me and I'll sort them out."

I'm bowled over by Simon's concern. He's not at all what I expected. People change, and whatever he may have done forty years ago in the heat of battle; a young man in a war zone on an island in the South Atlantic thousands of miles from home, he's not the same man now. And as for his alleged psychopathic tendencies, I have only one uncorroborated source.

"Tell me about Tommy Gibbs."

His face darkens instantly, and he averts his eyes. Ethel Hawley rubs the back of his hand.

"We stay away from the Gibbs," she says. "Him and Tommy were friends once, but the army changed everything. I feel sorry for Margaret and them girls, but he's got a black heart has Tommy."

My first impression of Tommy Gibbs, the truculence, the bitterness, and the accusation against Psycho Si, left me disturbed and wary. The insult against me should have confirmed it. I don't want to intrude on Simon's traumatic past, but now there's a new dimension and I need to know.

"I met Tommy by chance on the day of your dad's funeral. I don't even know why he was there, because he gave me the impression you and he weren't on speaking terms."

"He wasn't invited. He'd never be invited. He just turned up looking for trouble," says Simon. "Good job Arthur was there, or else God knows what would have happened."

"Arthur Needham?"

"Captain Needham. He was our commanding officer. Once a soldier, always a soldier. Even Tommy obeys an order from the Captain."

***

The world is spinning faster as each day goes by, throwing off pieces of a jigsaw I'm supposed to fit together without ever knowing the picture. The web of connections is growing larger and somehow, I'm being drawn to the centre. I've heard nothing from the police and still no arrests have been made, either in respect of George Hawley or Jeremy Jones. It's not my job to catch their murderers, but my continued presence in Farrier's Cottage is the common factor and that puts me squarely in the frame. Unless the perpetrator is found, I shall live in fear for as long as I remain in a place where no good fortune ever befell its occupants. I can't rely on Stride or his team. It's down to me.

I'm looking at the Fitzgerald family tree. It was drawn up in the late nineteenth century and ends with Julian Alexander Fitzgerald, his wife Mary and his two children Charles and Sophia, who sadly died aged twelve in 1914. There's little to add; Charles, having had two wives, was killed in Northern France in 1944 with Edmund his only offspring. He really is the last Lord.

I remembered amongst Eleanor's letters, a few that were signed J. Young. I hadn't read them at the time, simply scanned and filed them by sender and date, so hadn't realised their significance. I'm reading them now. Invariably, they start by thanking Lady Fitzgerald for her continued generosity and confirming the children are well, but all end the same way; a plea for more support together with an undertaking each is the last, each inevitably followed by another. The final one is the most disturbing, obviously in response to one from Eleanor. The language is desperate and upsetting and ends with an explicit threat if more money is not forthcoming, and also a key fact hitherto unknown to me. I wonder how

Edmund's memory is today and whether I'll set off another personal time bomb. Time to bite the bullet.

"I need to ask you something Edmund."

"Fire away," he booms, pulling up a chair next to me.

"This is going to hurt."

"Ha! You sound like a nurse about to rip off a plaster."

"Good analogy. Can I start with Jackie?" I pray he's not having a bad memory day and I have to explain who she is.

"Yes."

"She was doing pretty much what I'm doing, sorting out your affairs."

"Correct. I didn't ask her to author the family history though. You gave me that idea."

"I did?"

"Yes. Your instinctive knowledge and curiosity made you perfect for the job."

"Thank you. But did Jackie find anything that upset you, made you angry and want her to leave?"

"I don't think so."

"Did she have access to this drawer; Eleanor's private papers?"

"Only if Eleanor opened them up to her."

I show him the leather-bound file containing the bank statements. "Did you know Eleanor had a private account at Coutts?"

"Yes." There's nothing for it and no easy way to ask. *Light the blue touchpaper and stand well back.*

"Who's Jennifer?" There's no immediate reaction. I can't tell if he's searching for fragments of recollection or concocting some story. It's neither. It's sober reminiscence.

"She's someone with whom I had an affair. A long, long time ago."

"Did she live in Farrier's?" He nods. "And did Eleanor know all about it?"

"The affair? Yes, eventually. We had an open marriage. I think that's the term. But I ended it when she found out. Those were the rules."

"What's good for the goose?"

"Indeed. You're not too shocked, I hope. It should make excellent material for the biography." I have to smile. I'm pleased his memory is functioning, relieved he didn't explode, and his casual admission of adultery is further evidence of the trust he's placed in me. I can't imagine relating the sordid details of Lord and Lady Fitzgerald's open marriage whilst he's still alive. I'll cross that bridge another time, but there are more hazards ahead. "How did you find out about Jennifer?"

"Her letters. They continued to correspond after she left."

"Really? That surprises me. We were happy to waive the rent when she lost her husband but when she and I were rumbled, we thought it best she moved away."

"No hard feelings on Eleanor's part, then?"

"As I said. We tolerated each other's little dalliances, provided they were done discreetly. As soon as each was uncovered, they ended. But I can't imagine why they'd stay in touch." He really doesn't know. Bombshell is not the word. It's far bigger than that and I haven't got the courage. Yet.

"Did Jackie urge you to make a will?"

"Yes of course. We all knew Eleanor didn't have long and that only left me, and I believed all we had was this seventeenth century pile. I had no idea her investments had grown to such a value. If I had, then maybe I would have given some thought as to where it should all go."

"Did Jackie know about Eleanor's inheritance and the investments with Hollis Warburton?"

"If she did, she never mentioned it to me."

"Did she know about Eleanor's affair with Arthur Needham?" His face darkens immediately. I've seen it before. The volcanic rumblings are unmistakable, and I haven't even pressed the button.

"I may have lost my temper," he says, slowly, and with a hint of contrition.

"At Jackie?"

"It's all coming back to me."

Ordinarily, I would be happy Edmund's memory is working well, but I can't escape a sense of foreboding for what he may have remembered. "She got frustrated with me. I forget things you know, things that I find upsetting, I block them out of my mind, but only for a while and then something triggers a recollection, and it hits me with a vengeance and sometimes, I react badly. I don't mean to, it's just the way I am.

"Dissociative amnesia."

"What?"

"I looked it up. You deal with distressing experiences by forgetting they ever happened. Then when they do come back to you, the results can be unpredictable."

"See, you are a shrink."

"Hardly. You were saying?"

"It was late, and Eleanor was ill in bed. She'd had another stroke, her final one as it turns out. Jackie was trying to get answers and Eleanor was in no fit state and I couldn't remember, and she tied me in knots until one of us snapped."

"You?"

"No. She did. She berated me for being a stupid old fool. Both of us, in fact. She ranted about our sordid affairs, our vulgar and casual disregard for obscene wealth and an absence of humility or appreciation for our privileged position. And finally, she praised Arthur Needham for all the time and effort he'd put in to helping Eleanor. I had no idea she was talking about investments."

"So, you gave her short shrift."

"That's all it was. She stomped off and I never saw her again." It was the night Jackie had returned to the cottage to find it had been broken into and vile abuse painted on the mirror, the exact sequence of events still in question. The last straw, but one. Sara Lee comes to the rescue, comforts Jackie in her heightened state of anxiety, seduces her and, in the cold light of day the poor girl realises it's all too much. "I forgot that's all. Another bad memory." *Now or never Kate.*

"And Jennifer? Is she a bad memory?"

"No. I liked her very much and I think she liked me."

"Even though you were Lord of the Manor, her landlord, and she couldn't pay the rent."

He looks at me soberly.

"I didn't take advantage if that's what you think. I'm not Julian. I made no demands."

"But they were understood."

"No. It wasn't like that, although you may find that difficult to believe."

"That's how it looks."

"Damn how it looks!" he says, slapping the desk with his hand. "I'm not perfect, I'm just a flawed human being at the end of a life full of regrets. Regrets I couldn't have been better, more worthy, more faithful, more deserving, but I could not have been more loving, I never knowingly abused anyone and never shied away from the truth."

Silence hangs in the air like the dust suspended in the rays of sunlight streaming through the French windows. It's broken by a robin, chattering at a rival, guarding its territory. I can see fields of luxuriant grass and cattle, heads down, doing what they know best.

"I'm sorry." I'm chastened and I want to hug him but it's premature. Edmund's sensitivities are not my priority.

"Do you feel threatened? By me?" he says calmly.

"No." The storm has passed, but I fear it's just circling.

"You can leave whenever you want. You do know that."

"I'm not leaving Edmund. I want to help you do the right thing."

"And what's that?"

"Set your mind at ease. Organise your affairs, ensure your assets are put to good use when you're gone; something you and Eleanor would both approve of, and write a colourful history of the Fitzgeralds, from Cromwell to the Last Lord of Oakdale," I say with a flourish. It's also meant to give me an opening. I can't delay any longer. "But there may be a problem we didn't foresee."

"Go on."

"Jennifer already had a daughter when she lived here."

"I remember."

"She left Oakdale pregnant with her second child." I let the words sink in for a moment. "Eleanor knew, and paid her to go away. She paid her for almost three years until Jennifer's increasing demands became too much to tolerate." Edmund looks shell-shocked, numb with incomprehension.

"Good lord. And you think I'm the father?"

"It's possible, but you'll never know unless the child comes forward."

"Or Jennifer. She'll only be seventy."

"She's dead, or so I understand."

"Oh no. When?"

"Shortly after Eleanor stopped the payments. Apparently, the kids were taken into foster care."

Edmund lets out a moan and rubs his forehead with one hand. "How do you know all this?" His reaction so far, is mercifully restrained. That would all change if I tell him most of it came from John Lee.

"It's all around you. You just can't see it."

"And how can you?"

"Because I'm being attacked, and because I'm defending myself instead of running away, my attackers are slowly getting closer, and in the fullness of time, will reveal themselves."

He looks at me, suddenly anxious. "The child? My child?"

"A boy."

"Heavens. I may not be the last Lord after all."

CHAPTER 26

Margaret Gibbs is at the counter in N&N's in deep discussion with Naira. I hover between aisles, attempting to eavesdrop while pretending to survey the shelves for something interesting, but they lowered their voices when I came in and only the odd word breaks through. I pick up a magazine and saunter up behind Margaret. Naira looks up.

"Hello Kate, I'll be with you in a minute."

"No rush. Hello Mrs Gibbs."

Ma Gibbs turns around wearily as if showing any interest requires supreme effort.

"Alright?"

"How are the newlyweds? I hear they're off to Dubai."

"Not 'til January. Can't afford it anyway. These young folks think nothing about spending money they haven't got. Think it grows on trees."

"Steve kindly painted my door. Did a good job."

"He's a good lad. One down, one to go."

"Sorry?" It sounds like she's alluding to abusive graffiti.

"Daughters. Hoped to have them both married off by now. Get a bit of peace at last."

"I know what you mean," says Naira, laughing. "We found nice young men from rich families for our two."

"Our Mel prefers horses."

"You have horses?"

"The vicar's horses. She goes up there, mucks 'em out, grooms them and gets to ride around their paddock. Can't keep her away. Real tomboy she is too." Margaret Gibbs is being coy, but I understand if she won't discuss her daughter's sexuality in public. It wouldn't be right. "Saw you in church last Sunday."

"Yes, but I can't promise to be there every week. I'm not that religious."

"Me neither. I just go to ogle the dishy vicar," she says with a cackle. "Nearest thing to Brad Pitt we'll get round here.

Saw you having a chat. You watch yourself, dearie, that's all I'm saying."

"Sara was there too," I say, irritated I've allowed Margaret Gibbs to pluck one of my strings.

"Her as well. No matter which way you swing there's a shoulder to cry on, if you know what I mean. Ain't that right Naira?" she says, winking. Naira looks embarrassed and makes a show of tidying the counter.

"Sorry, I don't know what you mean." I do, but I want her to continue.

"Come on love, you must know Mrs Vicar's tastes by now. Turned my girl's head so she has."

"Mel?"

"More than twice her age and all, but Mel's grown up now so she can do what she likes. As long as my Tommy doesn't catch them. He'd have something to say, that's for sure." I take it back. Ma Gibbs is more than happy to gossip about anything, even her own offspring. I think she's worth pushing.

"Sara said she and John have been here three years."

"About that. But she was here first. She and her horses. Lived in your cottage for a while before he showed up."

"I didn't know that." This is getting better. I'm developing a taste for village gossip. I can imagine Stride trying to ply Ma Gibbs for information like this and getting nowhere.

"She took over playing the organ in church and our Mel was in the choir. Asked her if she liked horses and that was it. Best friends ever since."

"I don't understand. Where was John?"

"Some church in Essex. He was drafted in to replace that creep Fenton."

"The previous vicar?"

"Yeah. Touched up our Mel did Fenton. Sara witnessed it and that was that. He was history and trendy John took over, then before you know it, him and Sara's got married."

"I thought they were already married before they got here."

"No. We were all there, weren't we Naira? At the Lees' wedding?"

A head bobs up from below the counter. "Oh yes. Very nice it was. Pity they had no family there, other than the two children."

"He's divorced you know," says Ma Gibbs. "The kids are from a previous."

"I didn't know that." I do of course, but if Ma Gibbs wants to be the fount of all knowledge, then I'm happy to drink from it.

"Don't stop either of them doing what they want though. That's why I'm telling you to watch yourself. He had a thing going with Lady Eleanor when she was alive."

"No! You're not serious?" Ma Gibbs is preening, her boundless wisdom and perspicacity on full show.

"And that Sara was always round the cottage when that other girl lived there."

"Jackie?"

"That was her. And there's Mel, of course, but the less said about that the better. That's why I'm saying, watch yourself." She lays a hand on my arm. "You don't want to get sucked into something you'll regret. That's all I'm saying."

"Thanks."

***

I bump into Arthur Needham outside as I'm leaving.

"Morning Arthur!" I say breezily.

"Hello Kate. Are you well?"

"Yes indeed." *Time to rattle his cage.* "I'm sorry about Sunday, barging in like that. Wrong time, wrong place."

"That's quite alright. I hope you understand."

"Yes of course. I know you and Edmund are not on speaking terms and to be honest, I haven't told him we've had a conversation as I don't want to incur his wrath." I say, embellishing it with an ironic chuckle. "You know what he's like." Arthur doesn't respond, his expression inscrutable. He's not a stupid man by any measure. "But I do want to pick your brains a little. I'm trying to complete some work Jackie Thomas did for Lady Eleanor before she died. Sadly, it's of no consequence to her Ladyship now and Edmund himself seems ambivalent, but in the interests of completeness… you know."

"I'm not sure I do."

"I know you were close to Lady Eleanor." *No reaction. He's good is Arthur.* "And you were her financial advisor." *Nothing except a blink.* "You advised her on investing a sizeable inheritance from her late aunt." I pause to give him a chance to dismiss me again. He doesn't.

"Go on."

"Well, the thing is, Lady Eleanor's files contain documentation from Hollis Warburton going back many years; valuations and so forth, but the latest communication is about three years ago. I'm sure it's just been misfiled but I've looked everywhere and haven't been able to find any. I wondered if you knew what happened and whether her funds are still there?"

"Have you contacted Hollis Warburton directly?"

"Not yet. Edmund is waiting for probate so we can make arrangements to have the portfolio registered in his name."

"Then I suggest the best thing to do is wait for probate to come through and speak to them. I haven't had contact with Hollis Warburton for many years, certainly not on behalf of a former client. I would have no reason."

"Perhaps Lady Eleanor appointed another advisor after you retired?"

"Perhaps. Now I must be getting on. Have a good day." He makes a move towards the door.

"Tell me about Belles Fleurs Investments," he stops abruptly, "the owners of Farrier's Cottage," I add, in case he needs reminding. Arthur Needham turns slowly to face me.

"I can see you are very thorough in your work, and a very persistent young lady. But I don't think this is a suitable place to be discussing the affairs of the deceased. Come to the house on Thursday morning around ten. Marjorie goes to her fitness class. We can talk privately then."

***

I'm used to entering the Manor without knocking; I didn't need a key because Edmund only locks the place at night, but today when I try the heavy oak door, it remains stuck fast. I press the bell and wait. After a moment, it opens to reveal a severe looking woman in a housecoat. She's tall and thin, with short, cropped hair coloured an unnatural jet black. I guess immediately.

"You must be Marian."

"And you must be Miss Duvall," she says without a glimmer of welcome or grace.

"Kate."

Edmund appears behind her, beaming with delight. "Ah, you've met. My two guardian angels, together for the first time." Marian rolls her eyes and stands aside to let me pass.

"Very pleased to meet you, Marian. Do I take it you have resumed your position in the service of Lord Edmund?" Marian opens her mouth to speak but Edmund gets in first.

"I telephoned Marian to apologise for my intolerable behaviour and begged her forgiveness. I persuaded her to come back, and she has agreed to extend her scope of work to cover a range of household duties. We reached a negotiated settlement in respect of her remuneration. Am I right?"

"Yes, your Lordship," she says with barely concealed irritation.

"You have more than enough on your plate at the moment Kate, so I decided it would be unreasonable to drag you away from your primary tasks just to do menial work," I flash a look at Marian who's now simmering with rage, but manages to keep it under control, "and now I understand so much more about my financial situation, I can do so without worrying about the cost." Edmund rubs his hands together, evidently pleased with his analysis of this new business proposition.

"Marian has worked here for almost ten years, so knows a fair amount of what goes on. I'm sure she'll be a great help to you in your research. I've asked her to co-operate fully."

"No holds barred?"

"Warts and all."

Marian rolls her eyes again whilst fiddling nervously with a gold ring on her right hand. I see her left is bare.

"I look forward to having a chat," I say, and she appears to soften a little.

"Would you like some tea?"

"Splendid!" says Edmund. "Bring it into the study will you?"

***

I've had a predictably unsuccessful conversation with an advisor at Hollis Warburton. They acknowledged receipt of Eleanor's death certificate by post, but before they will discuss the account of a deceased client or even confirm one exists, they demand a grant of letter of representation, to confirm Edmund is authorised to deal with her affairs. This process is in train, but may take several more weeks, so establishing the status of Eleanor's funds will have to wait, unless Arthur Needham is willing and able to shed some light on the current position. I may find out more on Thursday when I see him, but I'm not hopeful, so in the meantime I've returned to studying the Fitzgerald family tree to reacquaint myself with Edmund's ancestors.

I begin to despair at the enormity of the task Edmund has set me. It's taken three weeks to acquaint myself with Edmund's financial affairs and there are still unanswered questions. As far as researching 400 years of Fitzgerald family history goes, I've barely scratched the surface. I've decided the best approach is to conduct a series of lengthy interviews with Edmund and start with his own life story; pick his brains, as far as his memory will permit, and go backwards in time. I should be able to supplement this with material sourced online and by ploughing through his extensive library. I would be interested to hear Marian's take on the Fitzgeralds' relationships, not only with each other but with their respective lovers, but would be surprised if Eleanor shared intimate details with her housekeeper. I remind myself this is a project which will take years to complete. There are no quick fixes.

I'm examining the contents of Edmund's bookshelves for inspiration. I do a quick survey of the several hundred books on display, noting three quarters of them are fiction and probably irrelevant. That only leaves around two hundred volumes of commentaries, diaries, political observations, and historical reference works, some of which may yield useful background information.

My eye is drawn to an edition of Burke's Peerage dated 1912. I wrestle it loose, judging it hasn't been moved for decades and notice an incongruous bulge in the centre. Two folded pieces of paper slip out onto the floor. Newspaper cuttings, flattened like pressed flowers and just as delicate, but otherwise perfectly preserved, as if they have never seen the light of day since the moment they were put there. I take them to the desk and carefully tease open the folds, spreading out the dry, fragile paper. Whole pages from *The Times.* The first is dated 17th February 1912 and carries a long commentary on the conflict in the Balkans, stories on the Chinese opium trade, the discovery of diamonds in Canada, and extensive coverage of Parliament's deliberations on Irish home rule. Alongside are large display adverts featuring Harrods furniture, Mazda drawn-wire lamps and one I know Edmund would like; Grand Chartreuse Liqueur now proudly made in Spain by the original Chartreux monks following their expulsion from France.

Overleaf are several reports from the Church Congress, commenting on the falling birth rate, the virtues of town planning and the Church's developing attitudes towards gambling, theatres, and music halls. Alongside, the latest ladies Spring fashions direct from Paris are advertised including *'Specialité'* riding habits. It's all fascinating stuff, but one article stands out, my eye drawn instinctively to a familiar name.

HEINOUS MURDER OF A NOBLE LORD

It is with profound regret and sadness your correspondent must report the tragic demise of one of the most esteemed and industrious members of the House of Lords, Lord Julian Alexander Fitzgerald, who yesterday was cut down in a callous and despicable act of villainy. It seems Lord Fitzgerald and a fellow member of the upper chamber who, for the purposes of this report will remain anonymous, had, after a strenuous session in the House, spent the remainder of the evening relaxing and dining at the Berkshire Club. Upon their departure, weariness set in and in their confused state the Noble Lords mistakenly stumbled into a side alley in a disreputable area of Soho whereupon they were tricked into entering a house of ill repute. The manager of said establishment known as "Angel's Delight", Mr Frederick Sykes, purported to offer the Noble Lords warmth, shelter, and refreshment until such times as a hansom cab could be summoned. Little did the Noble Lords know a shocking and wretched fate lay in store. After being forced to imbibe copious quantities of the cheapest gin, Mr Sykes, along with two unprepossessing accomplices took the Noble Lords to an upstairs room where they were forced to disrobe and were then robbed of their valuable possessions. It was shortly afterwards that the deadly incident took place. An anonymous but credible eyewitness recounts he heard a woman scream "you are the devil incarnate, Julian Fitzgerald!" and fearing for her safety, felt obliged to rush to her assistance. Amongst further screams and cries of "she's killing me! she's killing me!" he burst open a locked door to find the source of the hellish commotion and was confronted by a monstrous sight. Through a cloud of burning opium, he was horrified to witness the hapless and naked form of Lord Fitzgerald writhing on a blood-soaked bed, pinned down by a buxom, naked, wench who was stabbing him repeatedly with a six-inch knife. The bedlam continued as Mr Sykes and his accomplices arrived to restrain the demented trollop, beating her unconscious. They attempted to revive his Lordship, sadly to no avail. The police duly arrived and arrested Mr Sykes and three others, including the assailant who has been named as Lily La Muse.

The entire incident, as I imagined it several weeks ago, now confirmed in black and white as if it were yesterday. Julian indulging his perversions in a brothel, as was his habit, the real facts distorted to protect the reputation of the aristocracy, the verdict already reached in the press and by extension, the court of public opinion. I'm struck by one fact. The improbably named Lily La Muse knew her victim because she called out his name as she stabbed him, which meant either he was a regular or she knew him from the past. I spread out the second page and scan it feverishly. It's dated 24th February, exactly one week later and it all becomes clear.

PROSTITUTE GUILTY OF MURDER TO HANG

The jury in the trial of the harlot Lily La Muse took less than ten minutes to find the defendant guilty of the murder of Lord Julian Fitzgerald. The court heard of her abominable act of violence against a highly revered and respected member of the House of Lords, through the testimony of several members of the public who witnessed the crime and had no hesitation in reaching their unanimous verdict. Judge Lord Justice Reynolds donned the black cap to pass sentence on the convicted murderess under her real name, Edith Hawley. The condemned woman will suffer death by hanging, sentence to be carried out at Holloway Prison forthwith.

I want to weep. Younger than me when defiled by Julian Fitzgerald, a man in power, rejected and reviled by her own family and separated from her children. Poor Edith was cast out and banished forever for the most despicable of crimes; sacrificing her body, her pride, and her self-respect to preserve and protect those she loved. That much I already knew, and it would perhaps have been merciful had her life and that of her unborn child ended in a ditch. But somehow, she survived, made her way to London; a one-way ticket from destitution to prostitution her only option. Twenty years later and now in her forties; bloated, diseased, degraded beyond measure, she encounters her nemesis, the strutting, swaggering, debauched Julian Fitzgerald, a man devoted to satisfying his depravity through the subjugation of others. She does what any woman would do in the circumstances; exacts revenge, even though she knows it will be her final act.

I can only speculate on who preserved these pages and why; Julian's mother Winifred, his wife Mary, or even his son Charles researching the downfall of his family. And even though Edmund knows the story, he can't know these exist, or he would have mentioned Edith was responsible for Julian's death. But what drew me to this book amongst hundreds of others? I feel a chill; as if the ghosts of Jackie Thomas and Edith Hawley, both innocents, are watching me, here in this room, where Julian Fitzgerald once breathed. *There are dark forces at work.*

CHAPTER 27

The ominous words of Jackie Thomas remain at the forefront of my mind. I have known for a while there's something badly wrong, and it may just be I'm less susceptible to the fear and anxiety that ultimately drove Jackie to her death. On the other hand, with each new shocking revelation, I come closer to the point where even I might be tipped over the edge.

I feel a bond with Edith. I try to imagine what she looked like and how her life had been before that fateful card game in The Crown sowed the seeds of destruction that continue to this day. It raises another question I hadn't considered. Edith was pregnant with Julian's child when her pleas for succour were spurned by Mary and Winifred. I don't believe she made the story up, given its drastic consequences, and it's possible she had a back street abortion or induced miscarriage and never gave birth at all. But if she did, and it was a boy, then there is potentially, another branch to the Fitzgerald family tree Edmund knows nothing about. The chances of tracking down the descendants of Edith Hawley aka Lily La Muse are, however, beyond my comprehension.

The woman's voice I've heard at night calling for Jacob, I'm now certain, is Edith, even though I refuse to believe in ghosts. I can't resolve that dichotomy other than to dismiss it as a figment of my imagination. Edmund tells me I have an uncanny perspicacity when it comes to the Fitzgeralds, but so far, it's limited to what happened to Edith. I did correctly recount Edmund's vitriolic attack on Arthur, but subsequently found the letter in question, dismissing the episode as one of those mental aberrations we all get from time to time.

I think back to the day Clare and I viewed the cottage, Jeremy Jones showed us around and we both found it enchanting. If we had known of its sordid past, I may never have agreed to rent it, we may have left early, Clare may not have been late for her yoga... *leave it Kate*. But there was something else. Something I couldn't rationalise or explain.

A feeling I belonged here. I felt at home, and despite the strange goings on, the noises in the night and the efforts of person or persons unknown to make me leave, I have not once considered it. Ethel Hawley alluded to it. *I hope you get what's rightfully yours. Don't want you disappearing as well. Not now you're finally here.* She's obviously on my side, but I have no idea why. Edith would have been Ethel's grandmother-in-law and Simon's great grandmother. Neither are afflicted with the curse of Jacob and Julian, that finally died out with George, yet someone else has picked up the baton. I owe it to Edith to find out.

***

I dial and it takes her a long time to answer. Her phone is usually glued to her hand when it's not stuffed in her back pocket so she's considering whether to pick up. She does, but she's nervous and guarded, I can tell something's up.

"Mandy? Are you okay?"

"Yeah. Just surprised to hear from you that's all. Been a while."

"Just a few weeks."

"Is it? Seems longer. I have been thinking about you though."

"That's nice."

"Mark's getting married," she almost blurts it out. I now understand why she's uncomfortable.

"Is he? What's her name?" I ask for no reason other than to be sure it's not another Kate. That would be a humiliation too far.

"Chloe."

"When did he meet her?"

"Not sure." Mandy was, is, my best friend but even she can't tell me the truth sometimes.

"Ah well, something for you to look forward to. Good excuse for a new frock." I try to make it sound humorous but she's not in the mood. "Good for him and good for Chloe. I hope they'll be very happy. Please send them my best wishes."

"Yeah. I will."

"What else is happening? How's Phil?" I'm working hard but don't feel like I'm getting anywhere.

"I have to go."

"Okay."

"I can't handle this."

"Okay."

"I do miss you; you know."

"I miss you too Mand. I hope you can come and visit me sometime."

"Yeah. Bye."

Lives drift apart. Circumstances change and new norms are established. I was the one who abandoned them. There's no reason they should try to preserve something I chose to leave behind. I wouldn't be human if I didn't feel a sense of regret and inadequacy that Mark found what he wanted so soon. Yes, part of me wanted him to come running after me, tell me how much he loved me and beg me so reconsider, to try again. But only so I could stand my ground, reassure myself I was right all along. He'd change, he'd say but it wouldn't be true. Maybe I did both of us a favour. Maybe he'll be grateful for that.

But now I've split with Mandy too and that's fine. I'm here to make new friends, have new experiences, start a new chapter. It hasn't got off to a good start, but I'm not giving up. I dial home.

"Hello mum."

"Hello?"

"Mum, it's me."

"Who?"

"Your daughter."

"Clare?" She sounds distraught.

"No, mum. Kate. Are you alright?"

"Where are you?"

She's never been this bad before. Dad must be really getting her down. I'm beginning to wish I hadn't bothered but tell myself she's probably just having a bad day.

"I'm at home."

"Where?"

"In Oakdale, where else?" I need to change the subject. "How's dad?"

"He's…having his dinner."

"Yes, but how is he? You know, how is his mental state?"

"Getting worse. He's getting angry." I've been dreading this. It was inevitable and I just shoved it to the back of my mind, hoping it would resolve itself, but knowing it will eventually come to a head.

"Angry at you? Has he been violent?" There's no answer. "Mum?" I can hear her sobbing. "Mum, I'm coming back. Everything's going to be okay. I'll come back and we'll get some help, find dad a nice place so he can rest, you can get some respite and then we'll work out a plan. I can be there in couple of days. I just need to make some arrangements."

"Oh Kate, darling. I wish you were here, I really do. But we know that's not possible."

"Of course it is!"

"No dear. It's a lovely thought, but this is something I must do alone. It's the only way."

"Mum?"

"Your dad and I are going to be fine. Don't you worry."

"But I do worry!"

"You should have nothing to worry about. That's the whole point, isn't it?"

"Not when you need help."

"Look darling. I love our little chats. It's all the help I need. But I don't want to talk about current difficulties. I just want to remember the good times, that's all."

CHAPTER 28

The clock at St John the Baptist shows ten as I stroll up West Street and turn into the Needham drive. I know I struck a nerve in the churchyard referring to Arthur's role as financial advisor. His curt response was intriguing, at odds with the genial host I encountered in our previous discussion. But it was the mention of Belles Fleurs that made him think again and agree to meet me. I am not sure if there's any significance in Marjorie's absence; it might just be that she has no interest in Arthur's financial dealings. I gave no indication I'm aware of their past relationships with the Fitzgeralds and they could not imagine Edmund would be so candid with a stranger like me, so it can't still be a sensitive issue.

I don't expect Arthur to reveal much about Hollis Warburton or anything other than the general nature of his professional relationship with Eleanor. He has no obligation to discuss a former client's affairs with me; that falls on Hollis Warburton. Once probate has come through they will be obliged to provide all necessary information and documents regarding Eleanor's investments. At the moment, it's the cottage I'm interested in and the main reason I'm here.

I expect there's a simple explanation why the freehold was transferred to Belles Fleurs. There's nothing inherently sinister in the transaction especially as Eleanor was a director at the time, other than it's one of which Edmund would not have approved. The issue is that now Eleanor is dead, the loan is part of her estate and I want to know its terms for repayment. Arthur is the effective owner of the cottage and depending on how we get on, I must decide whether to tell Edmund. It could all get very messy.

"Good morning, Kate," he says, showing me into the conservatory where a tea tray is already laid. "Impeccable timing if I may say. Would you mind pouring? My hands are a bit shaky."

"Not at all. I see young Marcus is hard at work." Marcus Wilson is striding up and down the lawn behind a petrol mower, leaving neat parallel lines in the rich green grass.

"Yes. Beyond my capabilities these days."

"I'm sure Edmund would agree. I understand Marcus does the same at the Manor?"

"So I believe."

"Something you and he still have in common." It's deliberately pointed and something Arthur either doesn't hear or chooses not to respond to. He lowers himself into his chair.

"Does Edmund know you're here?"

"No. He doesn't need to know, for now."

"For now?"

"I'm just gathering information at the moment. I'll give him a complete report in due course."

Arthur puts down his cup and shifts in his chair. "May I ask what you do for a living, Kate?"

"I'm a writer."

"A writer? Really? I thought you might be an accountant or lawyer."

"Like Jackie Thomas?"

"I wouldn't know. Was she?"

I've never played bridge. In fact, I've hardly ever played cards of any sort, so if I need to maintain an inscrutable expression, I'll be doing so by instinct alone. Arthur Needham is a long-time bridge player and far more experienced than I am in many other ways. He needs to be, because unlike me, he has something to hide.

"Fresh out of a big city firm. She knew what she was doing."

"And you don't?"

"Complex financial arrangements, asset valuations, inheritance and wills are hardly my area of expertise."

"Then why did you agree to assist Edmund?"

"He asked me. I was reluctant at first, but I said I'd give it a shot. If I feel I'm getting out of my depth, I'll tell him, and he can appoint someone else."

"Appoint? You have a professional agreement with Edmund?" He's staring at me and a cocktail of conflicting thoughts and emotions whirl inside my head. *Whore!* I stare back and it's good to feel in control, even if I'm not.

"Yes. Until such time as one of us agrees to terminate." He nods his understanding, but I have no way of knowing what he's thinking or what conclusions he's drawn. He cuts to the chase.

"I should make clear, I can't discuss my advice to Eleanor, or indeed to Edmund, with a third party. I appreciate you may be his advisor…" he lets the words hang, conveying more scepticism than respect, "… but without written authorisation from one or the other, it would be a breach of client confidentiality."

"I understand."

"So if you would like to have Edmund give me that authorisation, then I should be happy to help, at least in respect of those matters that affect him personally. As regards any advice I gave to Eleanor, I'm afraid that will have to wait for probate."

"I understand that too." What I understand is that Arthur Needham is playing for time, relying on my inexperience to dodge questions about Eleanor's estate. It's no more or less than I expected. He will need persuading.

"Jackie Thomas not only lived in the cottage before me, she was also retained by Edmund and Eleanor to review and tidy up their… affairs." I pause to allow the last word to sink in, but the bridge player is unreadable. "I'm just carrying on where she left off."

"I see."

"I expect they might have asked you to do it had you and Edmund not fallen out over the cottage."

"Possibly."

"I remember you said at the Parish Council Meeting that ownership of the cottage was a matter of public record."

"Indeed. Anyone who was interested or prepared to take the time would easily discover the freehold was owned by

Belles Fleurs Investments, something you or your predecessor have clearly already done."

"But not who is behind the company."

He gives me a patronising smile and sits forward in his chair. "That's Jersey for you. The authorities there are far more discreet than those in the UK. That's why they're so successful in attracting investment and wealth. But in terms of who is the beneficial owner, then I suspect you already know the answer."

"I do. I just want to know why."

He won't sidestep this one. He knows it will simply fuel suspicion. He also knows that neither Jackie nor I could have found out he was behind Belles Fleurs without professional help, so he's not dealing solely with a naïve young woman.

"It's quite simple really, and totally innocent."

"I never had any doubt."

"Some time after I wrote to the Fitzgeralds concerning the dilapidated state of the cottage and received Edmund's, er, impassioned riposte, Eleanor came to me and said she and Edmund wanted to dispose of it once and for all. It had brought them nothing but bad luck and they were tired of endless harassment by the Hawleys. Edmund's mind was going, and he was reaching the end of days, or so he kept saying and he wanted to make things easier for Eleanor when he was gone. Little did we know that Eleanor would fall seriously ill and predecease him."

"Why would that matter?"

"It matters, my dear, because Edmund had no knowledge I was helping them. He's such a stubborn old stick he would have refused any help from me. Hence the sale to a Jersey based investment company."

"Why not sell it on the open market?"

"Because Edmund made it a condition precedent that no buyer, present or future would ever sell the property to any person or entity owned or controlled by the Hawley family and its descendants. I told Eleanor that such a condition would have a severely deleterious effect on the value of the property, and whilst we both knew that was of little concern to Edmund, who was not long for this world and had no interest in money, it was an important issue for Eleanor. So I recommended it be sold to Belles Fleurs, a small, Jersey based investment vehicle that belonged to me."

"Without Edmund's knowledge?"

"Technically, he didn't need to know. Eleanor was the owner and anyway, he would never have agreed to it. And I wanted to help Eleanor." I can see he's getting irritated by my persistence.

"How did it help Eleanor?"

"I offered ten percent over the valuation. She would not have secured a better price at the time and," he says, stabbing the air with a finger, "it meant they could dispose of the damned place and get on with their lives without worrying about blasted George." I do believe Arthur sounds defensive. He's losing his composure

"But no money changed hands."

He sighs and sits back in his chair, regarding me intently. My first impression of Arthur Needham as an affable and decent old gentleman is rapidly receding. It's understandable he feels frustrated if he believes his motives are being unjustly questioned, but this is not just about a business decision or financial advice; this is infinitely more complicated than that. I know about the tangled relationships between the Fitzgeralds and the Needhams, which must have played a role in the decisions they made. Arthur does not know what I know about their personal lives and will not admit to any of it unless forced.

"I said 'small' investment vehicle. At the time, Belles Fleurs did not have the liquid resources to buy the cottage outright, so Eleanor was issued with a loan note, interest to accumulate at six per cent and a right to be paid in full on Edmund's death. I made Eleanor a director so she had a legal interest in Belles Fleurs."

"But not a shareholder?"

"It was too complicated. We would have had to value the company's assets, engage accountants and lawyers, it would have been much too expensive for something of relatively little value."

"And when Edmund died?"

"She could either call in the loan or leave it to grow."

"While you rented out the cottage."

"Or sold it on. With Edmund gone Eleanor would have happily waived the condition precluding its sale to a Hawley."

"And in the meantime, you weren't bothered by George harassing your tenants?"

He waves a hand in the air. "George was as old as Edmund. His days were numbered. It was only a matter of time before he dropped dead."

"Sooner than you imagined."

Arthur gives me steely look. "I rather resent the inference, young lady."

"I'm not inferring anything Arthur. I'm just pointing out that unexpectedly, Eleanor has gone, George has gone and it's time for Belles Fleurs to repay the loan to her estate, so Edmund can have quiet enjoyment of the proceeds. Why have you waited four months?"

"Why do you think? I'm not in charge of Edmund's affairs and since he terminated our friendship it's not for me to go and tell him what Eleanor did without his blessing. I fully expected someone to contact me at some stage and make enquires."

"So you'll repay the loan?"

"Subject to Belles Fleurs getting sight of probate and having available resources."

"Does Belles Fleurs have available resources?"

"Of course, I just may have to liquidate other assets to raise funds."

"Is the loan secured on the property?"

"No."

"Why not?"

"We didn't think it necessary."

I'm not convinced, and I don't believe it was ever discussed. The strategy was flawed, predicated on Edmund dying first. It would be standard practice to take security over the cottage in the event Belles Fleurs was unable to repay the loan. Eleanor may not have even thought about it, and meekly followed Arthur's advice. If they had even considered the possibility Edmund would outlive her, Arthur would surely have insisted she made a will or incorporated some safeguard for Belles Fleurs into the loan agreement. It's possible their judgment was clouded by personal history. Their affair ended twenty years ago, but its legacy might have influenced their actions. I'm prompted to consider what would have happened in my absence. Edmund, in his fragile mental state, oblivious to the underhand dealings of his wife and her ex-lover, unaware she had an asset approaching four hundred thousand pounds and Arthur, keeping his head down until someone opens the can of worms, hoping Edmund dies before they do.

In the fog of theories and possibilities and suspicions, I sense a drumbeat approaching, a lone voice warning in the all too familiar silence. I look through the glass and can see Marcus and his lawnmower still at work but making no sound. *It's right in front of your eyes, Kate.*

Arthur and Eleanor never ended their affair. The cottage was sold to appease Edmund; sold to a company owned by her lover who persuaded her to take a loan so Edmund didn't get his hands on the cash. He didn't want it and he didn't need it, so there's no merit in bothering him, is how it would be explained. Her financial advisor, whom she trusted completely, who had invested her inheritance for her, making her the millions she craved, all without her husband's knowledge, knew what was best for them both. It's not that Edmund forgot, he never knew, and the cottage is just the tip of the iceberg. Belles Fleurs has assets of twenty million; more than the value of her supposed investments with Hollis Warburton and the cottage combined. Intimidation, ghosts, and dire warnings from demented hippy priests don't bother me, but for the first time, I'm actually scared.

Arthur is looking relaxed. He's either relieved to have unburdened his conscience on a sensitive matter or has swiftly formulated a new strategy. My own voice echoes in my head.

"Who did the original valuation on the cottage?"

"I'm sure you've already worked that out."

"Jeremy Jones."

"Yet another tragedy linked to Farrier's Cottage." he says. He's calm now. The die is cast. The cottage is a sideshow. I know where Eleanor's millions are, and I know how they got there despite having seen no documentation to prove it.

"Eleanor granted you power of attorney, didn't she?"

"It was prudent. She'd had a stroke and felt vulnerable. Edmund was clearly incapable of making decisions for them, so she turned to the only person she could trust."

"And Edmund too?"

He doesn't answer. He's actually enjoying this now. He was defensive at first but now he's revelling in the power he once wielded over Eleanor and still wields over her assets, and he's more than content to demonstrate how clever he is. I have until now assumed they're Edmund's assets by right, but without a will there's no way of proving it. I consider the possibility Eleanor knowingly and willingly handed her wealth over to Arthur, her lover; they were, after all, hers to do with as she wished. In the worst case it would leave Edmund with nothing more than Oakdale Manor and a modest pension. Hardly penury, but as these thoughts whirl around my head, I sense there's something wrong and even my slimmed down assessment of Edmund's estate might yet dissolve into thin air.

***

I leave the Needham residence despondent. I've been focussing on the cottage and it's only a small part of the picture. I wanted to find the proceeds of the sale, and I've confirmed the existence of a loan held by a Jersey investment company owned by Eleanor's lover, who was not only her financial advisor, but also her attorney, a blatant and shocking conflict of interest. I believe she was manipulated or at least persuaded into handing over all her assets to Belles Fleurs shortly after her first stroke. Arthur could not risk them automatically reverting to Edmund, with or without a will. I can only imagine how he sold the plan to her, but key to it was their relationship, plus the assumption she would outlive Edmund. Meanwhile, the hapless Edmund remains blissfully unaware not only of their financial chicanery, but the resurgence of his wife's affair, if indeed it ever ended.

It's clear that, even if it were all above board, I'm hopelessly out of my depth. It will require legal and financial expertise I simply don't have to investigate and unravel the mess, and if Arthur chooses to resist or procrastinate, Edmund may not live long enough to benefit. The irony is that Edmund has no interest in wealth and no one to leave it to, facts which may have influenced both Arthur and Eleanor, so it's difficult to see what would motivate him to spend huge sums on professional advisors other than to wage war. Even if paperwork can be unearthed that demonstrates the transfer of funds from the Fitzgeralds to a company owned and controlled by Arthur Needham was suspicious, it could take years to gather enough evidence to prove there was fraud, despite the obvious impropriety.

In any event, Edmund needs to be told. He needs to be told that the proceeds of Farrier's Cottage, together with Eleanor's original inheritance, since grown to a vast sum, are under the control of Arthur Needham, and in respect of her investments, virtually out of reach. It may kill him, and I'll be partly responsible. I told him of Eleanor's substantial wealth and went looking for the money. I may have been acting at his request, but I opened the can of worms; the same can of worms Jackie opened and for whom it had fatal consequences.

But whatever Edmund decides to do, I can't let it go. People have died due to their connection to this sinister world that has the house of Fitzgerald at its core. Three murders in the last six months, not to mention the deaths of Eleanor herself, Jennifer Young, Edith Hawley and, the architect of all their misfortune, Lord Julian, male power, and male greed the common factor. I need time to think.

I walk back towards the Manor and I'm halfway along Horse Lane when a white Range Rover pulls up alongside. The passenger window rolls down and the woman in the driving seat leans across.

"Get in," she says nervously glancing in the mirror and then at the road ahead.

"Who are you?" I say, mildly affronted at being given orders by a stranger.

"Please," she says. "I'm Felicity Jones."

CHAPTER 29

She puts her foot down and we flash past Oakdale Manor heading towards Thurston.

"What's this about?"

Felicity Jones is an attractive woman in her early forties, with a gold Omega on her wrist and expensive rings on her fingers. She's dressed for a day off; no power suit or tied back hair. Her jeans and tee-shirt scream designer, but they don't prevent her looking pale and haggard.

"I need to talk to you. But we need to get away from Oakdale."

"Why?"

"We can't be seen together."

"Why?"

"Please, humour me."

Humour is the last thing on my mind. Her husband was brutally murdered two weeks ago and to my knowledge no one has been arrested. I can't imagine I can be of any help in finding who did it, but if she's relying on Stride and his flunkeys, then she's right to be desperate. Despite the circumstances, I'm pleased to meet her and at least express my condolences.

"I'm sorry. It must have been awful for you."

"You could say that, but then shit happens to everyone doesn't it?" Despite the stoicism, she's struggling to hold it together, fidgeting with her sunglasses, scratching an arm, tapping the wheel impatiently.

"Where are we going?"

"Not far. I know a quiet spot."

I shouldn't feel threatened, but I do feel uneasy. She knows who I am, must know I've been in touch with her office asking questions, and she made sure no one saw me get into the car. She knew Jackie Thomas and must know what happened to her, if not who was responsible, and now she's taking me to a quiet spot with no mention of a return trip. I need to take the initiative.

"I have to be back soon. They're expecting me at Oakdale Manor."

"Won't take long," she says, then catches my eye and realises my concern. "I want to help you, that's all."

"You too?"

"I don't understand."

I'm not going to tell her about the lecture I got from the Lees, Sue Jenkins' warnings about my safety, nor Ethel Hawley's genuine concerns for my welfare, but it sounds like I'm about to receive similar advice.

"Why do I need your help, Mrs Jones? Are you sure you're not the one who needs it?"

A sharp intake of breath is her only response. I may sound abrupt and uncaring, but it's born from recent experience. She turns off the road and into a car park set in a clearing amongst some trees. There are a dozen empty cars scattered around, owners and dogs gone for a walk. She finds an open area and parks. The car goes quiet, and we sit in silence for a moment until I notice she's burst into tears, head tipped forward, sobbing. I open the glovebox and find some tissues, take out a couple and hand them over.

"Mrs Jones…"

"Felicity, please."

"Okay, Felicity. You have every right to be upset. I can't magine what it's like for you and your child. Is it a boy or girl?"

"Girl. Samantha. She's ten."

"How is she coping?"

"Badly." *Stupid question Kate.*

She didn't ask me here for sympathy and there's nothing I can do. Best get on with it. "You want to help me?"

"Oh God, it's such a mess," she says sniffing and wiping her eyes.

"What is? Tell me." I expect she'll calm down once she tarts talking, the cathartic effect of counselling.

"You wanted to know about the cottage."

"Your partner answered that. It was sold to Belles Fleurs Investments."

"And do you know who's behind the company?" I could deny it, pretend I'm just a simple soul and allow her to tell me, follow it up with the appropriate degree of shock and concern, but it's not going to add anything. If I'm wrong and it's all some big mistake, her reaction will give it away.

"Arthur Needham."

She nods. It's neither controversial nor any surprise to her I know the answer.

"Jeremy did the valuation. He had to reduce it because of a condition regarding the Hawleys. Lady Fitzgerald said her husband demanded it."

"I know all this."

"Are you a solicitor?"

"Writer."

"Oh. Are you an investigative reporter?" she says, suddenly concerned.

"No, but I may as well be. To be honest, I wish I had never come here but now I have, I can't let it go. There's something badly wrong; I know it, you know it and lots of other people know it. I'd be happy for you tell me what you know provided you're not going to warn me about Lord Fitzgerald."

"I hardly know him. I knew his wife, obviously, and she was a colourful character, but he's not a client."

"But he was a client of Jackie's."

"Yes. She declared it. That was the deal. She worked for us as an associate, and we fed her some of our work when we were pushed. She could take private clients provided she cleared it with the partnership. Just so there was no conflict."

"Did she specialise?"

"Family law, inheritance, wills, mostly non-corporate stuff."

"I can see why Edmund would retain her."

"But you're working for him now."

"Looks like I'm carrying on where she left off."

"That's why I need to warn you."

"Felicity, look. I've heard all this before and I'm tired of it. I'm being hounded and intimidated just like Jackie was, I've had insults and threats and been warned about dark forces and Edmund Fitzgerald's fierce temperament and it's not going to work. Not until I find out the truth."

"Jackie found out the truth and they killed her."

"Who?"

Instead of simply answering the question, she asks another, as if she wants to prepare the ground. "You know about Eleanor's investments?"

"Yes. Belles Fleurs holds them in Jersey. It looks dodgy, but so far, there's no reason to believe Eleanor was either coerced or defrauded."

"And Oakdale Manor?"

I turn my head to look at her. This is new; an alarm bell is ringing somewhere in my consciousness. I need to know about this. "What about it?"

She takes a breath, as if composing herself before the revelation of some painful and shocking memory.

"Jeremy wasn't a bad man, Kate. He had dealings with several dubious people, men with bad reputations, but he always kept them at arm's length. We discussed it and I told him not to, but he was driven; couldn't resist the big deal even though deep down he knew some of them were villains. I tried to make sure he stayed out of it, for our sakes, but it was only a matter of time before he went too far."

"Do I know any of these villains?"

"Jackie had been trying to get the Fitzgeralds to make wills and did some research on their assets," she says, side-stepping the question. "She discovered what you did. The sale of the cottage…"

"For a loan."

"…and the transfer of Eleanor's investment funds to Jersey, neither of which Lord Fitzgerald knew anything about. When she confronted them with it, shit hit the fan. Eleanor berated her for a breach of confidentiality and his Lordship accused her of lying, impugning his wife's integrity, and trying to steal from two elderly, infirm people."

"What does this have to do with Jeremy?"

"She found out Oakdale Manor didn't belong to them anymore."

"What?"

"She did a search. It belongs to English Trust. The house, the grounds, the family heirlooms, oil paintings worth a fortune, about ten million in total, all belong to English Trust."

"I don't understand." It's another bombshell landing in the world of Fitzgerald and it sends my imagination into a frenzy. "How could that happen?"

"The same way the sale of the cottage happened. Eleanor persuaded her husband it made sense because she was ill, and he had no one to leave it to. They may as well have the money now and enjoy it and it would help pay the bills. Jeremy valued the house and he got experts to do the artwork, contents, and historical artefacts. He bribed them to inflate the value knowing English Trust would only agree to pay sixty percent."

"Why sixty percent?"

"Because the Fitzgeralds kept their right to live there until they died. It's like equity release but in this case, it leaves the property to the nation. English Trust don't get it until they're dead."

"So, where's the money?"

Felicity Jones stares through the windscreen. I follow her gaze, fixed on a couple, hand in hand, returning from their walk with a ten-year-old girl and a dog. It could be the Jones family, but not anymore. The tears have started again.

"Jeremy took a massive fee for brokering the deal, way out of all proportion to the value, said the Fitzgeralds didn't need it and English Trust could afford it."

"Where's the money, Felicity?"

She wipes the tears away from her eyes as she watches the family climb into a black 4x4.

"Jersey."

"Belles Fleurs?" She nods. "It wasn't Jeremy's idea, he was just an agent," she says, pleading for understanding.

"Arthur Needham," I say, thinking out loud. "Did you do the conveyancing?"

"No. Needham used a firm in Bradford, well known for their association with local gangsters. Jeremy asked me, but I warned him against it because I thought they were being badly advised by Needham. You don't park ten million in an offshore fund when you're that age and in poor health; these are long term investments that take time to grow. You take the cash and blow it on cruises. I never once imagined the funds would be stolen. Nor did Jeremy. He wasn't a thief, Kate, you must believe me."

"What happened when Jackie found out? Who did she tell?"

"The Fitzgeralds wouldn't talk to her, and she was being harassed at home. She told me she was leaving and why, and said she was going back to London, and I told Jeremy…oh God." She starts sobbing again, reliving the whole sorry episode. "He flew into a panic; thought she was going to the police. He confronted Arthur Needham who told him to calm down, the funds were all invested in a company of which Eleanor was a director and he had power of attorney anyway and it was all legal and above board. We didn't know what to do. We had no evidence, just Jackie's accusations the funds had been diverted. All Jeremy was guilty of was being involved in a questionable transaction."

"So what changed?"

"You."

"Me?"

"You asked for Jackie's number and said you'd met Lord Fitzgerald. Eleanor had since died and Jeremy puts two and two together, thinks you're helping Fitzgerald look for his funds and you're going to blow the whistle. He warns Needham his new tenant is asking questions and wants to contact Jackie Thomas and is bound to discover what happened, but Needham again brushes him aside, tells him

Fitzgerald is losing his mind and Jackie Thomas is dead. Case closed."

"How would Needham know she was dead?" I ask her, but I already know the answer. Word never got back to Oakdale about the death of one its former residents. She didn't come from there, hadn't lived there long and the Dales police didn't make any enquiries, content to write it off as an accident. No one in Oakdale gave a damn about Jackie Thomas, any more than they give a damn about me, apart from those who considered us a threat.

"Exactly. Jeremy was shocked and said he would have to refer the matter to the police in case there was some connection."

"And he was stopped."

Felicity Jones breaks down again, shoulders shaking, forehead on the steering wheel. I place a hand on her back and give it a rub, the limit of my ability to ameliorate her grief. I want to ask her why she doesn't go to the police herself, but she'd be too frightened, as I would, especially with a young daughter. I wouldn't place my trust in Stride and Gerrard being able to protect me. If they have an ounce of intelligence, they'll find the link themselves in due course. Jeremy Jones dealt with wide boys and was one himself. He never imagined his association with Needham would come to this and in the end, he tried to do the decent thing, but he was way out of his depth. Money buys power, and with all the Fitzgeralds' money, Needham had the power over life and death. He may even have helped hasten Eleanor's death, it would have further simplified matters for him by removing a source of evidence, but I can't think how, other than by drugs.

"What are the police doing?"

"They're wading through his client list; a rogues gallery if ever there was one. There's no shortage of potential candidates. I have no evidence, but I know it was Needham and I'm sure they'll reach the same conclusion eventually."

"Just because he's a fraudster?"

"It all fits. And he has ex-army pals, men trained in violence."

"Who?"

"Barry Wilson, he's a director of Belles Fleurs. And there's Tommy Gibbs. He suffered from PTSD after the Falklands and never had a proper job since leaving the army, so needs the money."

"What about Simon Hawley?"

She shakes her head. "Don't know him."

"George Hawley's son. He was in the same platoon as Gibbs and Wilson with Needham as commanding officer. I've been told he's a psychopath, but I've met him, and I can't see it."

"God Kate, how did you know all this?"

"Asked around. You said you wanted to help me."

"They killed Jackie and they killed my husband, and they'll kill you too, if you carry on. You know too much already."

"I have to carry on. I have no choice."

"Why, Kate?"

It's a good question. I could walk away and have nothing to lose and nothing to fear other than regret I should have done something. If I stay and pursue this course, only danger lies ahead. I want to tell her my motivation, the one thing that impels me to put my life at risk, but I can't.

"I don't know."

***

She drops me at the iron gates and I walk up the drive to Oakdale Manor. There's a small hatchback parked on the drive in front of the house and Edmund is standing on the porch, talking to a man with a clipboard and briefcase. They see me coming and shake hands.

"Thank you for your hospitality, Lord Fitzgerald," he says. "I'll be back in twelve months." He jumps into his car and waves at us both as he sets off down the drive.

"You're late!" says Edmund, grinning broadly, but I'm in no mood for banter.

"Who was that?"

Edmund looks suddenly confused.

"Er, forgotten his name. No, wait, Johnson, that's it! From English Trust."

"Study," I say curtly, marching straight past him and into the house. I know it's rude to treat him like a child but I'm on edge. Marian is in the hallway, but I'm in no mood for pleasantries and brush past her. Edmund follows me into the study, and I close the door behind us, straight into the face of a bewildered Marian.

"Tell me about English Trust."

"Well, they're a charity that own lots of historic buildings..."

"I know that! What are they doing here?"

"Annual inspection. Checking the inventory. I forgot it was today."

I want to scream or break something. Edmund looks worried, perplexed at my reaction to something that to him, seems of little importance.

"Why didn't you tell me?"

"I forgot they were coming that's all."

"No. Why didn't you tell me you had sold the Manor?"

"Didn't I? Sorry, must have slipped my mind." He looks genuinely contrite, as if some minor detail had taken on huge significance. It's written all over my face. "My memory is not what it was," he says, staring into a void, and I crumble at the sight of the lost and lonely old man in front of me, wrestling with an affliction that's eating away at his consciousness slowly taking control.

"Oh Edmund," I say, putting my arms around his neck and giving him a hug.

"What on earth's the matter?" he says, patting my back gently. "I can't bear to see you unhappy."

I release him and step back. His eyes are glassy and moist and so are mine.

"There's something I need to tell you."

"Sounds ominous. You're not leaving, are you?"

It hadn't crossed my mind, but the mere suggestion makes me think. I now know Edmund's financial position and it's not what either of us imagined. I'd like to think that, given time and money, much of it could be recovered, but he has neither, nor does he have any incentive. In his current situation, he does not have the resources to fulfil our agreement and pay me to write and publish his family history, and I simply can't afford to devote several years to the project with no income and no guarantee of publication, never mind royalties. If I decide to walk away, I have to give him an explanation, but if I reveal the conspiracy between his late wife and her lover that has left him virtually penniless, it may well kill him. He might be sanguine about the loss of his wealth, but the manner of its misappropriation will break his heart. *Justice Kate. Justice for all.* I have no choice.

CHAPTER 30

Jackie Thomas had been here already. Edmund was becoming increasingly confused, unable to grasp what Eleanor was telling him. Deep down he knew they had more money than they needed and that, with or without a will, it would all go to Eleanor when he died. What other outcome could there be? She was fifteen years his junior, in a good state of health, active in the Church and still able to indulge her desires; she lived life to the full. That all changed when she had a life-threatening disability and he realised he needed to take responsibility for their futures, finding he was woefully ill-equipped to do so, both physically and mentally.

Although Eleanor had largely recovered from her first stroke, he began to have nagging doubts, suspicious something was afoot, especially when she persuaded him to sell firstly the cottage and then the Manor. There was no one to inherit so they may as well simplify the estate by liquidating those assets that were rapidly turning into liabilities. The estate agent had found a buyer for the cottage; one who accepted the condition the cottage would never fall into the hands of the Hawleys. He also introduced English Trust, who would take on the Manor after their death or at a time of their choosing, releasing most of the equity to fund a comfortable, if not lavish lifestyle in their twilight years.

Edmund had no idea the funds would end up in Jersey, nor that Arthur Needham would become not only the custodian but ultimately, the beneficiary of the estate. In Eleanor's mind, none of this would have mattered if Edmund had done the decent thing and predeceased her. The estate would have come to her anyway, at least that was what she believed. She may have imagined a new life in Jersey with Arthur Needham or given his age, perhaps even sought the affections of a younger, more virile candidate like Gigolo John. Eleanor's motives could only be a matter for speculation, but what was clear is that she unwittingly lost control of her own fortune due to her long-standing relationship with her financial advisor.

Edmund asked local solicitors Franklyn Jones to cast an eye over their affairs. They had acted in the sale of the cottage, so already had some knowledge, but given her husband's connection to a dubious transaction, Felicity Jones declined to get involved and introduced freelancer Jackie Thomas instead. Through the course of her work, she discovered the potential for fraud and most likely, the unconventional relationship between Eleanor and Arthur. This brought her into conflict with Eleanor and by association, Edmund too. She was suffering harassment in the cottage, resistance from Lady Fitzgerald and the unpredictable irascibility of his Lordship, all of which she found impossible to cope with. Her dreams of finding peace and tranquillity in the Dales after the intolerable pressure of her city career, were roundly shattered.

To my amazement, Edmund was philosophical. He wouldn't have anything bad said of his beloved Eleanor. He always knew of her infidelity, it was intrinsic to her character, part of her appeal even, so he was not surprised that her affair with Arthur had eventually been rekindled. He berated the duplicitous scoundrel for manipulating his wife but had to accept she may well have been a willing participant. His biggest grievance was that his dream of publishing a full history of his colourful family might not come to fruition.

"There's even more scandalous material than I could ever have imagined, right up to the present day!" he announced, with curiously misplaced enthusiasm. "We must find a way you can continue with your work, provided you are willing and able?"

It touched me and I didn't have the heart to refuse, asking for time to think it over. We decided tea was in order. I opened the door to the hallway and startled Marian, polish and duster in hand. She made a pretence of working, but I know her ear had been pressed to the door.

"I just wanted to tell his Lordship," she stuttered, a clumsy attempt to cover up her eavesdropping, "My boy won't be coming this afternoon, he has to help his Dad with the herd."

"My boy?" I asked Edmund when she'd gone. "Who's she talking about?"

"Marcus. You know Marcus?"

"She's his mum?" Edmund nodded. "Marian Wilson, married to Barry?"

So here I am, late evening in front of the fire, thinking it over. Unlike Edmund, who is living out his last few years and probably has a different perspective, I don't have the inclination to let things lie. He would go tomorrow if he could, anticipating a happy reunion with Eleanor. I briefly consider the notion of couples reunited in the afterlife, having affairs with other departed souls, amused to ponder whether the rules are different. I can accept the possibility that Eleanor knowingly and willingly entrusted her fortune to Arthur Needham. It was her inheritance and but for his advice it may have withered or been frittered away. She gave him power of attorney; the right to make decisions on her behalf, regardless of how those decisions look from the outside.

The proceeds of Oakdale Manor are different. The property belonged to Edmund and even if he agreed to sell, he would never have agreed to invest the money with anything connected to, never mind owned by Arthur Needham. Unfortunately, there's every likelihood that, intentionally or otherwise, he signed some authority that makes it legal. I feel desperately sorry for him. On the surface he copes well with his diminishing mental health, but he's fading fast. Others saw that and he was cruelly exploited. It makes me angry and tearful. I thought about my own dad and resolved to call mum when I got home, only to find that, following the day's events and the toll on my own emotional wellbeing, I had left my phone behind in Edmund's study. Tomorrow will do.

Inevitably, Farrier's Cottage returns to centre stage. The proceeds were originally converted to a loan and Arthur has not denied it, even offering to repay it to Edmund once probate is granted. I now know Belles Fleurs has the assets to do it. It would deliver four hundred thousand pounds to Edmund, enough to fund both my continued work on the Fitzgerald biography for a good while and keep his wine cellar stocked. I must expedite his making a will to protect what's left.

In the light of the flickering fire, I look around the sitting room; the chipped and worn stone floor, the cracked, uneven plaster on the ceiling, the ancient wooden staircase and creaking floorboards of Farrier's Cottage, largely unaltered since Jacob and Edith Hawley lived here. *There are dark forces at work.* Jackie Thomas was killed because of what she knew, what she found out about the Fitzgeralds and whom she told. Jeremy Jones knew what happened to her, tried to do the decent thing and it cost him his life. It won't be over until justice is served. A rap at the front door startles me and I glance at the clock. Nine p.m. Given all I've learnt today, I'm suddenly apprehensive. I pick up the poker and conceal it behind my back.

Sara Lee is holding a bottle. She's had her hair done, the grey-flecked brown now a deep copper. She's dressed up for an occasion, applied make-up and the scent of her perfume washes in through the open door.

"Peace offering?" she says, brandishing a bottle of white. It's unexpected and I don't have the heart to send her away. *A quick glass before bed.*

"Come in."

She steps over the threshold and throws her spare arm around my neck, kissing me sensuously under the ear so I feel her hot breath, her pungent aromatic fragrance filling my nostrils. She marches straight to the kitchen, bottle in hand. "Do you know where everything is?" I call after her, replacing the poker on the hearth. The clink of glasses and the familiar sound of the bottle opener says she does.

"I've been here before, remember?" she calls from the kitchen.

"Yes, but I didn't know you lived here yourself."

Sara reappears with the open bottle and two large glasses and we sit together on the sofa as she pours.

"My, you have been doing your research. Don't tell me, Naira?" I shake my head. "Ethel Hawley?" Wrong again. "Margaret Gibbs?"

"I never reveal my sources."

"Ma Gibbs then. She's never liked me."

"Maybe she didn't like you seducing her daughter."

"Ouch! Don't believe everything you hear."

"I don't. In fact, I struggle to believe anything I'm told in this village."

"And how do you separate fact from fiction Kate?" She raises her glass. We clink and I take a sip, noting she's from the Edmund Fitzgerald school of wine drinking. The bottle won't last long.

"I'm working on it."

"I wanted to say sorry. Sorry about John. He gets a bit wound up sometimes. He's very intense you know, very passionate about things that matter to him."

"Why do I matter to him?"

"Everyone matters to him. It's his job to look after his flock. He just gets carried away."

She takes another mouthful and sits back on the sofa, drawing her legs underneath, resting her head on one hand, just like she did at The Vicarage. Making herself at home.

"I've come to tell you the truth, the whole truth and nothing but the truth," she says, with fake solemnity. The wine has already hit home. I suspect she started earlier.

"Go on."

"But first you must do something for me." She fixes me with a lascivious grin. It's meant to distract me, but unlike John, she's no threat, just a flirtatious predator with a fantasy prey. "You must promise me you'll stay away from Lord Fitzgerald."

"Why?"

"Because you're in danger that's why. I couldn't bear it if something happened to you too."

"You're not still peddling that tripe about Edmund being responsible for Jackie's death? It won't work. I know Edmund better than I know you and John. He's more than earned my trust." It's pointed, I know, but I've had a drink now and she doesn't look offended. In fact, she looks increasingly relaxed.

"John did everything he could to reach out to Edmund Fitzgerald, respect his vehement atheism, tolerate his vitriol, make light of his lurid accusations, make peace with the man, but he just wouldn't have it. He was convinced John was trying to seduce his wife."

"And was he?"

"Of course not. It was the other way round. Eleanor Fitzgerald was a seasoned cougar. She was insatiable, especially when it came to younger men. No man was safe and John especially so. His position and her devotion to the Church was a real turn on. She said things, did things, touched him in ways no man could do to a woman and hope to get away with it."

"You mean like Reverend Fenton touched Mel Gibbs?"

"Ooh, naughty vicar!" she says, laughing, then taking a swig that almost empties the glass. "I suppose Fenton had to do something to satisfy his lustful tendencies after her Ladyship dumped him."

I don't rise to it. I already know about that affair, but she doesn't need to know that.

"So he went for someone younger and more vulnerable; someone confused by her sexuality."

"Mel wasn't confused."

"Not after she met you." I find I'm grinning at her even though I believe she's dangerous. Sara Lee laughs out loud, delighted at the compliment, backhanded or not. I'm still smiling when I decide to burst her bubble. "You made it up." The humour begins to dissipate, and she looks at me intensely, asking for more. "You wanted to get rid of Fenton, so you persuaded your girlfriend to come on to him. I don't know whether he wanted it or not, but you just happened to burst in on them and next thing, there's scandal in the church,

Fenton's despatched and John moves in. It was all set up." She doesn't deny it. She doesn't want to deny it. "You weren't married before you got here, or if you were, you went through with it again so people thought you didn't know each other. Problem is, I haven't worked out why you and he wanted to be in Oakdale of all places."

"Charming country village. A great gig for a trendy vicar, somewhere I can keep horses. There are lots of attractions. And they keep coming." She's eyeing me up and down, grinning suggestively again. I find it all very amusing but also very tiring. I'd like to go to bed, but I need to stay awake. I want to dig deeper into the Lees' background and my best chance is when I have Sara Lee alone with a bottle of wine to hand. I excuse myself and go into the kitchen to splash cold water on my face. When I get back, the glasses have been refilled. "Drink up," she says, raising hers and I find I can't help but go along with it.

"What do you and your husband want, Sara?"

She swirls the wine around her glass and holds it up to the light. "We want you to stay safe."

"You've done that already. I'm perfectly safe with Edmund Fitzgerald." Edmund's name comes out wrong. I've said Fizz not Fitz. It's the wine.

"John and his first wife were cokeheads, rich and vulgar and out of control, but they broke up when he found God and she had twins. Don't know what Amber's excuse was, but he blamed his addiction on a tortured childhood, no father, alcoholic mother, separated from his sister and given up for adoption, so he went looking for answers. He found me in rehab, fucked up just like he had been and I told him all about Jennifer." I must look blank because she raises her eyebrows and makes a face. "Can't you tell? He's not my husband," she giggles and waits for my reaction. The room was beginning to spin but I've been jerked awake.

"Brother," is all I can say.

"Yep. I'm his big sister. And not only that…"

"Edmund is his father."

"Correct!" she shouts with glee, holding her glass aloft as if proposing a toast. "He tracks down Fitzgerald here to Oakdale so we manoeuvre ourselves into position and try to get into his good books. We don't want to spring the surprise on him because we don't know how he'll react. So we soften up her Ladyship first. John turns on the charm, not that he needs to because she's all over him, but it keeps her juices flowing, so to speak, and one night in The Vicarage I slip her a line of coke and the three of us… well… use your imagination."

"You gave her drugs? After she'd had a stroke?"

"It helped her! She felt much better for it and couldn't get enough… of anything. Don't know why we bothered after what she did to our mother, but it was only to get Edmund's attention. Trouble is it backfired badly. He wanted nothing to do with the Church and then Eleanor boasted about her delightful new young acquaintances and how wonderfully liberal we were, and Edmund went berserk, banning her from ever going to church. She ignored him of course, but the die was cast. There was no way John could inveigle himself into Edmund's affections after that, no way he could casually introduce himself as the son and heir of Lord Fitzgerald. No hard feelings and all that; you may have fucked up our mother and our lives, but we're prepared to forgive everything, for old times' sake and oh, by the way, who are you leaving your millions to?"

Sara Lee's smug diatribe has given me the stimulation I need. "That's what this is all about. Greed."

"Not greed, Katie darling. Justice. Justice for Jennifer."

"He's leaving everything to charity."

"Only if he makes a will and he only makes a will if you help him."

"And if he doesn't? If he dies intestate?"

"It's easy. John steps forward and makes a claim. There are no others, he's checked. It'll sail through."

"You can't prove it."

"Oh yes we can. DNA. We got some of his hair."

"When?"

"When Eleanor was dying. John was up in their bedroom, holding her hand, sending her on her way. He went to the bathroom, found his hairbrush. Perfect match."

I have an urge to laugh. *Gigolo John and that drug-addled lesbian masquerading as his wife.* Edmund was bang on target. Sara Lee is loving this. She loves the sex and the danger and the intrigue and she loves being in control. She controlled Mel Gibbs and made her fabricate a story about Fenton, she and John controlled Eleanor trying to get close to Edmund and she controlled Jackie Thomas, making her fearful then calming her down before taking advantage. I'm probably next on the list, but the difference is, I know what she's up to.

"Anyway," she says, "don't give me that bollocks about charity. I bet you've got your sticky little fingers all over his assets. Know what I mean? Beautiful young woman like you? He'd be mad not to want you. 'Kate, sweetie, look after me in my dying years, be my companion and give me everything a man needs and it's all yours'." *Whore!* The childish, mocking tone. I should be outraged and offended, but I'm happy to let her fill in the blanks.

"It was you. You are the demon graffiti artist. You had a key and you let yourself in and violated my space, just like you did to Jackie."

"Aw don't take it personally, Katie." She reaches over and squeezes my arm. "It was just a bit of fun. A gentle nudge. I thought it fitted in quite well with the haunted cottage thing," she says, opening her eyes wide, feigning fear and horror, "and good old George got the blame."

"Until someone killed him."

"Yes that was inconvenient. We lost our stooge." She sees me staring at her. "Don't look at me! We had no problem with George and no reason to hurt him, although if we inherited the cottage, we'd have had to calm him down."

"You know the cottage is gone?"

"Of course. We'd just sell it anyway. Better off with the cash."

"Did you run Jackie off the road?"

Her irritating smugness disappears, replaced by sadness.

"No, of course not. I liked her a lot. We wanted to frighten her off but I never wished her any real harm. Very sad. I like you a lot too."

"And you tried to frighten me off, but it hasn't worked. So now what?" She grips my arm again and looks excited, all thoughts of Jackie Thomas consigned to history.

"Let's work together. You, me, and John. We don't mind sharing, everything," *did she wink at me?* "and you can steer Fitzgerald in the right direction. He seems to trust you."

"You mean just like Eleanor? I don't do coke and I don't do three in a bed."

"You should try it sometime. Broaden your horizons." She's taunting me, provoking me. "Look, even if his Lordship names you as beneficiary, we'll fight you and get our fair share. No point paying bloody lawyers to sort it out when we can manage the situation in a civilised fashion. What do you say?"

I want to tell her she's missed the boat, Edmund's riches are gone, there's nothing to inherit and I want to laugh in her face. But she wouldn't believe me and anyway I'm overwhelmed by fatigue.

"I say, see you in court."

Her face drops for a moment and she forces a smile and puts her hand on my shoulder.

"I respect that. I hope we can still be friends."

"And I'm not leaving the cottage, not after all this time."

She nods her head slowly in understanding, then fixes her eyes on a spot below my chin. It's my necklace that's caught her attention. She moves closer and reaches out towards it.

"May I?" she says, without waiting for an answer, she rubs the stone between two fingers. "It's very beautiful."

"Pearl. Birthday present from my parents," I try to say through the haze of tiredness and intoxication. The backs of her fingers are touching my chest. She releases the stone, but her hand is still there, in contact with flesh, but I can't be certain as my senses are confused.

"You have very soft skin," she whispers. Her fingers turn over and caress my chest, moving slowly in a circle. I look dumbly at her, not quite knowing what to do or say. She has the same sultry look she had in The Vicarage, eyes like deep, dark, pools of water, beckoning me to dive in. I find her behaviour strange, but gentle and friendly. Friendly, and sensitive, yes, that's what it is. Sensitive. I look at her circling hand. The nails are painted a deep scarlet, the same colour as the paint daubed on my mirror. I watch as they drop out of sight, inside my blouse and I feel a squeeze on my breast. I giggle. She's made a mistake and her hand has slipped. She can't realise what she's done or she'd say sorry.

"Oops," she says, or is it me? I'm chuckling at the absurdity and the room is spinning and something's unfastening the buttons of my blouse, one by one and pushing the cotton aside and I feel the warmth of the fire on my bare skin and hot breath and a tickling sensation in my ear.

"John knows who you are." It's a whisper that fades into the distance as my eyes close and I slip away into the dark…

CHAPTER 31

NOW

Desperately thirsty. Hands free, swing legs off the bed and stand, unsteady, a residual pain from cramp threatening to return. Floor is gritty and hard. Slide each foot forward, arms stretched out ahead, wary of obstacles and hazards, inanimate or not, a bottomless well ready to swallow up the unsuspecting. Feet shuffle inch by inch, arms wave around and ahead like a zombie. The plip, plop taunts, ridicules the craving for water. It's very close. *Bistari, bistari!* the Nepali word for "slowly" a phrase invoked many times in the past to calm me and others. Knee hits something solid. Smooth stone, cold and unyielding. A trough.

Resist feeling inside, suspicious of what's there, and search blindly for the source of the drip, both hands swirling in the void performing an unintelligible sign language. Hand touches cold metal, a pipe, and it's wet, the drops on the fingers, nectar on the tongue. It's sweet, but it's only a drip. Shaking finger descends, following the drip, anticipating the open jaws and razor-sharp teeth of the water demon. It touches the surface.

Wait. *Bistari!*

Desperation prevails. Force a hand under the cold liquid and scoop. It's sweet. Scoop again, then use both hands and drink; once twice, three times, gulping air in between. Splash it on face and run hands through hair. Nothing felt or tasted so good. Dip again, feel an object in the water. It has fur.

Scream.

Wait. Calm down.

They brought me in; there's a way out. Resume the zombie shuffle, moving the length of the trough, one hand on stone, the other waving ahead, fending off imaginary predators. A foot collides, and a metal bucket topples over on the stone floor, clanging raucously, rocking and rolling to a standstill.

Reach the end of the trough, another obstacle at the feet, wooden, a box or crate, and above it, a solid wall. Chalky. Use both hands like a mime artist to expand the search area. Sidle left, moving along the wall an inch at a time.

Shivering with fear now, expecting impact, injury, and pain at any moment. Keep going. An object on the wall, a picture frame? It swings to one side then dissolves to the touch and there's a crash and the shattering of glass that crunches under shoes.

A vertical edge. Slide a hand down and touch another object, bulbous, spherical. Doorknob. Twist and tug ineffectually, and run both hands over the surface of a door. Rotten at the base, split in the middle, feel the remnants of flaking paint hanging loose. Drop to the knees and sense a draft through a crack that widens to a ragged hole, big enough for a rat. Stand and aim a cursory kick. Wood creaks and splits, but not much. Lie on the floor and kick with two feet. The impact jars ankles and knees but the wood creaks and splinters and with a dozen kicks, the hole is a foot high and six inches wide. Fine for rats.

Crawl back across the dirt floor to where the bed might be. Full circle. Touch metal frame and pull, rusty legs shrieking on the stone floor. Toss aside the fetid mattress and underneath, flat metal bars straddle the frame. One lifts without resistance. Run a hand along its length. Three feet of iron given its weight; surface coarse with decades of accumulated rust. Crawl back to the door, tool in hand and manoeuvre it between door and jamb. Three attempts, wood splinters, the lock gives in, the door opens inwards.

More blackness beyond, but it's cooler, the faintest breath of air suggesting an opening somewhere ahead. The air is musty and damp, a welcome change from the stench of the cell. "Hello!" My croak echoes. A wall to the right, another two metres to the left. A tunnel, the floor smooth, cobbled, the walls either side, jagged rock streaked with slime and tiny rivulets of water. Step by step, guided by a hand on one wall, stopping to listen for scuttling underfoot. Sense a gradient, mercifully upwards, the tunnel curves right. Peer into the void.

Tiny feet making tiny footsteps. Moan in despair. Terror of being taken down and eaten alive by a horde of carnivorous rodents. Moan in despair. Make a feeble gesture, stamp a foot, wave an invisible arm, say "Shoo!" but it doesn't stop, whiskery snouts twitching ahead of dead black eyes, waiting to pounce. Moan in despair. Walk on, the sound of scuttling recedes.

Increase pace, one hand on the slimy wall, the other outstretched in the void, the incline steeper, the floor slippery. Stumble and crack a knee on the cobbles. Leg goes numb with pain. Weep with frustration for a full minute, stand and resume. Wall curves left and right and left again. No way to measure time or distance.

Wait.

Impotent vision has stimulation in the infinite black, drawn to a tiny spot on the retinal landscape. Black, but not as black. Dismiss it as an illusion, but it moves as I move and grows bigger with each step until gradually the black takes on a shade of grey and feet hit an obstacle and stumble again, toppling forward, hands flailing to break the fall.

Stone steps.

Climb. Climb. One by one, step by step, each step less black and more grey, more visible than the last. Dark walls glisten, feet and hands move in rhythm to a beat that propels me slowly upwards. Legs ache, flesh burns, but sight is restored and sensitive ears identify the rustle of leaves alongside running water. The last step. Ground flattens, stars twinkle through rusty wrought iron gates. Light from a distant galaxy guides the way.

Free.

***

I've been here before. I know the way. The ruined buildings of Fitzgerald's abandoned lead mine bathe in the moonlight. I drink from the river, it's even sweeter than prison and not as cold. The dark sky says it's after midnight, but for eyes conditioned to ultimate black, it's a bright summer's evening.

I follow the path I know well, shivering in the cool night air. I'm wearing only a short sleeved cotton blouse and jeans and now, with nothing to fear, physical discomfort makes itself known. It's three miles to Oakdale; if I maintain a steady pace, I'll be back in less than ninety minutes; before dawn.

For the first time since I blacked out, fragments of memory return. The uninvited guest, the make-up and fragrance, the alcohol, the flirting, the candid disclosures, the thinly veiled threats, the seduction and the irresistible fatigue. My drink was spiked. She knows about drugs does Sara and has form as a sexual predator. She was the last person I saw. She assaulted me while I was semi-conscious and afterwards, who knows? She violated my home, and now my body too, but apart from a natural revulsion, and the lingering effects of prolonged isolation, I feel no ill effects. But when she was done, when she had done what she wanted and had no further use for me, what then? Disposal. It was always the default. If I succumbed to her advances all well and good; if I refused to cooperate, so be it, she'd have her pleasure anyway.

Disposal would need help. She would call John, as agreed. It makes me shudder. Did his perversions match those of his sister? Can I rely on a man of God to take pity on the weak and vulnerable or is John Lee inherently depraved like his sister? He has lineage. The great-grandson of Julian, the devil who's the cause of it all, for the calamity that followed and the chain reaction that never ends. I tell myself, as a woman, I'd know, I'd be in pain, but apart from the general discomfort of forced imprisonment, I'm still in one piece.

But even with two of them, how did they get me here? How did they carry a dead weight in the middle of night three miles to a remote spot in the countryside and deposit it half a mile underground? The practicalities are debatable but secondary to the real facts. I was left to die. Perverted sexual predilections aside, they took time and effort to ensure my demise would be calm, undramatic, and natural. Nothing violent or tasteless. She's already comatose, allow nature to take its course, hide her from view in a place of solitude where she can make peace with God. Hell, I bet he even said a prayer. But as I continue to think about the Lees and the scenario they acted out, I begin to doubt. Something else might have happened.

Sara Lee indulged her pleasures and left. She left me sleeping, intending to call back the next day and continue where she left off, this time with my conscious participation. In the night, Arthur Needham and his cronies, came to visit. Marian Wilson had overheard me and Edmund. I was a risk too far. They came while I slept, strong men took me away, never to be seen again. No blood-soaked body this time, another violent murder would be careless and unnecessary, albeit unsurprising given previous threats to the latest resident of the haunted cottage. The Whore of Oakdale demanded too much money from a deranged client threatened with exposure, and paid the ultimate price, Stride and Gerrard might usefully, for them, conclude.

No, not that either. A simple disappearance like Jackie Thomas is all that's required and this time, with no evidence, no body. The practicalities are a better fit, but the probabilities less so. One of them likes physical violence. One of them likes to use a knife. One of them likes killing even when the victim is already dead. One or more could not resist the temptation of a young woman, barely conscious, tied down, helpless and hopeless, and for whom death beckons. Yet, here I am, striding purposefully towards home. I feel for my pearl necklace. It's gone. Inherited by Sara Lee.

The path beside the ever-dwindling river weaves its way between trees that rustle their leaves in friendly applause, urging me on, celebrating my return. I need to plan, form a strategy. There's no way back to normality. The Lees are poison and must be neutralised. I would never have been found in time. It would be days before any alarm was raised and then it would be treated with little concern and no urgency. She found the pressure too much and fled, just like those before her. Edmund would be unhappy, but impotent to do anything. *They all end up a disappointment.* My mother doesn't call; it would be weeks before she noticed. *You have a new life dear; this is something I must do alone.* Yet, here I am, shaken, stirred but more motivated than ever.

I can see the lights of Oakdale and to the east, the faint glow of a new day in a new sky. I can't go back to the cottage, not yet. One field from the road, I turn left and cross behind the village, wading through the lush dairy pasture, wet with dew. A dry-stone wall, drainage ditch and verdant hedgerow attempt to bar my way, but I won't be stopped. I clamber out onto the Thurston Road and turn right along Horse Lane, back towards the village.

***

The sky behind me is streaked with pink and amber beneath graduated shades of blue. I've pressed the ceramic doorbell twice now and still there's no sign of life. I consider the tool-shed. It would be shelter at least, but reminiscent of prison. A last resort. *Where are you Edmund?* A light comes on in the hall. Bolts, locks and chains shatter the peace with their metallic din. The door swings open.

"Good God!" Edmund is in his dressing gown, tousle haired, bleary eyed, mouth agape. "Where on earth...?"

I want to speak, but my throat is dry and cracked, bleeding lips sting at the slightest movement. I feel faint and begin to sway and he rushes forward to catch me as I fall. I'm more worried he'll notice the smell, but he swings my arm around his neck and carries me inside and lowers me onto a chair. A glass of water is pressed to my lips and I drink greedily coughing and then laugh.

***

I'm in a heavenly place, submerged in luxuriously warm water, silky smooth bubbles tickling my nose, the heat slowly restoring physical and mental strength. Edmund had half-carried, half-dragged me up the stairs, the black eyes of Lord Julian tracking our stumbling, erratic ascent. He filled Eleanor's cast-iron roll-top bath, enveloping the room in a cloud of steam, while I watched dumbly from a boudoir chair.

I declined his offer to help me undress, more embarrassed by the fetid odour than any misplaced sense of modesty. I had no doubt his motives were wholly altruistic but equally, he seemed content to spare us both the indignity. I succeeded, with difficulty, tossing the filthy rags into a pile on the floor and stood naked in front of the full-length mirror. Hair, lank and filthy; eyes, sunken in dark pools of grey; arms and wrists, bruised and red raw with abrasions; knees and shins, skinned, dark red scabs like tattoos, dried and hardened. Between my legs, no obvious bruising or tissue damage, the soft white flesh of inner thighs, merely chapped, angry and pink. The hot water stung at first, gradually soothing wounds, reducing the pain to a dull ache. There's a tap on the door, a pause, and the sound of the latch.

"Are you decent? May I come in?"

I smile without answering and the door opens tentatively. Edmund is dressed, balancing a pile of garments on one hand, the other covering his eyes. He shuffles across the floor towards the dressing table, averting his gaze and I'm so pleased to see him I want to chuckle with delight at his charm and chivalry.

"I brought you some of Eleanor's things. I had them all cleaned. Just in case," he says, looking studiously at the wall.

"Just in case of what?"

"Don't know. Just in case. You should find something suitable. I've got breakfast on the go if you can manage it."

"I'm starving. Fifteen minutes."

"Take your time."

I watch with amusement as he turns away from me like a robot and shuffles back towards the door.

"Edmund? Please turn around." His eyes eventually meet mine. "Thank you."

CHAPTER 32

Eleanor and I were of similar build. Pale blue cashmere and black trousers are a good fit. I thought twice about the underwear, but a quick sniff-test confirmed they were freshly laundered and fragrant. I descend the stairs carefully in her Ladyship's sumptuous sheepskin slippers, the smell of coffee and toast teasing my nostrils. Edmund is seated at the table, reading a crumpled copy of *The Times*.

"What time is it?"

"Six-fifteen,' he says, removing his glasses and folding away the paper. "Come and sit."

He brings toast and eggs and marmalade and coffee and watches me eat, waiting patiently for an explanation. A thought occurs to me.

"What time does Marian come?"

"Nine-thirty."

"Can you give her the day off? Call her and tell her something has come up and she's not required today?" he nods without question, leaves me to finish and I hear his muffled voice from the study. He's back within two minutes.

"You left this behind," he says laying my phone on the table. I press at the buttons, but the battery is flat. It's no matter. When I get back to the cottage, I can recharge it and change into my own clothes.

"What about Marcus?"

"Not here today."

I need more time to think, but I'm desperately tired. I don't know whether to go home or stay here for a while. I'm nervous about returning to the cottage so soon. Life can't go on as normal; there has to be a reckoning, but I don't know where to start. Edmund is still regarding me with concern, but there's something else. Despite his ministrations, he's not the same Edmund I saw yesterday.

"What happened Kate?" It sounds formal and detached, a hint of suspicion rather than natural concern for my welfare.

"The honest truth is, I'm not sure. I need to get some sleep. Would it be possible for me to stay here a while? I'll go back to the cottage when I'm rested."

"I'm afraid that won't be possible."

"Oh."

It's the last thing I expected. He tried to persuade me on several occasions to move into the Manor, so his change of heart is upsetting.

"I mean, you're welcome to stay here, of course, but you can't go back to Farrier's."

"Why not?" Alarm bells are ringing. "I need to change. All my things are there." He's shaking his head and I feel the first stirrings of panic. "What's wrong?"

"I thought you'd left. Everyone thought you'd left. Disappeared just like the other girl. One day you were here and the next, you're gone."

"Gone? But… it's only been a day, maybe two. I'm still a bit confused. I was here only yesterday… or the day before…" But he's still shaking his head.

"Kate, listen. You've been gone for over a month. When you stopped coming, I came to find you myself. The cottage was empty. All your things are gone. All your clothes, furniture, bits and pieces. All gone." Now it's my head that's shaking. He's gone mad, and he's still talking. "I was quite upset, but thought you'd just had enough, what with all the money and the business with the Manor. You'd decided to get away from it all. Get away from me."

"I would never do that Edmund."

"That painter chappie Marshall and his wife moved in three weeks ago, so you can't go back. But you can stay here as long as you like."

I reach out for his hand and it's warm and I feel tears welling up. He takes my other hand.

"Your hands are cold."

"Tell me what's going on. Please."

"Get some rest. It will all become clear."

***

I collapsed into Eleanor's bed and fell into a deep sleep, despite the madness overwhelming me, but there was little respite from the real world in dreamland.

"Jacob!" Edith Hawley is still calling plaintively for her husband, begging forgiveness, running up the stairs to her room to evade his blows. "That cottage belongs to me", screams George as he walks off into the mere, blood streaming down his face. "There are dark forces at work." Jackie Thomas, soaked to the skin, is smiling while Sara Lee looks on, arm around Mel Gibbs. "I'm about finished," calls Steve Marshall standing back from his handiwork. "Lovely," I say, admiring 'WHORE' he's painted in white. "Who the devil are you?" bellows Edmund before handing me a glass of champagne. Eleanor is on the couch snogging Arthur Needham while Marjorie Needham watches with disinterest. Tommy Gibbs and Psycho Si have squared up to each other pointing and pushing, ready to come to blows, and Gigolo John tries to separate them whilst repeating "I know who you are." "I don't remember," says Edmund. "Julian Fitzgerald, you are the devil incarnate!". "She's killing me! She's killing me!" Plip, plop…

I'm wide awake, sweating, heart pounding, tugging at tethered wrists, but they're already free and where there was blackness, now there is just gloom. I can see mahogany wardrobes, walnut dressing table, embossed ornate wallpaper, dotted with framed oils and prints, crystal chandelier suspended beneath a plaster rose and floor to ceiling velvet curtains, a hair's breadth of sunlight bisecting the fabric like a laser beam. I wipe the sweat from my brow with a cotton sleeve. I'm wearing a nightdress, one of Eleanor's, but I don't remember getting undressed. I can't resist a wry smile; Edmund may have felt compelled to assist, eyes shut tight.

I lie back on silk pillow covers and stare at the ceiling. A new sense of purpose beckons. I get up and push back the curtains. Sunlight from the western sky floods the room.

***

He's still where I left him, but the newspaper is gone and he's poring over a dog-eared paperback, spine creased and bent with age. The inevitable bottle of Veuve and two Bohemian crystal glasses lie in wait.

"What are you reading?"

He closes the book and looks at the front cover as if he's forgotten that too. "*Cromwell – The Rise and Fall of The Lord Protector.* We get a mention."

"Lord Sir Gerald?"

"That's the chap. What would have happened if he'd stayed on his pig farm and kept his head down?"

"We wouldn't be here now."

"I've been looking at this chilled champagne, getting worried. Thought I might have to wake you up or worse, drink it alone," he says, grinning mischievously. "But your timing is impeccable. Assuming you're in the mood of course?" I sit down beside him and take his hand. "Warm hands. That's much better. Shall I?" I nod my consent and he removes foil and cage and pops the cork like the seasoned expert he is.

It still feels like only yesterday, but he told me it was over a month. I know he's prone to misjudgement, but that's beyond any conceivable margin for error. And it's no trick. I know he would rather I stayed here but duplicity is not in his nature. We gently clink glasses. It tastes as good as I remember.

"I got the deli to deliver coq au vin. Hope that's fine with you?"

"We need to talk Edmund."

"I know."

CHAPTER 33

He called Marian to say her services were no longer required, nor those of her son Marcus. He felt little compunction about dismissing her, once he realised her husband was not only one of Arthur's business associates, but also a director of the secretive company he'd used to misappropriate all the Fitzgerald assets. He was more sombre about firing young Marcus. The lad had always done a good job, but there was no room for sentiment. I needed to stay out of sight for the time being and that precluded regular visits by any of the Wilsons, however innocent.

I shared everything I knew, and we debated the strategy throughout the days ahead and long into the night. Edmund's motivation was clear and had nothing to do with wealth. He had never sought any more than he needed to keep his wife happy and stock his wine cellar. He continued to express disappointment that I showed no interest in inheritance and tried to persuade me otherwise. I reminded him there was precious little to inherit, but even if there were, I would respectfully decline and insist on making make my own way, thank you very much.

As regards the outstanding loan for Farrier's, we would press for repayment as soon as possible. This would provide funds enough for Edmund to live out his final years and for me to complete the work on the Fitzgerald biography. In those circumstances, I would move into Oakdale Manor. Alternatively, we may be able to negotiate with Arthur to waive the loan and interest and return the freehold to Edmund. If Edmund needed the funds he could sell and lease the cottage back to me, either way I had my own space in which to live.

Despite the considerations we gave to normalising lives to come, a dark cloud continued to hang over us, its foreboding presence a stark reminder of unfinished business that took precedence over everything else. Three people were murdered, I was left to die, and Eleanor was helped on her way. The perpetrators of these crimes had to be brought to justice and until they were, things would never return to normal.

***

The weather is set to turn wet today, so I'm wearing Eleanor's waterproof jacket and Dubarry boots. Edmund didn't want me to go and when I insisted, demanded he accompany me.

"How do I know you won't go missing again?" he pleaded but we both knew he wasn't fit enough to do the walk. I assured him I would be fine and back for dinner. It's just something I must do.

The path is virtually deserted, the few people I encounter, strangers to me, but I pull up the hood and keep my head down, passing by with barely a murmur. I reach the ruins by midday and with some trepidation, slide between the iron railings and the wall that mark the entrance to the tomb. The first few yards are illuminated by the sunlight seeping in from outside, but soon, I'm plunged into darkness and switch on the torch Edmund gave me. The steps are damp and slippery and my boots echo around the cave as I descend into the void, swinging the torch left and right. It's a long way down and I count over a hundred steps before I reach the bottom and the familiar cobbled path that snakes downwards out of sight.

The first of my rodent friends make an appearance, snuffling in the dark, sensitive to the sound, oblivious to the light. The torch is my protector and I have spare batteries, just in case, but I try not to imagine it failing; I can't go through that terror again. I reach a fork, another tunnel disappearing off to the right. If I had gone that way instead, would I ever have got out alive? But then, I was gone a month. How can that be possible?

Rivulets of water that leave slimy streaks on the walls, sparkle in the torchlight. Rats scurry under my feet, but they're no threat to my heavy leather boots. Left, right and left again, the tunnel snakes, ever descending and I begin to wonder whether I've missed a turn and should go back. I've lost track of time and distance but convinced I'm moving faster than when I escaped, increasing the anxiety and fear I may be lost. But eventually, a familiar sight greets me. A battered, panelled door with flaking paint and a hole near its base. To the right of it, the tunnel continues down and out of sight. I push tentatively at the door and creaky hinges reawakened, complain.

Plip, plop. I shudder at the sound. The trough is there, filled to a level where an overflow outlet takes the excess away. A rat floats face down, its body bloated to double its size, the surface of the water around it, oily and contaminated. Glass crunches underfoot. I pick up a picture, dislodged from its frame; man standing, woman sitting, two children at their feet, dispassionate, unsmiling, composed for the camera. Jacob and Edith. She looks vaguely like me. I roll it up and stuff it inside my jacket. Rusty bedframe, filthy mattress spilling horsehair entrails, hessian rope the colour of straw, fresh and new. Upturned chairs, wooden barrel table, tankards, tin plates, opaque glass bottles, some still intact.

It's an office, or a room for miners to rest and refresh before the next shift and no one has been here for a hundred and seventy years. The mine closed in the 1850s before Jacob was born, but the family photo of the Hawleys must be around 1890, just before their calamitous confrontation with Julian. There's no explanation I can see. I return to the empty picture frame and the broken glass. It's dusty but modern.

An arched brick fireplace is set into the wall, the hearth three feet off the ground, fireback blackened by decades of soot. I lean across and point the torch up the chimney, but the light dissipates in the blackness, and it must be capped as there's no visible daylight. In the corner, there's a circular hole in the ceiling, two metres in circumference. The torch reveals another brick-lined tube like a chimney, a ladder fixed to one side, bottom rung just visible. An escape route, or a convenient way to lower supplies.

The ladder is out of reach, the first rung a metre above the ceiling. I lay the torch down and position the barrel-table beneath the hole, stack the only serviceable chair on top and drag the bed across. Three attempts to climb the makeshift platform and I'm balancing precariously on the wobbling chair, hand on the bottom rung. I stuff the torch in a pocket, beam pointing upwards. It severely restricts the light but allows me to place both hands on the rung. I take a breath and hoist myself up, one hand reaching for the second rung. The chair topples off the barrel and clatters onto the floor leaving me swinging, legs dangling in space, but I manage to get another hand on and pull myself up hand over hand until my foot can rest on the bottom rung.

I stand there panting with the exertion then begin a steady climb into the darkness. I stop to retrieve the torch, but fumble and it drops out of sight. I hear it hit the floor with a crash, extinguished in a second. Plip, plop. Total black. I've lost a lifeline. Make a decision, go up or go back. I can't make that journey again even though I know the way. If I go up, I can still go back, but if I go back…

The ladder is solid, but iron, rusty and coarse, tearing at my hands. Up and up, one rung at a time, stop for breath, look up into nothing. I'm progressing vertically so it should be shorter, but the entrance was at the base of a cliff, so I may not even be at ground level yet and there's still a hill above me. The shaft has to be vertical or would be useless as a drop for supplies, so eventually there will be a chink of light. Nothing. Up and up, thighs burning, legs wobble under the strain, hands are cold, losing their grip. If I fall now, I'll die. Go back? No. Up and up the endless ladder, each step harder than the last, each rung draining my strength until I reach the point where I don't have enough to get back. I've climbed five hundred, how many more?

An object strikes a blow to the head and one foot slips, then the other and I hang in space on torn hands, the pain searing through arms and shoulders. Feet find support and I cling on, gasping. An age passes and I raise my head slowly, feeling for something solid. Wrap an arm around the ladder and reach with a free hand. It's wood, a base or more likely a cover. It won't budge by hand, so I climb until I'm bent over, the cover on my shoulders. I push with both legs and feel it move an inch and fall back again. I push again and scream with exertion and I'm rewarded by a flash of light. Light! Breathe deeply and push. Another flash, but now it stays there, a sliver of light that stings my eyes. Push! It gives and sunlight floods into the shaft, illuminating the rust on the ladder and the blood on my hands. But I'm not out yet.

Two rungs more and I can squeeze my body through the gap, squinting in the light. The cover is wood, fashioned from straight planks, the surface a mixture of turf, moss and dead vegetation, and mostly rotten. A large piece breaks off with little resistance and tumbles down the shaft, hitting the floor fifteen seconds later with a distant echo. I'm at the top of the ladder but still a metre from ground level. I reach up and around for something to grab hold of, aware its only one metre up but at least two hundred down. I can't afford to make any mistake.

Fingers land on a thin wooden post, to the left and out of sight. I tug and it feels damp with some lateral movement, but it's all there is. I transfer weight gradually from ladder to post and it holds. *Don't look down.* I stretch, feet on the ladder, hands on the post, body at forty-five degrees, a leap of faith is all that's required. I close eyes and step off, swinging a leg up and over the edge, rolling onto my back.

It's raining steadily and the grass is sodden, but it's joyous to be out in the fresh air and I now remember why I came. I get to my feet, careful not to stumble and fall back into the shaft. A barbed wire fence guards the hole, the grass covered hatch there to prevent the exceptionally curious or just plain stupid from going further, unaware that anything heavier than a rabbit would fall straight through to their death. I quickly find what I'm looking for; a section of fence recently repaired and, on the ground, a deep groove cut into the grass that extends over the edge of the shaft.

I follow the groove. It gets shallower as it crosses the field and I find hoof prints. Horses have been here, the prints extending in a direct line to the hedgerow at the other side. They carried me here, comatose, wrapped in a horse blanket or shroud, tied one end of a rope around my feet or under my arms, the other end to a horse, and lowered me down the shaft. One of them waited below, tied me to the bed and climbed the ladder or was pulled out by horse and rope. A lot of trouble to hide a body that's still breathing and allow death to take its natural course. But then disposal was the prime objective, not death; disposal in a space that's impermeable or from which toxic energy cannot escape. Shielded by fifty metres of lead. *I know who you are.*

John and Sara Lee have horses, motive, and ambition, but lack the psychopathic tendencies that predicate violent murder. She would much prefer to enact her sexual desires with a willing participant, but once the truth was laid bare and I became the enemy, disposal was the only option. Murder would be futile, counselled John, devotee of reincarnation, believer in the holy spirit. He's as deluded as his peers, but I already proved him right. I was gone a month. *I know who you are.*

CHAPTER 34

My phone's still useless, and my laptop, somewhere in a landfill site with the rest of my belongings so I'm forced to use Edmund's antique contraption and find the number some other way. Surprisingly, it works well, and I derive a childlike pleasure from the tactile sensation, spinning the buzzy wheel with one finger. I thought long and hard, and when I eventually connect, I want to explain fully, but it would take too long and it's far too complicated. The telephone is unsuitable for relating more than the bare bones, but a meeting would reveal more, I suggest. There's no question, the offer was made sincerely and whatever I want, I can have, that's the deal. There'll be no charge, the opportunity for an emotional reunion will be payment enough. Tomorrow would be excellent, when more details can be discussed, with a follow up on Saturday for the main event.

"Don't you think it would be better if we simply called the police?" says Edmund, tucking into the gourmet Irish stew he bought in from the deli.

"We've been through this. I don't trust them not to mess things up. They'll stomp their boots all over it and achieve nothing. They won't do anything without hard evidence, and they won't get that by plodding and poking around the way they do."

"But you do have evidence."

"I have testimony but that's not worth much. Mere allegations of impropriety and dodgy dealing won't galvanise them into action. There's no obvious link between the theft of your wealth and the murders of three people, but I know it's there. All we have to do is to get them to admit it."

"And then what?"

"Then we bring in Stride and his flunkeys."

"Why don't we invite them as well?"

"The murderers are hardly going to confess while plod is standing around."

"How do you know who are the murderers?"
"I don't."

***

It's a full-time job, wading through old records, researching four hundred years of history and scribbling notes with paper and pencil. I admit, I do it to avoid the household chores. When I'm bored hoovering, washing up, ordering in supplies and cooking, I take myself off into the study and pick a dusty tome off the shelf, panning for gold amongst the turgid text. It's only temporary. As soon as we can resolve matters, Edmund can hire a new housekeeper and I will emerge from my place of hiding to continue working on my magnum opus.

We've rehearsed it a hundred times, my playing devil's advocate, taking each of the protagonists' roles in turn, ensuring he has a response to every denial, coaching him in trickery.

"I thought you were a bridge player?"

"Gave that up years ago. Never very good at it, always happy to let the other side win. Drove Eleanor mad!"

"You have to win this one Edmund. If not for you, then for Eleanor. This is not what she intended."

"No, you're right about that. I'll do my best."

***

We're all set up. Edmund checks his watch again.

"Are you nervous?"

"Not really, but it's a long time since I entertained so many guests. Just like old times." He smiles ruefully. "Except this lot aren't friends."

"There's nothing they can do to you now Edmund. They've taken everything. Time to give it back."

"Nothing will bring Eleanor back."

The doorbell rings and we exchange looks. He kisses the back of my hand and I throw my arms around his neck.

"I'm right here remember?"

He goes to let them in and I run upstairs to the spare bedroom immediately above the study. He's sitting in front of a bank of monitors, headphones on.

"Clear as a bell," he says. "Are you and the old boy…?"

"No. He's eighty-five. He could be my grandad for goodness' sake!"

Psycho Si shrugs. "Just wondered."

"Doesn't mean I don't love him," I say without thinking. The grandson of Julian Fitzgerald, about to lay the past to rest once and for all. Simon hands me some headphones and I scan the monitors. Six cameras, six angles, three microphones. All bases covered. The drumbeat has started. Act one is about to begin.

"Thank you for coming," says Edmund.

"Not at all," says John Lee. "We're always available to our parishioners, aren't we Sara?"

"Always," says Sara unconvincingly.

John Lee is in trademark denim and dog collar, the colourful tie restraining his long hair and revealing his shiny gold ear studs.

"But I am surprised. I rather got the impression you never wanted to see me again."

"Did you?" says Edmund.

"The night Lady Eleanor sadly passed, you said something like 'er, 'I never want to see you again'". Gigolo John can't resist the clever quip, but it shows he's wary. He's not as familiar with the amnesiac Edmund as I am.

"Well then, I owe you an apology. Forgive me if I was rude but I may just have been overwrought."

"That's understandable. But you also denied me the honour of conducting her funeral."

"Really? Dear dear. You must forgive me again. I confess my memory is not what it was. But I'm being rude. Let me offer you a drink. Champagne alright?"

John and Sara exchange looks but she's the first to respond.

"Thank you, your Lordship."

"Oh, please dispense with that formal nonsense, my dear." I'm proud of him; he's resisted the temptation to address Sara Lee as a drug addled lesbian. "Edmund is fine." Like a magician, he's opened the Veuve in quick time and hands them his precious Bohemian crystal.

"Why did you ask us here Edmund?" says John, still not ready to relax.

"Please sit. I have something to tell you." They perch on the edge of the leather sofa while Edmund takes a strategically positioned chair by the desk. "You will be aware that a young lady has been helping me with my financial affairs, that is, until she suddenly disappeared. Packed up and left without as much as a word."

"This is Kate?" says John feigning uncertainty.

"Yes indeed. Kate. She wasn't the first you know. I had another young woman before that doing something similar. Now what was her name…?"

"Jackie," says Sara.

"Well remembered my dear. Funny that. Both of them living in my cottage, both disappearing, must have been something I said." Edmund chuckles but his guests remain impassive. "It's a shame because both offered similar advice but then left me in the lurch, so to speak. They each pointed out that neither Eleanor nor I had made a will and that this was a grave omission."

"How so?" says John. "If I understand your position correctly, you have no heir and no surviving family. There would only be merit in making a will if you had a firm desire to leave everything to charity, or some third party."

"My view entirely, John. May I call you John? The truth is, I really don't care enough to go to the trouble. All Eleanor's assets come to me automatically, as would mine to her had I done the decent thing and died first. I'm sure Eleanor would have made arrangements for her own family to inherit, but fate got in the way, everything's left to me and frankly, I don't give a damn."

"I fail to see your dilemma Edmund," says Sara. "No one is going to force you to bequeath your millions to anyone else. If I were you, I would just enjoy them and live life to the full!" She raises her glass and empties it. Edmund refills it and resumes his seat. I note he has hardly touched his own drink.

"Then I had a bright idea. I'll offer it to Kate!"

"Kate?" says John. "Why would you do that? I mean, it's very generous but, she's not family. Is she?" He's rattled.

"No, not at all. But there is no one else, and I rather liked her."

"How do you know?"

"Know I liked her?"

"No! How do you know there's no one else?" says John with evident frustration. I want to laugh out loud. Edmund is playing the silly old duffer to a tee, or just being himself, I really can't tell, but it's winding up Gigolo John.

"Well, I didn't. Until she enlightened me." Edmund takes a small sip of champagne and washes it around his mouth. The pause is enough to make them both shift in their seats uncomfortably.

"In what way?" says John, clearly afraid Edmund has lost the thread.

"Patience, my boy." I want to clap. We agreed he should refer to John as 'my boy' at some point and he's remembered. "She's a writer you know. Writes all sorts of things. Articles, press releases, novels. She wrote in *Dales Diary* once, but that was before your time. I asked her to write a history of the Fitzgerald family, from Cromwell right up to the present day, to the Last Lord of Oakdale. It was a project that would take a few years to complete but she was up for the challenge. I was going to pay her very well."

"Then why did she run off?' says Sara, who's getting bored, probably wondering how she's going to cope when the bottle is empty.

"You tell me."

"How should I know?" she says with a little more aggression than necessary. John places a hand on her arm.

"It's just a figure of speech, my dear. It means I have no idea. I doubt very much you would have any idea either. May I offer you a refill?"

"We're fine thanks," says John on their behalf. Sara glowers at him and holds out her glass.

"Thank you, Edmund."

"As I was saying. Kate was doing some research into my family history and found out something extraordinary." He stops to take a sip and John lets out a sigh. "It turns out I do indeed have an heir. A son and heir no less! And I never knew," he says, shaking his head.

John has gone white. I can't tell if he's excited to be on the cusp of wealth, fame and glory or about to be told some hideous fact about a rival to the Fitzgerald fortune. He clears his throat and puts on his best sanctimonious vicar's voice. "And, may I ask, who is the mother of this boy?"

"A lady by the name of Jennifer." John Lee visibly relaxes, but it's brief; one danger has passed but others may lie ahead. "It was a long time ago. An unfortunate indiscretion on my part, an error of judgement one might say. I'm not proud of it, but Eleanor and I, well, we had an eventful life together, you might say, a flexible marriage which suited us both. She forgave me and the lady concerned moved away. I had no idea she was carrying my child."

"A flexible marriage?" says Sara, her interest piqued by any suggestion of sexual impropriety.

"Yes, you know the type."

"Do I?"

"I'm sure in your line of work you encounter all kinds of unusual personal relationships."

Gigolo John looks increasingly nervous. He tries to steer the conversation back to the subject at hand.

"Did you have feelings for Jennifer?"

"Oh yes. I seem to recall she was a beautiful woman, but it was such a long time ago, I can barely remember; another who lived in Farrier's Cottage and then disappeared. Extraordinary coincidence don't you think? You know, ol

George Hawley always put it about the place was haunted. He may well have been right," says Edmund chuckling.

"Cursed, more like," says John.

"Possibly, but as you know, I'm not one for supernatural or spiritual mumbo-jumbo, whatever form it takes."

"No. You made that very clear."

"When you were trying to inveigle your way into our lives?"

"Let's cut the crap Edmund," says John. He's had enough skirting around the issue and decided it's time to confront it head on. "You know I'm your son, and you know I'll inherit everything just as you did. I'm the heir apparent to the title of Lord Fitzgerald of Oakdale. All this should be mine when you're gone," he says, waving his arms in the air. "You either will it to me or I'll contest and the courts will side with me. Anyway, you've already said you have no interest in wealth, why should it matter to you?"

"It matters, my boy, for two reasons. The first is this, and it's one of the reasons I wanted young Kate to look back into the history of the Fitzgeralds. My grandfather Julian was a scoundrel. He flaunted his wealth and position, something he had done nothing to earn, and used it in pursuit of his carnal desires. He oppressed and impoverished many of his tenants, exploited women to satisfy his lust, reneged on his debts, disgraced his family and after his ill-fated death at the hands of a prostitute, left little more than an accursed cottage in the High Street and this decrepit roof over the heads of his wife and children.

"One of those was my father Charles whose name, I'm sure you are aware, tops the roll call of the fallen on the Oakdale war memorial. He grew up living with the shame of his father Julian and worked hard to preserve what little the family had left. He inherited this monstrous pile and all its problems and had to cope with the legacy of his father's debauchery in the form of a long running feud with the Hawley family. He forged a career of his own in the city and when war came, joined up and rose through the ranks, sacrificing his life for

King and country. He eschewed wealth, despised the notion of hereditary privilege and devoted his life to the welfare of his family and others."

"If he felt that strongly about it then why didn't he relinquish the title?"

"Good question. I believe if he had survived the war, he would have done just that. I was nought but a boy and he had already instilled in me a similar respect for privilege and the humility to go with it but stopped short of depriving me of something I myself might choose to live up to. The Lord Protector bestowed a peerage on Gerald Fitzgerald in 1652; it's not something to be discarded lightly."

"So, what's your point Edmund?" Sara, increasingly bored by Edmund's lecture, wants to push it along too. Worse, her glass is empty. "Other than to tell us your grandad was a shit, and your dad was a hero. So what?"

"May I offer you another refill?" he says, smiling sweetly. She holds out her glass and he empties the bottle into it. "The point is, my dear, that once it became clear Eleanor and I would not produce an heir, I had no reason or incentive to consider what would happen to the title. It would expire on the same day as I. But now, things appear to be different."

"Edmund…dad," says John in such a patronising tone I want to cringe. He's spotted an opening and wants to widen it. "I hope you understand, we totally respect you and what you and your father stood for. The Fitzgeralds are legendary in this village, and it would be much the worse off without them. It would be a huge honour to continue the line and pass it on to my son and he to his son. The title itself is academic, a fact of history, but one worth preserving in my view."

"You are of course, entitled to your opinion. For my own part I'm now faced with the dilemma of what to do. I don't think I can reasonably separate the title from the estate, they go hand in hand and as you know, I, like my father have no interest in wealth for its own sake."

"So you won't relinquish the title before you die?"

"No, and like my father before me, I acknowledge an obligation to preserve the lineage and the estate, which is inseparable, while there exists an heir apparent."

John and Sara Lee look at each other, barely able to contain their excitement, but it doesn't last because John has thought of something.

"So, where's the dilemma?"

"The dilemma, my boy, is whether my heir is a fit and proper person to inherit. I owe it to my father to ensure the Fitzgeralds do not inadvertently suffer a repeat of the disreputable and scandalous behaviour of my grandfather Julian which so tarnished the family's reputation."

"I'm a man of God," says John pompously. "Surely you don't think I would stoop to the levels of debauchery like those you've described. It's completely at odds with everything I teach; everything I believe in."

"Do as I say, not as I do?" Edmund is enjoying himself immensely. Simon Hawley is hooked. He casts me a glance and mouths "WTF?" but I press a finger to my lips and return my attention to the screens. The time reads seven-thirty. I hope Edmund is keeping track; he only has fifteen minutes.

"I don't follow."

"None of us is perfect John, not even vicars. I'm sure you would agree with that? What does your book of mumbo-jumbo say? He that is without sin among you…"

"…let him cast the first stone," mumbles Gigolo John.

"And in the interests of gender equality," continues Edmund, "I'm certain the same applies to vicars' wives, assuming of course, the vicar has a wife in the first placc." Sara scowls at Edmund. "So, if I am to agree your inheritance, you will first have to confess your sins. Only then can I reach the appropriate judgment."

John looks bewildered and nervous. He no choice but to cooperate.

"I admit that, before I became a man of the cloth, my first wife and I…"

"Stop!" says Edmund holding up a hand. "We could be here all night at this rate. Let's just assume God forgave you for being a vulgar, hedonistic swine before he allowed you to be one of his vicars and he's wiped the slate clean."

"Ok, well…"

"While you're giving that a bit of thought, let me ask your lady wife something?" Sara's suddenly alert. Her husband is floundering, but her resolve is fortified by drink and she's ready for a fight. "Soon after you arrived here, you seduced a young lady called Melanie Gibbs and between you, fabricated a story about Reverend Fenton molesting her, so he would get the chop and your boyfriend here could take up the position."

Sara Lee breaks into a smile. "I would have thought you'd be grateful given Fenton was shagging your wife at the time."

"Jesus, Sara," says John, beginning to panic.

"Oh, I knew all about that. As I said, we had a flexible marriage. I don't know what she saw in a man in a cassock, but it's just personal taste, I suppose, and unlike me, she was a devout Christian, so it gave the affair added spice."

"What was the question?" asks Sara, unperturbed.

"Do you think that's acceptable behaviour for a prospective Lady Fitzgerald?"

"No worse than Eleanor!"

"Yes, but she didn't marry her brother, did she?"

Simon's jaw has dropped open. Instinctively he turns up the volume in case he misses anything. Sara has been knocked off her stride, her smug arrogance dissolving instantly.

"Who told you that?"

"Why, she did."

"I don't believe you." Despite the drink, Sara is alert and suspicious. "She couldn't know that. Anyway, it's a damn lie." But she's challenged the premise before denying the fact.

"She was only repeating what you told her."

"I never…!"

"A bottle of gin and a line of coke tends to loosen the tongue somewhat, especially during the postcoital, three-in-a-bed phase." The Lees are stunned into silence. "Don't worry about it my dear. I'm partial to a drop of the happy juice myself, so I know how garrulous one can become."

"Edmund," says John, desperate to salvage something from the wreckage. "We didn't know. We only found out later and when we did…"

"Spare me the bullshit, my boy. I really don't care whether your incestuous union was based on desire or practicality. You will have to answer to your God for that, if not the bishop."

"You wouldn't tell the bishop? It was just an innocent mistake. We have separate rooms!" Simon lets out an involuntary snort of mirth and I wish I found it so amusing. John's plea may be risible and pathetic but I can't forget what they did to me.

"Of course not! My point is, you both exploited my late wife for personal gain, taking advantage of her libidinous tendencies to find out the extent of our wealth, hoping she'd use her influence to mollify her irascible husband and smooth the way to your inheritance."

"She wanted it," says Sara, unruffled, dismissing it scornfully.

"Thank you for your honesty my dear. That's all I'm asking; for you to confess your sins and then we can all move on."

"Good. I'm all for that. Now we've cleared the air, what about another drink?" says Sara, eying the bottles laid out on the desk.

"My pleasure," says Edmund. He mixes a gin and tonic and hands her the tall glass without asking. "I'm all out of champagne I'm afraid."

"Sara," hisses John.

"Shut up, bro'. I like this man." She's grinning inanely and beginning to slur her words.

"But you much prefer girls," says Edmund. "While Gigolo John here carried on entertaining his stepmother, you were turning your attentions to Jackie Thomas. You pretended to comfort the poor girl, whilst, at the same time, making her life a misery."

"Bollocks. She wanted a shoulder to cry on and got one."

"You broke into her house, vandalised it, caused her intense trauma and blamed it all on George Hawley."

"This is pure invention," says John, trying in vain to take back control, but Edmund is in full flight.

"Jackie encouraged both of us to make a will and we would have done had she not disappeared, terrorised by the very people claiming to help and protect her. I admit Eleanor and I played an unwitting role. Jackie uncovered some painful truths, and we gave her short shrift, but you had a vested interest. You needed Eleanor to die first so her funds would come to me, only then could you be sure of inheriting them. Are you willing to confess your part in her downfall?"

"Whatever, Edmund," says Sara. "She was a sweet girl, good at her job, but ill-equipped to deal with complex personal issues. And why shouldn't George take the rap? Silly old bastard."

"Sara!" I feel for John, unable to control his sister with or without a drink.

"And you fed Eleanor drugs, knowing she'd already had a stroke, knowing they could be fatal."

"Life's fatal, Edmund," drawls Sara. "She loved life and she loved being spaced out." I glance at the screen; ten minutes. I hope they're not early.

"Good! We're getting to the bottom of it now. Don't misunderstand me. I'm an old man who doesn't have long to live. I need to go with a clear conscience and I'm sure you feel better getting everything out in the open. There's just one more thing I need to know." Edmund waits for them to respond but John's body is rigid and Sara's, beginning to sag.

"What did you do to Kate?"

"What do you mean?" says John, a rabbit in headlights.

"Just tell me and we can all go home friends."

"There's nothing to tell."

"I offered to leave Kate everything and she declined. She insisted you were the rightful heir, not she. I was offended, we had an argument, and I haven't seen her since."

"Maybe she went back to London?"

"You went to visit her the night she disappeared," he says, looking at Sara.

"No I didn't."

"You arrived at around nine pm with a bottle in your hand."

"Rubbish."

"Don't lie. Kate took security measures after you broke in and vandalised her mirror. I say broke in, but you had a key, given to you by Jackie Thomas. She changed the locks and had a small camera installed over her front door." We're on dangerous ground here. It's a bluff. There was no camera, but Sara doesn't know that. We have to hope the fact that she knows it's true is enough. Astonishingly, Sara's face creases up and I think for moment she's going to laugh.

"It was an accident." She's blubbing, and it looks genuine. "We needed her help. We couldn't get close to you without her, but she refused," she says between sobs. "She got angry and over-excited, and I gave her something to calm her down."

"You drugged her?" asks Edmund.

"It was harmless, but she'd had too much to drink and went into anaphylactic shock."

I'm staring at the screen, shaking my head, marvelling at the performance. I glance at Simon, who's engrossed but confused.

"I couldn't wake her and didn't know what to do, so I called John and we took her out the back door so we wouldn't be seen."

Edmund is fixing her with a steely stare, taking in the lie, controlling his urge to challenge her, instead, handing her a clean shovel.

"Was she dead?"

"Yes," she whispers, through floods of tears.

Simon pinches the back of my hand to check I'm still flesh and blood, and I just shrug.

"What did you do with the body?"

"We gave her a decent burial," says John imperiously. He's been quiet and subdued but seems to have recovered his composure. "She was a troubled soul; believe me, I could tell. I tried time and again to warn her, to stay away from you, that she was in danger, just like Jackie, but she was driven, like a woman possessed."

I didn't plan for this, and I hope Edmund holds back. I can see he looks disconcerted.

"In danger from whom?" he says, and I suck in breath. He's being forced to go off script.

"You, Lord Fitzgerald."

"Me? Why would she fear me?" he barks. "It's you she should have been afraid of and with good reason," he says, stabbing a finger in their direction. I will him to calm himself, he has a long way to go. *The truth will out Edmund.*

"We did all we could to protect her, but to no avail. We then acted on impulse. We know we should have called someone, but it was too late. It's not the first time someone disappeared from that cottage. It's not such a bizarre occurrence, and she has no family as far as we are aware. It's sad, but it was all done for the best."

"Where is she?"

"We took her to the abandoned lead mine in Willow Dale. Thought it was appropriate and she would feel at home there. We left a family photo. She would have liked that, and the lead all around her will keep her soul at peace."

The family photo?

"I see," says Edmund. "Poor girl. It seems the Fitzgerald saga goes on and is likely to go on for generations to come."

"Does that mean…?"

"It means, dear boy, that I'm tired. I can't condone what you've done, we all have our faults, we all have regrets and soon, I shall be released from the burden placed upon my shoulders. It's not in my gift to determine the future of Oakdale's notorious dynasty, that's up to you."

"Thanks, dad," says John. "May we say a prayer?"

"Certainly not!" says Edmund. "Keep it for when I'm gone." John exhales deeply and looks at Sara who's beaming. The doorbell rings. Startling them both. The timing is perfect.

"That's military precision for you," I whisper to Simon. "Let Act two commence."

***

Simon and I watch Edmund go out of shot. John and Sara jump to their feet and hug each other, then indulge themselves in a passionate kiss, his hands squeezing her buttocks, one of hers rubbing against the front of his jeans. I squirm at the thought of the last night I spent in the cottage, unconscious, at the mercy of these animals.

"He's coming back," whispers John and they disengage. We hear muffled voices and then the mic picks up the conversation.

"So good of you to come," says Edmund, as three men come into shot. "I'm sure you all know each other."

"Evening Arthur," says John, shaking hands. "Tommy, Barry."

"Hello John, Sara," says Arthur. "This is a surprise. I didn't know you'd be here?"

"Gentlemen, I have a short announcement to make and a minor piece of admin to complete. Please take a seat." Arthur makes himself comfortable on a wing chair, Tommy Gibbs and Barry Wilson standing to attention behind. The Lees resume their places on the couch.

"Arthur and I go back a long way, don't we Arthur? I want you to be the first to know. John here is my son. He and his good wife will be the next Lord and Lady Fitzgerald of Oakdale."

"Well goodness me," says Arthur, guarded as ever. "Another surprise. Congratulations. How long have you been keeping this under your hat?"

"John and Sara have known for a while but were far too modest to make a big show of it. I learned only recently. It was young Kate who did the research and delivered the bombshell."

"Do you know what happened to her?" asks Arthur, unmoved by Edmund's familial revelation. "She was utterly charming. I do miss our little chats."

"Disappointing she should run off like that, just like the last girl." John and Sara remain impassive. I can almost hear their heartbeats. "You didn't kill her too did you Barry?" Edmund laughs out loud. John and Sara come slowly back to life and jerk their heads in Wilson's direction. Barry Wilson scowls and shifts his weight. No one but Edmund finds it amusing.

"Is that a joke Edmund?" says Arthur wearily.

"No," says Edmund, suddenly serious. "Just asking whether your henchman murdered Kate like he murdered Jackie Thomas."

"You're such an old fool. You've now completely lost the plot."

"Oh, there's life in the old dog yet, Arthur, I assure you. I should get your truck fixed Barry if I were you. It won't be long before the police match the blue paint to Jackie's car."

"What's the point of this Edmund?"

"I'm sorry. I've digressed. Apart from introducing my son and heir, and unmasking your murderous acquaintance, I wish to request repayment of the loan on Farrier's Cottage."

"As soon as I get sight of probate."

Edmund plucks a document from the desktop and hands it over. Arthur scans it and slides it into his jacket pocket.

"I'll attend to it tomorrow."

"I don't understand," says John. "I thought you sold the cottage to some outfit in Jersey?"

"I did. Arthur's outfit as it happens, although I didn't know it at the time"

"You kept that quiet, you rascal," says Sara. Arthur ignores them.

"I need the cash to see out my last few days. You can keep the rest."

John looks perplexed. "Don't tell me you're short of a few quid?"

"I'll come back to that." Edmund resumes his seat and makes himself comfortable. "You must think me extremely rude in not offering you a drink, but this won't take long and anyway, Lady Fitzgerald here has quaffed most of it already." Sara Lee's jaw drops open, but Edmund carries on before she can protest.

"We were talking about the untimely death of a young woman. In light of Eleanor's illness, I asked Jackie, who was a trained lawyer, to look into our affairs. She discovered something quite disturbing. She found out about your dirty, unprofessional dealings, didn't she Arthur? She threatened to blow the whistle on your little scam. Seduce Lady Fitzgerald into investing her riches in some offshore trust in case her befuddled old stick of a husband gets his shaky hands on them, then forge his power of attorney to make him hand over his house. It would all go to waste otherwise, wouldn't it? The old duffer can't be bothered to manage his own affairs, so may as well do it for him. He'll be dead soon anyway."

"Eleanor granted me power of attorney as was her prerogative."

"No doubt drugged up to the eyeballs at the time," says Edmund, staring at Sara, who looks away.

"As did you, but there were no drugs involved, you were just stupid."

"You see John, this is what you as a Fitzgerald will have to put up with. Every Tom, Dick and Harry wants a piece of your inheritance. Everyone thinks they deserve it more than you do and some of them are probably right. Talk about the damn cottage being a curse, just wait till you take the ermine!"

"Calm down Edmund," says Arthur. "You were perfectly content to sell this festering pile of rubble and invest the proceeds in a trust controlled by your wife. You were bound to die first and she didn't want to live here after you were gone but until you were, wouldn't risk having you evicted; hence the right to live here in perpetuity."

"What's going on?" says John. Five minutes ago, he was set up for life but now the foundations of his future are crumbling.

"This man," says Edmund looking at John while pointing at Arthur, "used to be a friend of mine, but he turned out to be a major disappointment. No doubt Eleanor boasted to you about her millions stashed in Jersey?" John nods dumbly. "He's got them. He conned her into handing them over, then conned me into selling Oakdale Manor and kept the proceeds. When Jackie Thomas discovered what he had done and ran off, hounded out of town because you two wanted all this for yourselves, he thought she was about to tell all, and had her killed."

"What are you saying? You don't have Eleanor's millions and you don't own this house?"

"Nor any of its treasures. English Trust."

"Jesus!" says John.

Edmund shakes his head in dismay. "You're certainly old-school Fitzgerald, my boy. More concerned about gold thar the demise of an innocent girl."

"You thieving bastard!" shrieks Sara at Arthur, the alcoho having suddenly worn off.

"He doesn't want any of it," says Arthur.

"True," says Edmund. "But I'll be damned if I let you ge away with murder. Jeremy Jones had a change of heart, didn' he? That was the sale of the century for him until he found ou who he was dealing with."

"The estate agent?" says John, white as a sheet.

"He warned them Jackie was asking questions and the nex thing she's dead, run into a ditch by Barry in his pickup. Jone panics and decides to go to the police, so Tommy here knife him in his car. Mission accomplished." Tommy Gibbs looks sideways at his mate Barry and smirks. "Arthur promises Tommy his daughter and her fiancé can have the cottage when they're married, payment for services rendered, but Jones has already signed up a new tenant. This is very inconvenient, but worse than that, she's not only asking questions about her predecessor, she seems to be pally with that silly old sod in the Manor who has retained her to carry on where Jackie left off. You all tried to chase her out of there, but she stubbornly refused to succumb to threats and when she dug deeper and blew the lid off your respective conspiracies, her time was up. Arthur would have sent one of his two hoods to deal with it if you two junkies hadn't got there first."

"Where is she?" says Arthur.

"These two deluded nincompoops; Gigolo John and this drug addled lesbian masquerading as his wife, fed her alcohol and drugs and buried her down a lead mine!"

"Bravo," says Arthur. "There's a weight off my mind. I had feelers out everywhere looking for her."

"Should have looked closer to home." All heads turn towards me. I've been standing in the doorway for a full minute, listening, all of them oblivious to my presence. John and Sara leap to their feet in shock, then John drops to his knees, clasping his hands together and closing his eyes.

"Our Father, who art in heaven… deliver us from evil…" he mumbles, sweat forming on his brow.

"Yes, yes, yes," says Edmund impatiently, "that's quite enough of that claptrap. Kate, my dear, do come in. I believe you know everyone here." I summon up the courage to walk straight past them and stand beside Edmund. Luckily, they're all too shocked to react.

"It's not possible," says Sara. "How did you…?"

"Ask your brother, he knows how." I look at Tommy Gibbs. His fists are clenched and he's red in the face. "How are Tiff and Steve getting along in my house?"

"Bitch! They moved out again, place is fucking possessed and now I know why. It was you!" he says pointing his finger directly at me.

"Well this has all been very illuminating," says Arthur, "but I must take my leave. Men," he says, addressing Gibbs and Wilson, "the enemy is at the gate. Make sure you don't leave a mess. And as for you two," he says, looking at the Lees, "best we all forget about this and have a chat later. I'm sure we have plenty to discuss."

Gibbs pulls a hunting knife from inside his jacket and Wilson, a thin metal wire which he wraps around his fingers.

"Stand down, boys." Simon Hawley is standing in the doorway holding a weapon in each hand. "The CO is relieved of command." Gibbs and Wilson lunge at him and he fires both tasers simultaneously, their bodies twisting and buckling before they hit the floor, writhing in agony. John leaps on Arthur, pushing him to the floor, hands around his neck as Sara kicks him in the ribs, screaming obscenities.

Edmund holds me closely, watching the mayhem as flashing blue lights permeate the study, throwing revolving patterns on the ceiling.

CHAPTER 35

My heels echo in the seemingly endless corridor that runs the entire length of the building. The place is strangely quiet, even late at night. I thought hospitals were frenetic places twenty-four-seven, but on this occasion, in this department, apparently not.

I find the ward I'm looking for and a lone nurse at the counter, huddled over a paper-strewn desk, bathed in the light of an old angle-poise lamp.

"May I see Lord Fitzgerald?" I ask, as she looks up.

"Are you a member of the family?" I'm reminded of John Lee in the graveyard at Oakdale the first day I ventured out into the sunshine, and I'm tempted to say yes, but Edmund would not approve of such disingenuousness.

"He doesn't have any family. I'm his personal assistant Kate Duvall."

"He's in room five," she points to a succession of closed doors. "Don't be long."

The police arrested the Lees together with Arthur Needham and his two incapacitated associates, Stride asking Simon to send him the full recording of the proceedings and asking us to be available to give further evidence the next day. I had alerted them the moment the Lees had arrived at the Manor and, by prior arrangement they were able to watch a live stream of events before arriving with armed backup. It was after they had all left and the three of us were halfway through the last surviving bottle of Veuve '82 that Edmund felt nauseous and complained of chest pains, the whole exercise having clearly taken its toll.

I open the door gently to avoid waking him and pull up a chair alongside his bed. The room is sparsely equipped and I'm pleased to see he's no longer wired up to drips, monitors and beeping devices. He senses I'm there and opens his eyes.

"Ah, it's my favourite daughter," he says, drowsy but conscious.

"You sound like my dad."

"Perhaps I can be an honorary dad," he says taking my hand and giving it a squeeze. "How's the cottage?"

"Lovely. It's good to be home."

"No more bumps in the night?"

"A few, but they don't bother me. Rather like old friends."

"And how are you getting on with my book?"

"It's going to keep me busy for a while, that's for sure."

"Well you just make sure you finish it, with or without me," he says.

"I've told you 'til I'm blue in the face, don't talk like that. What would I do without my fount of all knowledge?"

"You mean Mr Memory?"

"You were brilliant Edmund. I just don't know how you managed to pull it off without losing your place, scratching your head or once saying, 'I don't remember'."

"Neither do I. I was well briefed."

"Felicity Jones is investigating all the transactions between Eleanor and you and Belles Fleurs. She's hopeful she can get all the money back, provided it's still there, but it will take time."

"Well it's no use to me, so you'd better have it."

I laugh, but resist arguing only to keep him happy.

"Arthur and his cronies and the Lees have all been charged variously with murder, attempted murder, fraud, and embezzlement."

"Do they think old George was a victim of theirs too?"

"They haven't said."

They won't, I know. Simon confessed to me when I told him the whole story in the hospital waiting room. Ethel called for help and her son came running. He confronted a drunken George on his way back from the pub. They fought, George fell and hit his head on a stone. End of story.

"I don't expect to be here long enough to see them banged up."

"Stop it!"

"Oh Kate. I'm done. I shall miss you terribly, but Eleanor is waiting for me. I have to go to her. You do understand?"

"Do I?"

He grimaces and adjusts his head on the pillow.

"You know how you left your phone contraption behind, the day before you disappeared?"

"Yes."

"Well I was so worried, I thought it might be useful in finding you, but I have no idea how these things work so I asked young Marcus and he did it in a flash. He said you only had two numbers stored; your mum and someone called Mandy."

"Mandy's my best friend."

"I called your mum, wary of alarming her, and fearing I'd be given short shrift, but she was very helpful. I understand you father is unwell."

"She has a lot to cope with."

"She said she loved your little chats, hearing about your life in Oakdale, but she was determined to get over it."

"She's very independently minded."

"She told me about Clare and the accident. Clare seems to be showing signs of improvement."

"That's marvellous. I must call her."

"No, don't do that. Your mother has these dreams you see. Dreams about her second daughter Kate who rings her up, but it just distresses her. She said Kate didn't survive the crash. She was killed instantly."

"Oh."

"Your friend Mandy said pretty much the same, but for her it's a recurring nightmare. Time to let go Kate."

I'm distracted by a quiet tap on the door. It's the nurse.

"Sorry to disturb you Kate, but the undertakers are here."

"Fine. We're done."

I kiss Edmund on the forehead. He's cold and stiff but peaceful.

"Say hi to Eleanor."

EPILOGUE

LATER

English Trust have two reasons to be happy I continue my work. They are not only looking forward to publishing the story of the Fitzgeralds from the time of Cromwell to the present day, they're also pleased to have a knowledgeable volunteer on site who can meet and greet visitors and guide them around their latest acquisition.

I'm showing an American couple the Fitzgerald family tree, updated to include Edmund, the Last Lord of Oakdale. Another recent addition, in dashes, shows a line from Julian and his mistress, Edith Hawley, through their illegitimate son Frederick. Fred grew up in a workhouse and was given the name Perks. He married Anne Devlin in 1925 and had one daughter Helen who married John Duvall in 1950. Their son Graham, my father, was born in 1955, married Jean in 1985 and had two daughters, Clare and Catherine.

"Oh my God!" shrieks Wanda from Idaho, pointing at my lanyard. "Are you *the* Kate?"

***

On this hot sunny afternoon, I'm in the graveyard of St John the Baptist, having a chat with Edmund, telling him of all the people who've visited Oakdale Manor and giving him an update on the book. He tells me he and Eleanor are blissfully happy together.

At night, alone in bed at Farrier's Cottage, I'm often awoken by a commotion and sometimes have to remonstrate in order to get some sleep.

"Edith! For God's sake give it a rest."

"Jacob!" My great, great, grandmother is at it again.

Printed in Great Britain
by Amazon

78999063R00171